SHATTERED COLORS
STACIA GARLAND

Cover Design: Corey Light
© 2017 by Stacia Garland
www.exquisite-minds.com

ISBN-10: 0615448798
ISBN-13: 9780615448794

ACKNOWLEDGEMENTS

Thank you to my mother, Paula Gleason, who saw my vision and spent countless hours editing. This story wouldn't have been told without you. And to Parkie Gleason, a kind father and talented glass artist, I apologize for making artists controversial in this book. Thank you to my husband, Rick, for all his support, he is my biggest fan.

Dedicated to my students—the gifted, the creative, the quirky—you were all a blessing to teach.

SHATTERED COLORS

Colors, like features, follow the changes of the emotions.
-Pablo Picasso

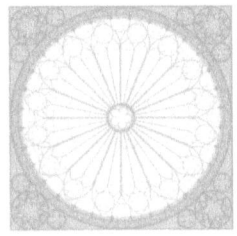

CHAPTER ONE

IN THE QUIET dark of my room I lay very still and considered the meaning of my dream. I had suffered another nightmare that left my heart pounding and the sheets tangled around my legs. As my pulse slowed, I let my thoughts circle around the room in random orbits until the effect of the nightmare receded into the dawn.

I squinted at the numbers on the clock radio and saw it was nearing time to get up. This was going to be a good day, a day I was looking forward to greeting. But my nightmare had left me feeling exhausted, and just as I started to drift back into a deep sleep, my alarm went off with the radio playing, "We had joy, we had fun" from *Seasons in the Sun*, as if to remind me what the day held in store.

Shadows blurred the outline of my parents' bodies as I entered the bedroom. Their natural colors were grayed by sleep as the day's first light seeped in through the edges of the curtains. Father snored softly against his pillow. Mom's face, partially submerged under the sheet, held the hint of a smile. Maybe she was having a good dream. I never had good dreams.

"Wake up, Mom, it's six already." I leaned closer and whispered in her ear, "I couldn't sleep last night because I had another nightmare—I thought I saw a giant owl outside my window—not part of the strigiformes species but a giant human size owl watching me in the dark." She didn't appear to be listening so I nudged her arm. "Mom—"

"Did you plug in the coffee?" she mumbled, barely audible, but I knew what she was asking because it was the same question every morning, even though the swoosh, kerplunk of the percolating coffee could already be heard.

"I always do because you're more lovable with coffee flowing through your veins." I turned to leave; knowing the perking coffeepot already had her attention, more than I ever could at that hour. Walking towards the bedroom door I heard my mom mutter, "Good grief Bree," into her pillow. She should've been grateful I didn't wake her at five a.m. when that so-called nightmare nearly scared me straight out of my pajamas.

I almost always shared my dreams with my mom, hoping she would be able to offer an explanation. While it was my nature to share much of my life with her, there were some thoughts we never discussed.

Like most people I possess secrets, all kinds of secrets. Some secrets are exciting to hold onto in anticipation of what may come later. Some secrets become unimportant and in time I forget their significance. Some I keep inside protected, their natural consequences might prove too disastrous if discovered. What I realized back in the summer of '76—the summer I saw a dead girl—is that the most dangerous secrets are the ones we keep from ourselves.

I loved my parents and until a few years ago, I thought our family was normal. When I was about nine, my mom started putting on weight and began speaking of herself in the third person as if some obese woman she did not recognize had moved into our house. My father, a well-known stained glass artist, began spouting Bible verses the way some men cuss even though he never went to church and besides, he cussed too. And Bree makes three. My teachers saw me as "unusually" gifted, my classmates saw me as weird, and I saw myself as a work in progress.

Over the years, the illusion of normalcy had been stripped away with each book I read, each movie I viewed and each intrusion from the outside world. Maybe things at home had changed or maybe I just saw things differently as I got older. I even found some measure of acceptance, or perhaps some small amount of pride in the fact we were not like everyone else. This was simply the way things were. Except, I really wanted to be normal.

Bree. My parents never gave me a reason for my name. I pictured my mom pregnant in the cheese section of the supermarket having an epiphany. Kids at school sometimes called me Bree Cheese. Father called me Breezy and I liked that. While my name didn't lack for uniqueness, the rest of me certainly was most ordinary. After my shower I stood looking in the mirror at an awkward girl with long dark hair. A girl with feet too big and breasts too small, I sure wish God hadn't got that one backwards.

As I crossed the hall to my bedroom, I saw a small red glow in the darkened kitchen and knew Mom was up, smoking her unfiltered Camels and drinking her coffee. After a couple of cigarettes and a few cups of coffee, Mom was able to face the day. She needed her two vices all through the day, fortifying her efforts to be a good wife and mother.

It is on this day, in 1976, that my story begins. And so that day began like any other day, waking Mom, getting ready for school, and listening to Father throw a tantrum over something she'd done or not done. I distracted myself with busywork by packing my lunch for the school picnic. One cream cheese and black olive sandwich, made the night before by Mom, one can of Snack Pack vanilla pudding, one grapefruit and a knife to cut it with, a spoon, and my thermos of grape Kool-Aid. I had just run back to my bedroom to grab my book bag when I heard Mom calling out from the hall and figured my bus must be coming down the road. I grabbed my bag and rushed toward the door.

Mom stopped me before I made it through the living room. She held a coffee cup in one hand, an unlit cigarette in the other, her robe was loosely tied around her ample waist, and her house-slippered feet were firmly planted too far apart as if she were seeking balance.

"Bree," she said in her softest tone, "sit down, honey."

"I can't talk right now, I'll miss the bus! Love ya but gotta run or Jason will take my seat." There was a pecking order on the bus and as a sixth grader I laid claim to the left side seat, second from the back—unless Jason got there first, then I'd acquiesce to the front of the bus because it wasn't worth the fight.

"There won't be a bus. Please do sit down." Mom gestured toward the gold velvet sofa in the living room.

A rush of uncomfortable words tumbled out. "School has been canceled; actually, yesterday was the last day. I heard all this just now on the news."

"No way!" I cried. "Today has to be the last day—they have to give us our Bicentennial picnic. I already put on the red, white and blue sundress you made just for today!"

She tried to suck a drag from her cigarette and only then seemed to notice that it was still unlit. Her shoulders sagged and she watched me guardedly.

"Bree, listen to Mom. I was in the kitchen having my coffee and watching the news. It's not fair, it's not right at all. It's not all right...but we didn't know the girl." She was rambling now, but seemed to regain her focus. "Evidently, a girl's body was found on the playground early this morning by some of the neighborhood boys. They had to cancel school. The whole area is roped off."

Hundreds of questions were colliding around in my head but only one careened out. "Who was the girl?" The sound of my own voice surprised me, and I felt tears well up in my eyes. I didn't really want to know her name. What I really wanted to know was how this could happen. Kids fell down and scraped their knees at school; sometimes, like when I was in the fourth grade and someone fell off the slide, an arm or wrist got broken, but kids weren't ever supposed to die at school.

Tears were running down my cheeks, but Mom held the same expression she always wore, a smile of resolute denial. "According to the report, her mom dropped her off at her grandmother's for a visit. The girl told her grandmother she was going for a walk and she just never came home." Mom said the last part like that was all there was. There was a lot more and I knew it—a lot more.

"Do they think she was murdered?"

Mom put her arm around me and pulled me close. "I don't know. Maybe. They've only just started investigating. I wish you wouldn't think about that. I know how much stories like this upset you. Try to forget your questions and enjoy an early start to your summer. Young girls don't need to think about sadness and death. Do you hear me?"

"Yes, but why do adults always think they can tell kids to put something out of their mind and just like that, it will go away? I mean, I understand what you're saying and I'm not going to overreact if that's your point. I didn't even know her, right?"

An irrational idea pierced my defenses and claimed my mind. I felt a sudden and strong need to go up to the school. I announced as casually as I could, "I'll change my clothes. I'm going to go ride my bike and maybe go over to Lori's house." I was hoping my mom believed me.

"That's right, just enjoy the day, and spend some time with your friends."

I heard the heavy sound of Father's footsteps. He appeared in the entrance to the living room and I sensed his anger before I saw his colors. The thunder in his voice confirmed this. "Bree, I will not hear talk of a skip day with Lori!"

Skip day? What was he talking about? Didn't he know school had been canceled? I opened my mouth to explain, I felt Mom's arm tighten around me. "But…Father, you're wrong! School has—"

His stride was long and he reached me before the rest of my words reached him. Father grabbed my chin and squeezed my mouth shut, bringing the tears before the sting. "You *are* going to school. You will not skip school with Lori and you will not backtalk! Understood?"

I nodded, my face burning with humiliation. He turned on his heel and left the room.

Mom's arm slackened, just when I needed to be held. "You shouldn't provoke him."

"Mom! I was only trying to explain!" Why hadn't she tried? She never defended herself, but why didn't she defend me?

"You make matters worse when you argue with him."

"I know, I'm sorry. I'll ride my bike up to the school. That way I can keep my word to Father and then maybe I'll go over to Lori's."

"I don't want you going up to the school. They'll have the whole area blocked off. Ride your bike. Go to the pool. Just put all of this out of your mind." Mom looked at me with an expression of love and concern. By not speaking up to my father she thought she was protecting me. I knew my parents loved me but I wanted them to love me better. I hugged her and told her not to worry, but we both knew what I was going to do.

Mom never was very strict. She tried to lecture me from time to time, but she always buckled when it came to actually enforcing the rules. This was a good thing in my opinion. I hated rules. Father, on the other hand, wasn't so easy. He demanded obedience, prompt and unquestioning and had even used his belt on me. Mom said I could save myself a lot of grief if only I would keep my mouth shut and not talk back to him. I thought she wanted me to be more like her. She just didn't understand how hard it was to keep my mouth closed when I knew he was wrong.

Pulling away from her soft, round arms, I avoided responding to her directive about staying away from the school and ran back to my room to grab my binoculars. While I sometimes justified lies of omission, I felt guilt wave over me as I snuck past the kitchen, where Mom was standing at the sink, her back lit by her colors.

One secret I tried to hide—not always with success—was how I saw the world. I'd learned to disguise my ability to see the colors surrounding each person; those shades and hues that form auras around each of us and go unseen by most of us. I'm not exactly sure when I began noticing this phenomenon, but it seems it's been with me all my life. When I was younger, I lay in my bed wondering why my brain never ceased its whirling, colors spinning like a kaleidoscope. Worries and fears—a rainbow of colors surrounding each thought. I learned to keep my secrets to myself, to hide both my ability and my fears.

The colors of my own family were very different, one from another. My mom I saw in shades of blue; peaceful, naive, unassuming. Sweet, quirky Mom who talked in the third person and smacked her lips when she got nervous. She even smiled when problems threatened to overwhelm her. My mom wore house shoes to the supermarket and sampled the fruits and vegetables in the produce aisle. I always felt very protective of my mother; she brought that out in me, even as a small child. She needed me more than either of us knew then. Mom touched me often and loved me always.

Father, on the other hand, radiated brilliant colors like the aurora borealis—colors that varied with his temperament. My father, acclaimed as a brilliant artist, had mood swings that frightened and confused me. Once, a long time ago, I watched him throw a cathedral window—one that had taken months to create—across the studio floor. Shards of stained glass shimmered at my feet, catching the light on the dusty hardwood, purples and violent shades of red.

My own colors? Like everyone, I can only see myself in a mirror. A reflection of who I am, distorted by glass—a cast-back image of broken colors.

I went out through the garage before Mom could speculate too much about what she knew I was going to do. I hopped on my ten-speed Schwinn and headed for the school, only mildly considering that I might be making a huge mistake. Like maybe children were not meant see the dead bodies of other children.

"I hate it when you ignore me."

"I'm not ignoring you, I'm upset. I don't want to talk about it anymore, that's all."

"You have to talk about it. I don't want you falling apart on me. That would be dangerous for both of us." He emphasized the "us."

I considered the implied threat. It was dangerous but it was too late to undo things. I had wondered all along why I had gone with him into those dark woods.

That night was still fresh in my memory… I had watched as he lifted the body from the vehicle. He was careful. She was moaning, she appeared weak. Her clothes had been removed. He laid her down most gently, combed her hair with his fingers, wiped away her tears. I thought maybe he cared about the girl, I thought maybe he was trying to help her. But I thought this only for a moment.

He wrapped something around her throat and pulled. She fought, she was not as weak as she first appeared. She was trying so hard to breathe, to live— but he would not give her that option.

"I can tell you're still thinking about it. You don't have to say anything. I can read your mind you know," he said with a smirk.

I remain silent, remembering...and I watched that beautiful girl die. I did not do anything to stop it, I did not attack him, I did not even go for the police. Why? Why was I paralyzed, helpless in that horror?

"Do something!" my mind had screamed. "My God, do something!" But I watched in morbid revulsion.

Why? The truth, I am afraid. Afraid of this man, this particular man.

CHAPTER TWO

I DON'T KNOW what I expected but it was not the controlled chaos I encountered at the school. There were cars everywhere; not just police cars, but all kinds of vehicles, including vans from our two local news stations. Mom was right. The whole area was roped off with yellow crime scene tape, just like in the TV shows: POLICE LINE—DO NOT CROSS.

People who lived nearby stood on their front lawns or gathered in groups of two or three in the street. Some were still in their robes. Some carried coffee mugs. I wondered if any of them knew the family or if they were just in a state of curiosity and disbelief like me.

My town was not without crime, but I couldn't remember a child ever being killed—and on my school grounds, close to my house. A college town, Englewood had a small town feel, even though 50,000 people lived there. It was the typical, Midwestern all-American town depicted in so many ways throughout the Bicentennial as America celebrated its 200th birthday.

With a mix of frustration and relief, I decided I wasn't going to be able to get beyond the cordoned area. A young girl like me would never blend into a crowd like this. Sitting on my bike, I pondered what I was doing there at all. At the very same time, I was devising a way to get closer. I lifted my binoculars from the strap around my neck and saw most of the important-looking people gathered at the woods on the edge of our ball fields. Teachers used to let us play there, before school, in the small copse of trees. When the boys started chasing the girls, some girls complained, and that was the end of hanging out in the woods.

I was determined to get closer, even though I really didn't know why I felt such a desperate need to satisfy my morbid curiosity. Deep down, I suppose I really wanted a glance at my first dead body. Someone I didn't know. Someone I had no attachment to. If my last day of elementary school had to be cancelled, I didn't just want to know why, I needed to *see* why. If it was a case of murder, of violence, it seemed that my knowing more would be the protection, the reassurance I was looking for.

I had read so many books, seen so many movies involving crime mysteries. Sometimes I stayed up and watched *Ellery Queen* with my father. I learned a lot about murder and crime work from that show. Since it was still fairly early, I thought the police might yet be taking pictures. My child's ego easily imagined finding that one elusive clue everyone else had missed, solving the crime and becoming a hero, my picture on the front page of the paper.

Riding my bike around behind the school grounds, I pedaled as fast I could to the row of houses that backed up to the
woods, to an old ranch, with no fence, perched on a ridge
at the outskirts of the area. I cut through that yard, putting
myself on the back side of the woods. Leaving my bike in the
grass, I crept closer to where the people were gathered. Still
I wouldn't be able to get close enough to see the body. And
seeing that body, a young girl's body, was all I could think
about.

A makeshift clubhouse clung precariously in one of the
trees. It was pretty rickety-looking but the location was perfect.
I crept over to the old tree and placed my foot on the bottom board nailed to the trunk. It was about three feet off the
ground, so I had to really stretch. Sometimes it paid to be tall
and skinny. Once both feet were on the first rung, I was able to
climb, limb by limb, up to the tree house, which was little more
than a plywood platform.

From my leafy hideaway, I could see the whole crime
scene with greater perspective. I imagined how it would be
if I could hear the voices from below floating up to me on
the light morning breeze, certain there would be hushed
murmurings of respect for someone who could no longer
hear. Most of the crowd was roped off several yards from the
woods, with policemen guarding the area. Only a few people
were huddled near the body, covered in black plastic. Something about that mound of plastic with its suggestive form
caused my stomach to churn and my breaths to come in short
alternating bursts.

The body would have been hard to come across, partially
hidden under a small rocky ledge. Had I not come from this
side of the woods, I wouldn't have been able to see it either. I
figured that if neighborhood boys really had found the body,

they were probably smoking pot—at least that's what I had heard the bad kids did up there before school.

A photographer stood stiffly as if he were waiting uncomfortably for his orders and I wondered if he was going to take pictures. If they were going to take more pictures, they would have to uncover the body. My heart hammered in arrhythmic beats of anticipation and fear. I tried to catch my breath, calm my heart. Then I thought about how that girl had tried to catch her breath too. How panicked she would have been as the horror had dawned on her.

I only saw one person I knew, my neighbor, Detective Hines. Sometimes I baby-sat for his wife and him. Mrs. Hines was a nurse and they had a new baby daughter, their first child. Detective Hines looked solemn and grave as he stood talking to some woman. He was a big burly black man who reminded me of every football poster I'd ever seen. He was the only black person I knew, personally. At one time I had been kind of afraid of him, but the more I got to know him, I noticed he was quiet and kind. He spoke slowly and softly, like he was putting great thought into each word. He looked like a linebacker and talked like a professor.

When the photographer stepped forward, I saw Detective Hines hesitate and then reach down and slowly pull back the tarp. I held my breath. Stretched out in the dirt, posed like the beautiful but lifeless dolls that lined the shelves in my room, was a girl I didn't recognize. Thank God. Her arms all akimbo, her body naked, vulnerable. Her long blonde hair fanned out around her head like a halo. I don't know what I had expected, but it was not all that beauty and ugliness in one space. I felt guilty looking at her naked body. I noticed that her breasts were bigger than mine. I felt a wave of jealousy and then shame for feeling jealous. She looked about my age but she was much prettier; how beautiful she must have been when she was alive.

The photographer began taking a lot of pictures focused primarily on the inside of the girl's mouth, which was being held open by a woman wearing gloves.

The girl's large eyes seemed to stare up at nothing and everything. The colors I usually saw surrounding a person weren't there. I stared hard, pressing the binoculars against my eyes until it hurt, but there were no colors, not even the slightest tinge. Was I too far away? She was the first person I can ever remember seeing who had no colors. My gift served me not at all now.

It was utterly disconcerting to see someone so young and beautiful without a trace of colored light, personality, or life itself. I laid down my binoculars and rubbed my eyes trying to erase the image. I wondered if she passed out before she felt any pain. My father's best friend had lost his only daughter in a hit and run accident a few years ago and I remembered how upset everyone had been at the time of her death. Her sudden death had hit our family hard and in response to my questions about that death, my father had assured me that she wouldn't have suffered, she wouldn't have known what hit her. But this girl had known.

Now, less than one hour after hearing about the murder, I was staring at the naked body and trying to sort through the emotions that writhed around in my brain like worms after a rain. The thought that she might have known what was happening to her made me feel incredibly angry—angry and afraid.

I was already familiar with adolescent angst and all the ego and paranoia associated with that dark anxiety. Frequent nightmares left me jittery for hours and my father's prevalent temper often left me feeling uncertain, and sometimes I felt apprehension for no reason at all. But this death unnerved me in a new manner and left my thoughts raw and primitive. I suddenly felt very vulnerable in my own neighborhood. Trees that had shown green with the vitality of a new summer's growth only an hour before, now took dark and sinister forms. The little group of people standing around the body could hide a madman. The familiar treehouse could be a deathtrap. A manic giggle nearly escaped my throat.

Once I had told my mom most everything, my every opinion on books and shows, every dream that crept through my sleep, every drama that swept through school. I could never tell her this. I would never crawl up next to her and share where I had gone, what I had seen. I could not share these unholy, terrifying thoughts. Why did I almost laugh when I truly felt so sad, so alone in my secret? Now there was a new revelation— out of all the friendly and familiar faces that populated Englewood—there was someone whose face masked dark secrets and evil intentions. Someone in my own town who would hurt me if they could.

Immune to the tingly prickles of splinters, I stayed still and spent an inordinate amount of time imagining this girl's last moments. I didn't know why, I just knew I couldn't stop visualizing what I thought had happened to her. My mind was fixated on what might have occurred during the dusky hours of the previous evening. This was a problem because I didn't know what *had* happened exactly and yet my imagination filled in the blanks with all kinds of horrible scenarios. A slideshow of pictures I could never unsee. Maybe the natural evolution to these thoughts was visualizing the murder happening to me. Envisioning my own life being stolen without sense or reason.

Lying on the rotting boards of my aerie, I foresaw the many different outcomes of such an encounter. When I was feeling brave and confident, I would emerge a survivor, a hero. When the fear gripped me, I imagined my death, a most brutal death, at the hands of a madman.

Having an overactive imagination made it more difficult to control these anxious thoughts and being in such close proximity to the body, made it impossible. Now every stranger would be a potential suspect. Every neighbor had opportunity, and in my child's eyes, every man had motive. Yet there was a clarity, a calming resolution in this fear. The only way to feel safe again was for this murderer to be caught.

What I didn't fully realize then is that my childhood had been changed, altered beyond repair. Whether or not the killer was caught, my neighborhood was no longer several blocks of idealistic Midwestern life and I was beginning to see that it never really was.

It was obvious from her nakedness that this was not an accident. It was murder in all its ugliness. I was determined now more than ever to find her killer. Anger fueled my courage; I retrieved my binoculars and doggedly resumed my observation.

At first, I didn't see any blood. Taking a deep breath, determined to find a clue that made sense of all this, I used my binoculars to carefully scan her body. I made out what looked like dried blood on her face and neck, but there was not a large pool of blood like they show in the movies. I didn't think the blood I saw could be the cause of death; there sure wasn't very much of it. Then I noticed her neck. It looked very dark—discolored, actually—compared to the rest of her pale skin. She must have been strangled and my own breath caught in my throat. I sat back against the tree, trying to imagine what that would be like, to have your life choked right out of you. She would have panicked, disbelieving what was happening to her. I placed my hands around my own throat and squeezed. I couldn't make myself squeeze hard enough to stop my breath, and yet it was hard to breathe.

A different kind of anger rose in my chest. Not the anger of my own righteous indignation at what had happened to this girl, but anger at her for letting it happen. I knew I'd never let something like that happen to me. I'd fight, I'd scream, I'd stab him in the eye with my finger and kick him hard in his privates, then I'd run faster than I'd ever run in my life.

I wondered why this girl didn't do that? I knew I could have gotten away. Why hadn't she? I had never felt such anger. And I was angry at this girl.

I wanted to stay and try to hear what the police and reporters and photographers were saying, but I was starting to feel dizzy, images were blurring and I felt really nauseous. I wasn't even sure if I would be able to get down the tree without falling. My brain was in overload and I felt like I did when I had the flu. This had been a horrible mistake. Just one big, huge, gigantic mistake.

Questions exploded in my head and I needed help. I knew there was one person I could talk to about what I'd seen and how I was feeling.

Half scrambling, half falling, I made an awkward landing at the base of the tree. I pedaled my bike as fast as I could, pushing back terrifying thoughts of violence and death, trying to leave the images in the woods behind. Faster and faster I pedaled, wanting to turn back time. Time before I went to the woods. Time before I knew about the murder. Time before it all began.

As I turned the corner behind the school and headed down Minor Road, a red car pulled in closely behind me, not passing, tailgating. A threatening presence following in the wake of my flight. I turned onto Maple, even though it wasn't the street I wanted. The red car turned too. Heart pounding, I pedaled furiously, turning onto the first street I came to. Glancing behind, I was flooded with relief as the car continued on down Maple. Don't murderers always return to the crime scene? Had I been seen spying down from my treetop hideout?

CHAPTER THREE

AS IF BY MAGIC, as if my bike could really fly, as if it were a time machine, I found myself in front of my Aunt Sharon's house with her green Triumph Spitfire glinting in the morning sun. I was so relieved and grateful she was home that tears sprang hot to my eyes. I leaned my bike against the carport and dashed to the front porch. Before I could ring the bell, she threw open the door and swept me up in her arms, her purple colors emanating from her like heat waves on hot asphalt. From the back of the sofa Sharon's three cats, Sparky, Elliot, and D.C. watched with squinty, disinterested feline eyes. I heard music playing in the background.

AND ALL THE GIRLS DREAMED THAT THEY'D
BE YOUR PARTNER. THEY'D BE YOUR PARTNER,
AND YOU'RE SO VAIN, YOU PROBABLY THINK
THIS SONG IS ABOUT YOU, DON'T YOU?

I started to cry and I could not stop crying. I cried sobs, hiccups, gasping chokes, and Aunt Sharon held me until I was empty.

"Bree, Bree…baby, what's wrong?" she asked, but I couldn't answer, I couldn't even look at her. I didn't know what was wrong. I only knew I felt an anger that threatened to consume me.

"Is it about the girl that died on your school grounds? Is it something else? Something I don't know anything about?" She took my tear streaked face in her hands and forced me to look at her.

She always looked me straight in the eye, smiling slightly as if she saw someone so interesting that she could not look away. Sharon taught psychology at the community college and held group therapy twice a week for abused women. As my mother's only sister she could not have been more different.

"The girl," was all I could say.

"I'm so sorry. It's always sad when someone dies, especially a child. It's not natural and it's easy to rage against the injustice," she said.

There it was. It was rage I felt. Rage that a girl my age was gone. She would never go home, never go on a date or laugh with friends.

"She didn't come back. She didn't come home." I said trying to explain what I was feeling.

"Look, honey," Aunt Sharon cajoled as she led me over to the sofa, shooing the cats away with the wave of her hand. "The girl was visiting her grandmother, she wasn't someone you knew. It's still so very sad and so unjust, but tears won't bring her back."

"Yeah, I don't know why I'm so upset, Sharon—I didn't even know her. I just can't shake this horrible feeling that somehow it all involves me—like I'm supposed to do something. And if I don't, another horrible thing will happen. What if the person who killed her lives in my neighborhood? What if he comes after me?" There. I said it. My real fear, if it could happen to that girl, why not me? Why not anyone?

I told my aunt the awful truth, all of it. I had gone to the school. I had seen the body. She didn't say anything for the longest time and I was afraid she might think what I did was bad. She had tears in her eyes when she finally smiled at me in a way that let me know she didn't think I was so bad after all.

Aunt Sharon shook her long braided hair and hugged me tight. "Sweetie, we don't know any of the facts yet. Just because one girl was killed, doesn't mean that it has anything to do with you. And you, young lady, will be careful in the meantime. Not because it has anything to do with you but because it's smart. Okay?"

"All the way here I felt like someone was following me." I hiccupped again.

"The odds of the same thing happening to you are one in a million, or even more. Remind yourself of that when you start getting a bit obsessive about that girl's death. Try to put your thoughts in perspective. You're fairly street-smart, and I think you pay a lot of attention to what's going on around you, maybe too much attention. Just don't take any unnecessary risks, like walking alone at night and you'll be fine."

She placed her hand on my shoulder. "Thinking someone was following you was probably your imagination at work. You do have a very vivid imagination, you know. I'm sure that's one of the reasons you're in the profoundly gifted program. We're lucky we're in a college town so you can get services. I can't imagine a child like you in a regular classroom."

I knew Sharon was bringing up the gifted program with some kind of aunt's pride, but it still embarrassed me. In the 4th grade I had been asked to take a letter home for my parents to sign. It was sealed in an envelope and I couldn't imagine what it contained. Was I in trouble? I hadn't done anything but I still wondered what private communication was being passed between my school and my parents. I think I remember being a little anxious when I handed it over to my mom. She seemed just as curious at first but when she had finished reading, she grabbed me in her arms and pulled me tight against her chest. After I pulled away, she took my face in her hands and said how proud she was of me. Completely mystified, I asked her what I had done. My mom's explanation was something about how my scores on a national achievement test had qualified me to be tested for a new program. She kept saying, "I knew you were smart. I just knew you were the smartest of the smart." She seemed so happy and I wondered why it made me feel kind of uneasy, a little uncomfortable. I wasn't sure I wanted to be smarter than everyone else, I wasn't sure I wanted to be in some program.

Later in the week, the school counselor, Mr. Reynolds, came to our classroom and called me out in front of everyone. On the walk to his office he explained that I would be given a "fun" test. I was still flushed from the embarrassment of being taken from class and of course I had many questions. When I asked him about the program I was being tested for, he told me that any qualifying students would be placed in a different class within the school and given more challenging work. While I relished the idea of more challenging schoolwork, I did not want to be pulled away from my friends and I definitely did not want to be singled out as different.

So, as the test began I decided not to try my best, if the questions were really easy I answered them so he wouldn't be on to me. But once the questions became more difficult I strategically threw in an "I don't know" every now and then.

However, as my interest in the test grew, I found it difficult to resist any puzzle Mr. Reynolds gave me to solve. He asked, "Explain how to measure exactly 2 pints of water if you have a 4 and a 3 pint container."

After thinking for a few seconds, I told him, "I think I'd fill the 3 pint glass and pour all of the water into the 4 pint glass, then refill the 3 pint glass and fill the 4 pint glass to the top. And now I'd have 2 pints in the 3 pint glass. Or I could just ride my bike to the five and dime store and buy a measuring cup, that'd be easier, wouldn't it?" He smiled so I knew I got that one right.

The vocabulary section started out boring until he started asking more interesting questions like could I describe the difference between character and reputation. That question made me think of my father.

So I said, "My father has a great reputation as an artist, a lot of people buy his work, but it really has nothing to do with who he is as a man. But he showed his character when he came home from work really tired the other night, and still went to my P.T.A. meeting to see me in a play and like the day he was already late for work but took the time to help me change the tire on my bike.

"Those things have nothing to do with his reputation as an artist. So, I think his reputation is who people think he is and his character is who I know he is, does that make sense?" I asked, looking for validation. Mr. Reynolds didn't smile that time but rather looked like he was having a deep thought, so I didn't know if I got that one right or not.

Later, when he told me I had qualified for the program, I had mixed emotions but then Mr. Reynolds told me he had never tested someone as good as me at solving puzzles. Basking in flattery, I agreed to give the program a try.

Aunt Sharon looked at me with a caring smile, but her comment brought back all the disappointment of losing my last day of school. "You know, when I got up this morning, I was really looking forward to today. We were supposed to have our Bicentennial picnic and bury our time capsule. Now I won't get to go back to the school in fifty years—when I'm 62 and really old—to watch them dig it up because it was never buried in the first place! I know it may sound selfish, but it doesn't even feel like summer yet."

I began picking at a loose thread on my shorts, hoping I didn't sound as immature as I felt. "What started as a fun day has turned into something so different. How can it do that? I woke up feeling all excited and now I only feel weight sitting on me. What's the point in making plans anyway?"

"Well, we make plans so we can try and control our destiny. Most of the time our plans work out; and when they don't we adapt. You missed a special day at school, but you have the first day of next year to look forward to and I know you like school, especially your gifted classes." She cocked her head and encouraged me to respond. What I liked about talking to Aunt Sharon was that she always acted like she wanted me to talk to her.

My anger had dissipated. I felt calmer, but weak and drained. I stopped pulling at the loose thread realizing I had caused the hem to unravel. Somehow the scene at the school and all its morbid curiosities seemed like a dream, a nightmare from another time. I knew Aunt Sharon was trying to change the subject and it felt comforting to allow her to lead me away from the murder.

"I like being in gifted better than the regular classroom. My old regular class teacher, Mrs. Nelson, always acted weird about any art project I did in class, like it wasn't good enough. Then one day, she slipped and mentioned Father's art. That's when I realized that the look on her face whenever I turned in a project was total disappointment, disappointment in my inherited traits I suppose."

My aunt shook her head. "How unfair, just because you're Geoff's daughter doesn't mean you'd inherit his artistic genius. You're a genius in your own right, with talents your dad will never have."

"Like social skills?" I said with a smile.

"Well, perhaps." Aunt Sharon put her arm around me and squeezed.

"Hey, don't worry about Mrs. Nelson. I took care of that problem."

My aunt looked at me skeptically. "I almost hate to ask, but tell me anyway."

"I told Mrs. Nelson I was adopted."

Aunt Sharon pulled away from me, "You didn't!"

"I did! And it was the smartest thing I did that year. She threw up her hands, and a big smile spread across her wrinkled old face and she said, 'Well, now, that explains it!'"

Aunt Sharon burst out laughing and I joined her, the morning's horrifying dreamscape fading with each shared laugh. "If your parents find out they'll kill you."

"They won't find out. Mrs. Nelson is always so excited to just be in the presence of the Great Geoffrey Grant that she can't put together a coherent sentence anyway."

"Actually, I doubt your parents could ever get too mad at you, even if you did lie about being adopted. I think they know how lucky they are to have a neat girl like you."

I felt my face redden, "Oh, Sharon! Father gets plenty mad at me, believe me!" Although I really trusted my aunt, I decided to change the direction of this uncomfortable conversation, maybe out of loyalty to my parents or my own ego, I had a strong need to portray my family as *Happy Days* perfect and that meant not discussing my father's temper.

I did not understand then why I cared so very much what people thought of me and my family. Maybe it was because the fathers on T.V. did not lose their tempers, or, if they were upset with Richie or Joanie, it was a controlled, watered-down version of what happened at our house.

Contrary to what my father would have said, I spent much of my youth trying to control my tongue and avoid rocking the boat. But try as I might I could not predict my father's outbursts. I saw myself as the peace keeper in our family, or at least I tried to be. In turn, I was feeling more and more uncomfortable expressing myself and, even worse, the fear kept me from being able to stand up for myself.

Hearing Carly Simon in the background, I asked, "Isn't that the same song that was playing when I first came in?"

She looked sheepish. "Buck and I broke up. This is my break-up song for the month."

Another boyfriend down the tubes. I couldn't help but feel sorry and elated at the same time. Aunt Sharon went through boyfriends like my mom went through a box of donuts. Neither ever seemed any better for the experience. I'd met Buck a few times, and he was no winner. Not particularly handsome, he was no great conversationalist either, just a guy with big meaty hands and a bad hairpiece. Surely Aunt Sharon knew she was better off without him.

A sudden thought occurred to me, "What if Buck is the one who killed that girl?" How in the middle of laughing and talking with my aunt, had my brain come up with the murder again?

"*What?*" Aunt Sharon's eyebrows furrowed.

"Well, you've told me Buck has a temper, and you said that guy you work with claims Buck cheats at golf..." I began to realize I wasn't thinking logically, maybe not even sanely.

She looked perplexed. "What does that have to do with anything? Lots of people cheat at golf, but that doesn't make them killers, Bree."

I was embarrassed. For a minute, it had almost felt logical. "I guess you're right. I was just thinking that if he isn't honest and has a temper...oh, never mind, there goes my dumb brain again!" I tried to laugh, but it came out as hollow chuckles.

"I don't like the way you're dwelling on this girl's death. I think I know you pretty well, and I want to help. When you're all worried or full of anxiety, please call me or come by. Will you do that for me?"

"Sure, Aunt Sharon. I like to talk to you. You always make me feel better." And that was the truth.

"Hey, it's almost eleven and that's close enough to lunch. I'll make us a couple of black olive and cream cheese sandwiches."

"That sounds yummy. Do you have any sprouts to go on them?"

"Yes, ma'am—and fresh pumpernickel bread." Aunt Sharon headed for the fridge.

I bent down scooping up Sparky, petting Sparky made me feel better, yet I couldn't get the image of the dead girl out of my head.

I yelled back into the kitchen, "Sharon, can I go turn on the TV and see if the news is on?"

"What's this sudden interest in the news? Oh, yes. I'd really rather you didn't, but...oh well, go ahead. Maybe, they've found the murderer—or found out it was just a horrible accident."

I wanted to explain, "I'm curious, that's all. I feel kind of a bond in some weird way to this girl. Maybe because I saw her body? Maybe because she was about my age?" But my explanation didn't ring true, even to me. In some way the dead girl and I were connected.

I went back into the living room, intent on finding out what that connection was. Aunt Sharon's decor kept your eyes traveling trying to take it all in. Her decorating style demanded attention. Her home was as colorful and creative as she was. She bought old furniture at garage sales and painted each piece in an explosion of bright colors. She said it was an expression of her inner child.

One of my favorite things was her Felix the Cat clock that hung by the TV, its tail twitching to the tick of the seconds. Usually, its novelty made me feel like smiling; today, it seemed to be reminding me that time was slipping away.

I sat down on the quilt-covered sofa and switched the knob on the TV. Scanning the channels, I looked for news about the dead girl. Channel 3 was just beginning a newscast. I leaned forward, hoping some of my questions would be answered.

The newsman looked theatrically solemn. "Welcome to NEWS-3 for the eleven o'clock report. Up first, we bring you the latest on the tragic story of a young girl reported missing last evening. Englewood police report that Rachel Carter's body was discovered early this morning at Brighton Elementary School.

"At the school now is Frank Martin. Frank, what can you tell us?"

I leaned forward, hoping Frank would have all the answers to my questions. Standing on the school grounds, looking slightly windblown and serious, he spoke.

"Well, Mark, the police aren't saying much at this point, but young Rachel Carter's death is being investigated as a homicide."

Frank glanced down at his notes before continuing. "Rachel Carter was at the home of her grandmother, Teresa Phelps, in the 3200 block of Monroe Street yesterday after school. Mrs. Phelps said Rachel's mom had driven the girl from Kennedy Junior High to her grandmother's house. Rachel went for a walk in the early evening. When she did not return for dinner, Mrs. Phelps contacted the police. It wasn't until two teenagers found the body on the school grounds around six this morning that the story turned tragic."

The camera shot back to Mark Costner, who said, "Thank you, Frank. NEWS-3 will keep you posted as we learn more about this sad story. Up next, we will have residents of Englewood's Nursing Home sharing a Bicentennial quilt they made honoring 200 years of American history."

The dead girl now had a name—Rachel. I was hoping for more information, I wanted to hear interviews with teachers and classmates who'd express their upset over Rachel's death.

People who knew her would be stunned and shocked that something like this could happen.

I wondered what would be said about me if I ever fell victim to a violent crime. My father's reputation as an artist would probably garner my death a whole truckload of attention. But what would they actually say about his daughter? "Bree was always a quiet girl. She seemed really nice, never caused any trouble." Something was definitely missing in my epitaph.

I could hear Aunt Sharon singing in the kitchen while she finished making our sandwiches. As we ate, she convinced me of the real therapy of getting back into a normal routine. I decided to run by home and get some money so I could buy a Slurpee at 7-Eleven and de-stress.

When I walked in the front door, I announced to my mom that I was going for another bike ride.

Mom tore her gaze from the Sears catalog. "Bree, your father wants you to work at the studio tomorrow. He has some projects for you and says he'll pay you."

If he wanted me to go to work with him, then he wasn't still mad. By now he had probably heard about the murder, knowing he had been wrong to make me go to school. Not that he'd ever admit it and I wasn't stupid enough to point this out. Besides, I was definitely getting low on money. "Yeah, tell him I'll do it if he cooks some Chinese food for lunch. Gotta make it worth my while!"

Mom smiled. "I will call and let him know. Oh, and Bree, I'm getting low on Camels. Would you stop by the 7-Eleven while you're out and get me a pack and a Snickers? I'll give you money for a candy bar for yourself."

I hated getting cigarettes for Mom, I felt like I had to explain to the clerk that they weren't for me, they were for my mom, although the clerk never looked like she cared one way or the other. "O.K., I'll do it but I'm gonna buy me a Slurpee instead of candy, much better on a hot day! I'll stop by after my bike ride; otherwise your Snicker's will be a soupy mess."

"Sure, that's fine." Mom pulled out a couple of dollars from her housecoat pocket and handed them to me. "Have fun. Be careful riding your bike, dear. There's a killer on the loose, you know." Mom's face looked odd—concerned and absentminded at the same time.

I knew what she said was probably normal for a mom to say—at least my mom. But it seemed strange in some way. Like, "Be careful, it's slippery," or "Be careful, it's hot." One more thing to worry about. I just nodded and headed out the door, telling myself, "Don't think about it, Bree. Just don't think."

There was a line at the 7-Eleven. I was juggling my Slurpee and Mom's candy bar when I finally reached the counter and was able to set them down. I mumbled, "And a pack of Camels, unfiltered please," while fishing the money from my pocket.

"So the famous Bree smokes cancer sticks, uh?"

Startled, I spun around in embarrassment, an angry retort on the tip of my tongue. Grinning back at me was Mike from my gifted class. Cripes.

"I don't smoke. I never will. They're for my mom." I watched as Mike balanced a Slurpee and carton of milk. I didn't see any snacks.

Mike replied, "Good for you. I'm kind of surprised to see you out running around by yourself after all the news about the murder. Of course, there's murders all over the world every day.

Just a few weeks ago, a woman and her boyfriend killed her entire family in Illinois. Murders are everywhere. In January a whole bus of people were murdered in Ireland."

His comments were not making me feel any better, so I shrugged like I didn't care, hoping he'd stop. He had a way of going on and on in class so I knew what he was capable of.

"Your mom must really need those smokes to let you come here by yourself."

The clerk was growing impatient and I was anxious to get away from Mike's bemused comments on my mom's bad habits. I was irritated but then I remembered Mike didn't have a mom. It was just him and his dad. Well, that was still no excuse for his rudeness. I paid the clerk and said a quick good-bye to Mike, before straddling my bike and hurrying back to the house.

At dinner that evening I was quieter than usual, still feeling confused and angry about the murder. My deep thoughts were interrupted by Father's comment to my mom.

"So, Dorothy, how was your day? Did you get everything done on the list I left for you this morning?"

Mom smiled and replied, "Yes, dear and I even had time to work on my needlepoint, sometimes I think that throw pillow will never be finished, I should have chosen an easier pattern, one with less colors."

Father didn't allow Mom to work. He believed a woman's place was in the home apparently this was in order to keep his child from becoming a delinquent. I wasn't so sure about his theory. Father was now recounting his day. "And now that idiot priest over at St. Michael's won't give me my window back!"

I thought I'd missed something. "Father, why would you want that window back? You just got it installed last week."

He laid down his fork, his manner tense, his tone condescending. "Because, after I installed the window and saw it in the sanctuary with sunlight shining through it, I realized the colors are all wrong!" Father's face was getting red as he spoke. "I tried to tell those idiots that their color choices were poor, but they had to have it *their* way. Now that I've seen the damn thing in situ, I hate it! I told that idiot priest that I needed to redo it, free of charge—even. But he told me—can you believe this—to go away and leave him alone! Can you imagine a priest treating anyone like that? And him, a man of God!"

Mom interjected, "Geoffrey, dear, I'm sure your idea was better. You always do know best, but can't you let it go and let them live with it? You don't have to look at it anymore. We hardly ever drive out to Greenview anyway."

"Damn it, Dorothy! Why don't you mind your own business! It's my name on that window, not yours! I'm changing the damn window. Just shut your mouth and eat your dinner!"

How was she supposed to eat her dinner if her mouth was shut? I looked at my father as he aggressively stabbed his pork chop. There was a white light surrounding him.

I stared at him harder and the light became more intense. There seemed to be little flecks of red and green vibrating within the light.

My concentration was broken when Father dropped his fork. "What in damnations are you looking at?"

I looked down at my uneaten food. "Nothing."

"Well then stop staring!"

I felt tears well up in my eyes. I continued to stare down at my plate as Mom reached out to touch his arm. He threw his chair back and knocked his plate to the floor. He stomped off yelling, "You two are no different than Judas! *'When Judas, who had betrayed him, saw that Jesus was condemned, he was seized with remorse and returned the thirty silver coins...'"*

What the heck did that mean? So much for our charming family dinners together. He acted so sure of himself all the time. And half the time I wasn't sure of anything. I didn't dare look at Mom. I wouldn't find answers there. I needed comfort and reassurance, but knew I'd only be disappointed. I was strangling. Why couldn't anyone see I was strangling?

I did not understand my father's bursts of temper. He had always been a bit moody but lately his demeanor was becoming increasingly unnerving. I searched to find patterns to his moods, to find some way to predict, pause, sway, or circumvent his triggers. Anything to keep even one dinner running calmly, one dinner where we could share thoughts about our day without worrying about saying the wrong words. Words that when phrased poorly or said with a misconstrued tone caused something in his head to combust and burst forth in rage. When this happened he was like a cornered cat with its fur on end, refusing to be soothed, storming off to be by himself and lick his imaginary wounds. It was confusing because sometimes I sensed he was mad at himself and sometimes I felt like he was truly mad at my mother and me.

Mom said, "Bree, why don't you finish your dinner and Mom will clean up this, uh...the dishes."

Father had already stormed off to the bedroom, his words and colors clouding the air. I was more than happy to finish my dinner quickly and go to my room. I needed to regain control of my emotions in the one place I could.

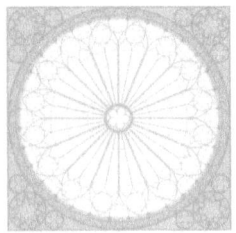

CHAPTER FOUR

MY CLOSET WAS extraordinary, because our house was extraordinary. My parents bought the house from a sculptor who had designed and built it for himself before moving to California. Maybe it reflected my father's artistic taste, but it stood out like a Picasso among Monets on a street lined with traditional homes.

The woodwork and stained glass in our house were extravagant. Also, each room was a different and unusual shape. The kitchen and dining area were an octagonal hub with four other rooms jutting off by way of small hallways. My parents' room was called the Pentagon because of its five-sided shape. My room was the Hexagon, for obvious reasons. There was also a living room with a small office in the corner known as the Trapezoid. The garage was quite an original shape—a square.

My room held all my treasures—all of my collections. But my closet, my refuge within the Hexagon, was my favorite and most secret place.

A year or so after we moved in, I had an inspiration and decided to make my closet into my own little secret room. It had sliding chrome doors and cedar walls. I made a humble sofa from my toy box, which was actually Father's old Army trunk. Over time, I plastered the walls with posters of crushes and idols of the moment. Beginning with Donny Osmond and working my way up to Evel Knievel, the greatest daredevil of all time. I also taped a sign to the outside of the closet, insisting people respect my privacy. The clothes hamper became an end table for my lava lamp and now held my most prized collection, my Bicentennial coins. This became my sanctuary—too young to even realize why I needed a secret place within my private room.

One day while I was lounging on my homemade sofa, reading Judy Blume's, *Are You There God, It's Me Margaret?* I noticed an indistinct square outlined on the ceiling. I thought about asking Mom if there was an attic they hadn't told me about. No reason to ask Father; as far as I knew, he rarely set foot in my bedroom. Sometimes when he yelled at me to clean my room I wondered how he knew it was messy. It didn't matter. I couldn't ask either one, they were out running an errand. I decided to explore this newfound mystery myself.

Reaching what I guessed to be the attic entrance was the first problem: I wasn't tall enough. I got a wicker chair from my room and placed it on the toy box; by doing this I could just reach the panel and push it out of the way. It looked dark. I got a flashlight from the kitchen drawer and decided I'd need more height to be able to hoist myself up through this door in the ceiling. Finally, I placed the clothes hamper on the toy box, then the chair on the clothes hamper. It was wobbly but it worked. I carefully pushed myself up from my tenuous perch, keeping the flashlight under my chin while raising my knee to get enough leverage to pull myself through the beckoning threshold.

With my heart beating like crazy, I switched on the flashlight. I felt something brush against my face in the dark. I flinched and gulped in stale dusty air. I waved the light in that direction. I thought it might be an old cobweb, but the beam from the flashlight revealed a string hanging from a bare bulb. I pulled on the string and the attic was illuminated seconds before my eyes could adjust and register what was revealed. I felt a strangled scream rise in my throat as I saw the bodies of several women caught in that first exposure of light. My eyes and brain were trying frantically to understand this vision as I clawed my way back down, toppling the precariously balanced ladder, and landing hard on the floor below.

A kind of sanity finally forced through the gushing stream of fear, insisting that what I had seen couldn't have been what I had seen. As my panic subsided, I carefully reconstructed the make-shift ladder. Coaxing my determination as best I could, I climbed again to the opening of the attic, feeling anxiety with every cautious step. I looked, suspending my disbelief, and saw the figures were not real women, but abandoned mannequins. Warily, I glanced around, searching for any other repulsive revelations. I saw a few old trunks and many cobwebs drifting among the rafters, but no live—or dead—bodies, thank God. There really was nothing to fear, but my body was still quivering in shock.

I found myself holding my breath as I edged closer to the mannequins. Breathe Bree, I reminded myself. I crept closer and knelt before them, spotlighting them with my flashlight. Each was dressed in elaborate evening clothes, as if posed for display in some Twilight Zone store window. The mannequins—I counted five—stared vacantly into the light. They were men! Male mannequins dressed in women's clothes. Lace, silk and feathers decorated ragged and torn, yet, the most beautiful gowns I'd ever seen. Their blank, staring faces wore makeup that was smeared and grossly misapplied. Where had they come from? Why would someone keep them in an attic? Why were they costumed so horribly?

I knew the sculptor was the only person who'd ever lived in the house besides my parents and me. I couldn't remember if he'd had a family. The mannequins' clothing was what Mom would call tacky. The outfits were silky and slinky, bold bright colors and with lots of accessories; they even wore high-heeled shoes! With some natural instinct I decided to give each mannequin a name. Finally, I decided on unisex names for each of them: Stacey, Jesse, Terry, Kelly, Gene. Giving these poor discarded creatures names made it seem less lonely, less sad. My fear and confusion had been replaced with pity for their loneliness and abandonment in the dark.

I decorated this special space with Christmas lights from Mom's stash of decorations. Later, I added incense and a Ouija board I bought with my baby-sitting money. Eventually I convinced myself they were merely life-sized Barbies, or actually more like Kens in Barbie's clothes. I was reluctant at first to touch them, in time I managed to mend their gowns, which had funny names on the inside tags, like Pierre Cardin, Yves Saint Laurent and Givenchy. I also reapplied their make-up and rearranged their limbs into more natural, comfortable poses. As a kid, I thought the mannequins might be real and wondered how they felt about my efforts to renew them. Then, as I redid Stacey's make-up, I could swear she winked at me! I began talking to the mannequins and telling them about my father's temper tantrums. Over time, the mannequins became my friends, my confidants.

On this particular evening, I escaped the anxiety of the murder and my father's temper in the only way I knew. Climbing into the attic, I lit incense and turned on the string of Christmas lights. The attic got hot and stuffy in the summer; I kept my visits short so I didn't suffocate in the heat. My mannequin friends stood next to me as I began what we called the "cleansing ritual". I had come up with the idea after one particularly upsetting confrontation with Father. We refined our ceremony until it was perfected to each of our satisfactions. We did this as often as necessary and I truly believed the ceremony helped Father regain control of his demons. Now that I was entering the 7th grade, I knew I was getting too old to play with dolls; my girlfriends had already put away their Barbies. Yet, these were more than dolls, they were my friends and I needed them. This was one of my many secrets I could justify.

I said hello to my friends and filled them in on Father's latest episode. My stories tended to upset Terry the most.

"You poor thing!" Terry exclaimed with his inner voice.

"Terry, will you lead the cleansing ritual this time? I think it's your turn." My mannequins tended to argue if we didn't take turns.

I bowed my head as Terry spoke. "Spirits, guide us to an understanding of Bree's father. Help him to understand himself and to regain his self-control. Give him a sense of peace, so that Bree's life may be easier."

I reached for Terry's hand, as we gathered in a circle and began to chant. The scent of incense filled the air. "Peace to Bree and her father. Peace. Peace. Peace…"

We did this as long as we had to, until we felt we had made a difference. We knew we had when our hearts settled to a calmness. So much of the time their colors were grayed like my parents in sleep. I thought it was from living in the dark, but they never asked me to leave a light on and I never offered.

I dropped my arms and asked for their attention, "There's still more work to do tonight, guys. There's been a murder, a girl I didn't know, but I feel like I'm supposed to do something. But there are so many unanswered questions, I need answers."

"Oh my!" they gasped in unison.

"Gene, I need you to guide this séance."

I looked up at Gene, the most serious of my unique friends. I could hear his inner voice. "You see something, don't you? Something only you can see?"

I looked up from the Ouija board. "Yes, I do. But I'm not yet ready to put my feelings into words." I hadn't told them about seeing the body. I couldn't, but they sensed I was holding back.

Handsome, blonde Terry shot me a glance. "When you are ready, you will talk to us, won't you? You know you can trust us, don't you?" We locked eyes.

"Definitely! You're the only friends I can totally trust, with the possible exception of my Aunt Sharon. Come on, let's get to work!"

I explained my plan to catch the killer, which I had made while spending the afternoon laying across my bed, making notes in my diary, and listening to my stereo. I had mapped out the neighborhood and school and made a list of people to interview.

The board began to spell out my first plan of attack. I decided to begin tomorrow morning. After the cleansing ceremony, I snuffed out the incense, turned off the lights, and shimmied down through the crawl space, using a pull-down ladder I'd discovered attached to the opening. I could only hope I'd spent enough time on the ceremony. I felt better and I didn't hear Father's angry voice when I re-entered my bedroom, so our ritual must have worked.

That night my mom came in and sat on my bed, she took my hand. "Mom knows your father scares you when he acts the way he did at dinner tonight. But he does love you so much. He just doesn't always realize how his actions hurt others."

We'd had this little conversation before. It was another ritual after each explosion.

I didn't want her to worry about me. "I know. I feel sorry for Father, that's all. I wish he didn't feel like he had to change that window. I'm sure it looks fine just the way it is."

"Regardless of how it looks, the people who ordered it are happy, so Geoff should just let it go. But… that's difficult for him."

"Yeah, I just wish he didn't seem so…tormented."

Mom patted my hand. "Your father is a very sensitive, caring man. That's probably his greatest fault. He worries so much about everything." She reached into her housecoat pocket and fumbled for her cigarettes. "Mom didn't want you going to sleep tonight feeling sad."

She lit her cigarette, she took a long drag and blew the smoke out through her nose. "Remember, dear, your father loves you, no matter how he acts." She walked out of my room, inhaling deeply and not really leaving me feeling any more protected.

"You know the definition of family?"

I knew he was messing with me, as he'd been doing since that night in the woods. I tried to ignore him. He was too confident and impossible to ignore. He waited patiently and finally I gave in and said, "What is it?"

"It's where you go and they have to take you in," he said and I knew he was having fun. "You and I are like a family," growing more serious now. "No one can separate us. We're bound together like those little oriental freaks. Ying and Yang or something."

"Eng and Chang," I corrected softly. "They were Siamese twins. I don't quite see us like that."

He glared at me. "Then just what do you see?"

CHAPTER FIVE

THE NEXT MORNING my radio alarm clock went off, blaring *Afternoon Delight*, waking me with a start. I trudged slowly to the kitchen, the shag carpet soft under my feet and plugged in the coffeepot for my parents.

I'd told Father I would help at the studio, but there were other things on my mind and I had important work to do. I dressed in my version of good spy clothes: a black T-shirt, jean shorts and a ball cap. I gathered items for my bag: binoculars, my diary, pencil, and a package of Pop-Tarts. What else did a good investigator need? A murder had been committed and I felt the self-important burden of moral duty.

Since my parents weren't up yet, it was pretty easy to sneak out of the house. I looked down the street, wondering where to even begin. My neighborhood was older, but nicely kept, for the most part. My home stood out with its alien shape, immense stained glass windows and varying seasons of tidiness. Sometimes it was embarrassing to live in this island of oddity. I left looking for answers.

Even though Mom stayed home, she had never been one to socialize with the neighbors. Anyone I knew was mostly from hanging out around the neighborhood. I decided Detective Hines' house would be a good place to start, since he was probably working the case.

Evidently Detective Hines had a good reputation in Englewood. Father repeated a story about some hoodlum who was in front of a judge and kept denying that he had done anything wrong. The judge asked who the arresting officer was. When the guy replied that it was Detective Hines, the judge said, "If Detective Hines arrested you, then I know you're guilty!" Father said that makes a statement about Hines' reputation.

I walked four houses down, keeping my eyes open for anything suspicious, pulling out paper and pencil, in case I needed to take notes. I began scoping out the neighborhood. I tried to recall everything I knew about these familiar, but until now, mostly unnoticed surroundings. The first house, across the street from us, seemed like an unlikely suspect. I reviewed my make-shift detective's diary:

The man, Mr. Kohler, is in a wheelchair and could hardly have killed Rachel. However, he does sit by his sliding glass door and watch the neighborhood most afternoons. He could have seen something. I will have to interview Mr. Kohler.

Mrs. Barker is a widow. She has nine cats, at least that's my best count so far. What would she know about the murder? I better interview her anyway.

I rarely see anyone at the brick house. They keep their curtains closed all the time. I will keep an eye on this house.

The old guy with the camera, otherwise known to me as "Cameraman", I should spy on him and see what he's up to.

Further down the street was a home partially obscured by overgrown shrubbery. I was particularly suspicious of the witch lady. I didn't know her name, but I knew she was spooky, just by looking at her. I caught rare, fleeting glimpses of her as she moved about the shadows of her yard in the spring and summer. I always avoided her, keeping to the far opposite side of the street. She made me uneasy with a familiar anxiety. She needed to be watched, although I dreaded interviewing her.

I arrived at Detective Hines' front lawn, noticing the well-manicured hedges led me to a thought. Detective Hines had a yardman come every week and take care of his lawn. I wasn't sure what he looked like, but he was around the area a lot, perhaps even maintaining other lawns in the area. I remembered an episode of *Police Woman*, in which Pepper stated, "In the absence of motive, what about crime of opportunity?" I had no idea what the motive was in this crime, but I could look at it as a crime of opportunity. Some crazy person who was around at the time and saw an opportunity. The yardman maybe?

Not sure what to do next, I decided to walk around the back of the Hines' house to get a feel for how I might approach the detective about the murder. As I came around the side, I heard a door slam. Detective Hines' voice called out, "I love you, too, baby. See you on the flip side!"

I casually walked back to the sidewalk, hoping he would not see that I just came from behind his house.

"Bree, is that you?"

I looked over and waved. His colors, blending with the early morning light, were a mix of gentle hues.

"I hardly recognized you in that hat! What are you doing up so early?"

"Oh, just, you know, getting a little exercise, I guess."

Detective Hines reached for the door of his car. "Take care, kiddo. Stay safe."

This was my opportunity; it was now or never. "Uh, wait. Detective Hines, I want to ask you something."

He paused and turned to me as I ran toward him. "Bree, what's up?"

"Everybody's talking about that girl they found up at my school, the one that was killed. If it was someone from around here—the killer I mean—well, it would be kind of scary, right? I mean, well, I was just wondering if you were working on the murder case."

Detective Hines hesitated for a moment. I could see the muscle in his jaw twitching. "Yeah, I'm working on it. I'm the lead detective, actually. Not a case anyone would choose to be in charge of. Why did you want to know, Bree? Did you see or hear anything I should know about?"

I shuffled my feet, thinking about what to say. "No, I haven't seen anything. I was just curious, since I knew you were on the police force. Do you think it could be someone from around here?"

Detective Hines touched my shoulder. "No one really knows at this point, kiddo. Murder or no murder, you just remember to be safe, O.K?"

"There is one more thing I was wondering about…"

"Yes?" He was trying to be patient but I could tell he was anxious to get going.

"I was wondering if I could baby-sit for your wife and you again some time. I just love your baby!" What *was* that kid's name?

Detective Hines rubbed his forehead and thought for a few seconds before his face broke out in a determined grin. "You know," he said, pointing at me, "that actually is a great idea! Gayla and I were just talking that we probably won't even get lunch together today, what with my caseload and all. I bet she'd love a surprise date next Saturday!"

"Saturday works for me!"

"How about you be at my house by six p.m., and we got a deal."

"Thank you! Oh, yes, I'll be there... I mean here!" I said, gesturing toward his house. I was elated! This was so easy. My plan was coming together better than I expected. Surely I could find some kind of relevant information in his home. I was almost too excited to continue on my spy route, but not quite.

I headed on down the street to the residence of my number one suspect. I opened my pad of paper and wrote:

The man with the camera, what do I know about him? He's old, in his fifties, I'd guess. He lives alone. I've seen him on his deck, watching people through his telephoto lens. He gives me the creeps, always spying like that. Does he watch me? My house?

I decided to pay him a little visit, perhaps even knock on his door. After my encounter with Detective Hines, I felt confident and unafraid. I was thinking up my excuse as I strode purposefully around the corner toward the back of Cameraman's house. Oh, my God. There he was. Leaning across the back rails of his deck, lenses, camera cases and rolls of film spread out all over the place. That pervert. He had his camera, of course, only this time it looked like he was watching the house behind him. It didn't even look like he was taking pictures. Just watching, through that big, fat lens. I wondered who lived in the house he studied so intently. A wave of fear washed over me and I hesitated, afraid to approach him. If he was indeed the killer, I might be setting myself up. I decided to watch him from behind the big maple tree in Mrs. Barker's yard.

I didn't know Cameraman's name, but I knew he was a solitary soul. I remembered noticing that on Christmas Day there were never any cars at his house. I'd even seen him out shoveling snow, all alone, on Christmas. I realized I never saw anyone at his house. I thought he must be a real creep not to have any friends or family that wanted to be around him.

He wasn't really ugly, just kind of pathetic looking. Rather tall with a wiry build, silvery hair framed a sad face.

I stared hard at Cameraman, trying to comprehend the colors swirling around him. He was too far away. What kind of excuse could I come up with to get close enough to examine his colors? I jotted a note on my pad.

I hadn't made it very far up the street when I noticed the sun had risen well above the rooftops, and decided I better get home before Father noticed I was gone.

I heard him in the shower as I came inside. I slid onto a stool at the kitchen bar, after making myself a glass of Tang and began munching on the Pop-Tarts I'd thrown in my bag. A lot my friends' parents made a big deal about too much sugar being bad for you, but not my parents. I worried more than they did, like the year before, they banned red M&M's, something about Red Dye #2 causing cancer or tumors. I worried about that for weeks, all the red dye I had consumed in my twelve years. Surely I already had a tumor, like those rats they tested the dye on. I flicked on the portable television, hoping for more news on Rachel Carter's death, but I became temporarily distracted with an episode of *Captain Kangaroo*, even at 12 years-old, that rabbit still cracked me up. I finally found a station that was talking about the murder when Father stepped out of the bathroom and into the kitchen.

"Bree, turn that crap off now!" He yelled so loud that he scared me right off the barstool.

"Father! I just wanted to hear more about that girl! It happened so near our house." I climbed back onto the barstool as Father turned off the television.

"There is nothing to learn! Have you got that? What's done is done!"

How could he say that? "But the killer hasn't been caught. There *is* a lot to learn. What if we're in danger? What if I'm in danger?"

Father stared at me blankly for a moment, then his face began to turn a dark angry red. "We're not in any danger. You're not in any danger! I'm not going to tell you again! Her murder doesn't concern us!"

The moment he uttered "doesn't concern us," I knew better. My obsession with solving the murder had less to do with my ego and more to do with the unwavering belief that there was an invisible thread tying Rachel and me together. All I had to do was find that thread and I would find the murderer. Staying on Father's good side was going to be necessary to having the freedom to continue my investigation.

I said in my sweetest voice, "Father, I'm all ready to go to the studio with you. Would you cook lunch for me? You haven't done that in a long time." I didn't realize I'd used Mom's technique to calm him.

Father's angry face relaxed with the change of subject. "OK, Breezy, I do need your help. Let me go tell Dorothy good-bye. Then we'll be on our way."

Father drove a 1934 Pontiac. He'd totally redone it himself; it was beautiful and complete with a CB radio. People always stared and sometimes they'd wave as we drove around in the old car. I kind of liked the attention; Father seemed oblivious to it. He also had a truck down at the studio that he used for deliveries.

Englewood had changed a lot in the last year, but then I suppose most towns across America had. Much of the town had been repainted to show our patriotism, from buildings and fire hydrants, to the locomotives on the railroad. The Bicentennial was a party that had taken several years to prepare and gallons of paint. America was invited to celebrate its patriotism in the most flamboyant and colorful style we could create. The spirit was competitive by the very nature of its enthusiasm. My father had advised me in a teasing way that if I stood still in one spot too long, someone would decorate me with red, white and blue paint.

Father was very patriotic himself, having served in Vietnam, but he felt most of the decorations were in bad taste. He had always been opinionated about how others chose to decorate, working with a wealthy clientele, creating stained glass windows for their huge homes. Most of his business, though, was creating stained glass windows for synagogues and cathedrals and churches. That was why he knew the Bible so well. Most windows incorporated scriptural references through symbols, pictures or actual wording etched into the glass design. He often sat and read the Bible in the late evenings. I had once asked him why he found the Bible so interesting yet we didn't go to church. That question prompted a long lecture on the problems with organized religion that I really didn't understand. When I asked my mom the same question, she explained that Father had lost his faith in Vietnam but was trying to find it again.

An old, historic building in downtown Englewood housed Father's studio. It had been originally built as a church, but hadn't seen a congregation in decades. The owners prior to Father had gutted most of the interior and used it as antique store, but they had left the leaded glass windows intact and so had Father. He repaired those that were bowed or cracked so that the sunlight penetrating the multi-colored panels made a rainbow of prisms dance across the wood floors.

The studio itself was a work of art. He was surrounded by beautiful stained glass windows and works of art from other artists that he admired. His work table was immaculate, his tools arranged in perfect order. A pegboard of hooks displayed soldering irons, foil and lead wrapped in neat circles. Because of the turpentine he used in mixing glazing for the windows, Father's studio not only looked artistic, it smelled artistic.

We entered through the back of the studio, which was more convenient to the parking lot. The massive front doors of the studio were made of ancient oak with beautiful, ornate carvings, but the back door was an ugly, heavy metal thing opening to concrete stairs leading down to a dank and musty basement. Turning right, we crossed the threshold into the main part of the studio.

Father flicked on the lights and his stereo simultaneously. His studio cat sauntered up and rubbed against my leg. Father had named him Van Gogh because one of his ears was missing, probably bitten off in a catfight before Father found him in the alley behind the studio. I reached down and scratched Van Gogh behind his remaining ear.

"O.K., Breezy." Father was already bent over one of the work tables. "I made a list of what needs to be done. Here's the deal: I'll pay you twenty bucks if you get everything done on the list before 4:30; otherwise, I'm only paying you $1.50 an hour minus an hour for lunch—after what happened last time."

Last time he didn't think I worked hard enough or fast enough. That was why no employee lasted very long with him. He expected everyone to work as hard as he did and that was nearly impossible. Aunt Sharon called him Frank Lloyd Wright on speed.

I looked down at the list. Jeepers, how was I going to get all this cleaning done by 4:30? One and a half an hour wouldn't be bad, but twenty sounded really good. I vowed to focus and work hard. Maybe I could do it. I grabbed the broom and began sweeping the hardwood floors. They got really dirty from all the lead dust and chips of glass. I started sweeping at the front of the studio, to stay out of Father's way while he was working.

The front of the studio was filled with large stained glass windows hanging from oak rafters; most of these were for sale. My favorite was of a pensive-looking little girl lying in the grass, looking at the clouds above her. I don't know why this one appealed to me so much. Maybe because I, too, daydreamed in the long summer grass, gazing up at the clouds, thinking about life and all its mysteries.

I have memories of sitting on the front steps of our house on warm evenings with my father, Mom inside bustling around in the kitchen while he and I talked about anything that popped into our minds. Father and I would look up at the sky and wonder aloud if there was life on other planets, if animals went to heaven when they died, if Aunt Sharon would ever get married, and whether lightening bugs were really fairies with flashlights.

That's what Father's art work was capable of doing. Like cathedral windows in medieval times, his stained glass creations told stories. Not just arrangements of colored glass suspended in an opening but designs enlivened in light to convey a mood or message to the beholder.

Two large Oriental rugs covered the well-worn hardwood floors, their colors fading with footsteps and time. I worked my way toward Father's table and saw that he was working on something besides a church window for a change.

Hunched over, assembling the mosaic of glass, the design laid out in front of him, I watched him work without his being aware. Instead of classical music, today he was listening to Paul Simon's *Mother and Child Reunion*. I leaned against my broom and asked, "Who are these windows for? They're beautiful!"

Father loved receiving compliments on his work. He smiled. "They're for a woman who's building a house. She wants these as a divider between her bedroom and master bath."

"Are those all different kinds of birds?" I was amazed at the detail going into each individual bird.

"Yes they are. She wants as many birds as I can artistically fit into the windows. And, she said each bird has to be different. She loaned me her bird books, so that helps. She's head of the Audubon Society or something."

"Wow! I mean, not wow that she's head of the Audubon Society, but wow, that's a lot of work for you!"

Father smiled again. "Yes, Breezy, it is. But that's all right, because I explained to her that the more pieces of glass I use, the more it costs."

I looked at all the pieces already scattered across the table. "How many pieces will it have when you're finished?"

"Oh, I'm guessing fifteen hundred."

"Ka-ching! Maybe I'll get some Izod shirts for school after all! So, how much do you charge per piece?"

"None of your business."

"If you charge, um, $1.33 per piece, you'd make almost $2,000, well, $1,995 to be exact. That would be plenty for you to share with me."

"Don't hold your breath. I have bills to pay, you know."

"Oh, those nasty things. Hey, are you going to hide anything in her windows for her to find?"

Father liked to hide little pictures, either etched or camouflaged within the pattern, and delighted in their obscurity—it was like a game to him. He once did an elaborate front door for a man that had the man's last name hidden in the foliage; it took the man four years before he discovered it. Father was always disappointed when his odd version of hide-and-seek was over.

Father looked down at his window and thought for a moment. "I suppose I'll hide something in this window. What do you think?"

"I think you should, definitely. Maybe you could hide some symbol from the Audubon Society or something."

Father intoned, *"Do not be afraid of those who kill the body but cannot kill the soul. Rather be afraid of the one who can destroy both the soul and body in hell! Are not two sparrows sold for a penny? Yet not one of them will fall to the ground apart from the will of your God!'*

Alright, maybe he was pulling my leg with that quote.

"Actually, I was thinking of hiding a fallen sparrow. Of course, if she's some Audubon Society freak, she'll probably get pretty upset if she finds a dead bird in her window!" Father snorted. I always thought he had a morbid sense of humor.

"Is this going to be *the* perfect window?" Father had been on a quest, as long as I could remember, to create the 'perfect stained glass window'. He had told me, many times, the only stained glass window that was truly perfect, was the Rose Window in Notre Dame.

Father studied the glass pieces before him. "No, I knew before I began. I always know before I begin. It will not be perfect, but, you never know, the next one may be the one."

I decided I better stick with my work and let Father deal with his bird windows. I shouldered my broom and went back to sweeping.

By lunchtime I was famished but hesitated to stop working. I really wanted to go for the whole twenty dollars. I could smell Father's Chinese food cooking in the wok in the back kitchenette, which pretty much cinched my decision to put down the toothbrush and Ajax I was using in the crevices around the window ledge.

I walked back to the kitchen, where Father was busy stirring vegetables and chicken, the delicious steam rising and swirling thick around him.

He barely glanced at me. "I invited Moose to come over and eat with us." It was a statement, and I could tell he wasn't waiting for my response.

I didn't mind, I liked Moose. He ran the Jennifer Sullivan Drug and Alcohol Center next door. He was a big scruffy-looking guy with a brown beard that looked dirty, like it could almost have something living in it. He always wore the same clothes; jeans, a T-shirt and motorcycle boots. Father and Moose were in Vietnam together. Father told me Moose was almost killed in Vietnam, and that he saved Moose's life. Maybe that's why Moose was especially friendly toward me.

I felt sorry for Moose and I think Father did too. Soon after the war Moose spent a few months in jail, although Father would never tell me why. His wife divorced him during his jail time. Moose left jail a broken man and still prone to alcohol abuse. Then, if that wasn't all bad enough, later his 17-year-old daughter, Jennifer, was killed in a hit-and-run accident. Like Popeye says, Moose had all he could stands and he couldn't stands no more. The pain of Jennifer's death sobered Moose. He joined Alcoholics Anonymous and eventually started his own alcohol counseling center, housed in the building adjoining Father's art studio. That made it pretty convenient for Moose and my father to keep in touch. Outside of Vietnam I couldn't see that they had anything else in common.

For whatever reason Moose had started collecting old coins, and sometimes he brought a new purchase over for me to see. Sometimes he brought me Bicentennial quarters and half dollars for my own collection. I think it made him feel good that I showed an interest in his hobby, especially since Father just blew him off. Moose thought Father just wasn't into coin collections, but I knew the real reason was that Father saw Moose's spending habits as a character flaw. I'd heard him tell Mom that spending money on money was as dumb as buying useless crap out of the Sears catalog.

"I'm glad Moose is coming for lunch. I like him." I decided to respond, whether Father wanted my opinion or not. I did like Moose, as far as I knew he was my father's only real friend, but mostly Moose made me feel special. I don't think I looked much like his daughter, but sometimes I would catch Moose looking at me and I knew he was remembering Jennifer.

Mom said Moose would never recover from the loss of his only child. I had seen real pain and fear in her eyes when she said this; I guess both imagining and denying that she could ever lose me. I wanted to tell her it could never happen, but she had changed the subject so quickly that the words of reassurance had never come out. Then cruel fate had stabbed Moose again.

I hesitated to ask but my curiosity was stronger than my trepidation, "Father, did they find his daughter's body yet?" Someone had robbed and desecrated Jennifer's grave the month before. No one knew who or why and, of course, Moose had been a basket case ever since. What kind of creeps would do something so gruesome? How could so much happen to one person? Could a person's life be cursed?

Father put down his spatula and turned to look at me. "Not that I'm aware of, but Moose sounded distressed when he called this morning. He might want to talk to me alone, so you'd better plan to eat in the studio and keep an eye out for customers. Moose and I'll eat back here in the kitchen."

I was disappointed, but he wasn't asking for my approval, so I didn't say anything. Maybe I was learning to hold my tongue.

I heard the front door chime and walked out to greet Moose. He shuffled in, big meaty shoulders slumped and head bowed like a man in prayer—or maybe weighed down beyond prayer. It was sad seeing the contrast between Father's confidence and Moose's despair.

"Hey, Moose! The food smells great, doesn't it?" I tried to sound cheerful, but Moose's colors were frayed and charred by burnt black edges. I remembered that I hadn't seen him since the grave robbery thing and I figured I wasn't such a great reminder of his daughter now.

"Hey, kid." Moose gave me a hug and I felt a little better about being there. "Yeah...oh yeah, smells good. Don't expect me to eat, now. I just came by to talk to your dad for a few."

"Well, OK. He's in the kitchen. I'm going to eat out here with Van Gogh."

Moose stroked my hair absently, then wandered back to the kitchen. He looked so sad I could hardly stand it. I knew I'd probably get in trouble, but I just had to know what they were talking about. I also knew my father would probably blow his stack if he caught me eavesdropping, but I really couldn't stop myself.

In the kitchen Father handed me a plate piled high with his steaming hot concoction. I said thanks and headed back to the studio. I paused just around the corner so I could still hear. Sitting on the floor, I gingerly sampled Father's sizzling, spicy, delicious lunch. Rice, onion, bacon and egg all squashed together and fried in peanut oil. This was comfort food at its best. I thought Moose should try it.

I heard Father's voice first. "So, Moose. Talk to me."

Moose was quiet for a moment before he answered, "A detective came by the office today. They... they've found my baby," he groaned. "Jennifer's bones, over by Brighton school." His voice cracked. "Why would somebody do that? What kind of animal would... I can't... I don't get it!"

Silence again. Moose roared, "And the damn cops think I did it! They think I'm just another dopehead vet. They're trying to frame me for that little girl's murder!"

I was too shocked and surprised to eat. That was completely nuts. Rachel's body was the only body I had seen at the school. It made no sense. Did the police think Moose had killed Jennifer, or Rachel? It must be some kind of terrible mistake.

I could hear Moose cussing up a storm, which wasn't uncommon for him even on a normal basis but this time he was pounding his fists and yelling so loudly, that I could barely hear Father's voice. "That's asinine! What would *you* know about the kid's murder?"

"You tell me! I'm so angry they did nothing to find my little Jennifer's body, and they're sure not looking for whoever it was that stole her. And now they treat me like a criminal. Me! I'm the victim! I'm the victim here!" Moose's voice shook with anger.

"They wanted to know where I was the night of the murder. I told them I was with my girlfriend, Lisa, at her pad. Stupid cops. They're only looking at me because I have a record. Dammit, why can't they leave that be? All I ever wanted is another chance. I've kept my nose clean—they ain't got nothing on me, those pigs.

"Aaaahhh, Jennie, my sweet baby... I just... I want her back..." Moose sobbed and coughed. "I just want my baby back and bury her properly, all over again. But no, those pigs said my sweet Jennie has to stay with them—for evidence, they said."

I thought, okay, so the police think Moose murdered Rachel. I doubt if he even knew Rachel. And what did Jennifer's remains have to do with anything? This wasn't fair or logical or good investigating on Detective Hines part at all. Moose had every right to be furious.

Moose continued, "You know what else those stupid pigs did? They took my coin collection! They, like, destroyed my office; God only knows what they thought was in there. So what's that all about? My coins were the only things I had of value. Just a simple little hobby to occupy my mind and maybe build a little something so Lisa and I could have a future. They kept asking questions about my coins, like there was a problem with them, or something. No way I was going to tell them anything without a lawyer! Then they totally threatened me—told me they'd, like, haul me in!

"Geoff, they wouldn't even, like, tell me what they were looking for! I reckon I can't talk to them without a lawyer. I can't afford this right now. Why me? Why is God trying to destroy me?"

I could hear Moose crying, big harsh sobs. Normally that would be impossible to imagine, but after seeing Rachel's body, I guess not much shocked me anymore. Aunt Sharon had once said women cry and men get angry, but I knew now that was chauvinistic.

I didn't believe for a minute that Moose could have anything to do with Rachel Carter's murder. Sure, he was a giant-size guy, but he was a creampuff. He was like the sweetest man ever, and usually he had soft, almost sad colors all around him. My stomach was starting to cramp and hurt really bad. Why would someone use Jennifer's bones in a murder scenario? And what did that have to do with anything? Why would the police question Moose, of all people? He was a victim, not a criminal.

Father spoke, "Moose, I'll stand with you. I'll be a character witness for you. I'm writing down the name of a great attorney—his name is Leonard, he's an ethical wolf. My family used his firm when my dad was killed. I want you to call me if you need anything, anything at all. Dorothy and I'll support you, man. We know the kind of human being you are."

Good! Father was going to help Moose. That made me feel a little better. If Father didn't think Moose did it—and I knew Moose couldn't do something like that—then surely the police would figure it out too, regardless of some little jail time. A thought flashed into my mind; all the more reason to spy on Detective Hines. I needed to keep my investigation going, so if the real killer was in my neighborhood, I could find him and save Moose.

The whole thing about Jennifer's remains being there was too crazy to even consider. I couldn't get my mind wrapped around the idea. Grave robbery was ghoulish. I wouldn't think about it; I would concentrate on helping Moose instead.

I suppose at this point I should have trusted my father, at least to some degree, to fix this mess Moose was in. But I was determined to help, just in case. Father had saved Moose once before, but could he do it again?

Confusing feelings floated through my mind. I was remembering the time when I was six, and climbed an oak tree in our backyard. Higher and higher I climbed, only looking up, not thinking about consequences, like how I was going to get back down. When I ran out of branches I finally looked down. The ground seemed to fall farther and farther away.

I began crying; louder and louder, tears streaming down my cheeks, until Father finally came running. He tried to coax me back down, talking softly and urgently, but I was afraid and wouldn't move. He couldn't come up after me, because he was too big for the branches that my skinny little body had been able to shimmy. I remember so clearly how he kept telling me to trust him. Just trust him and that he would catch me if I fell. This man—my father—was telling me to trust him, but I couldn't. The fear of letting go was too great. I trusted myself to hang on more than I trusted him to catch me.

Eventually, with much coaxing, I finally closed my eyes and let his soothing voice guide me back down. When I got to the final branch I jumped into his arms.

That was exactly what I wanted to do right now. Just trust him and fall into his arms. Let him handle getting a lawyer for Moose. Let him protect us from the real murderer. It was just this morning Father had argued that Rachel's murder had nothing to do with us and now, here we were, involved with the accused. I had no choice but to continue my investigation. There was too much to lose and I decided to trust my own vague instincts. Knowing in this case, I'd better not let myself fail.

When Moose left I stayed out of Father's way, moving the broom around absently while he cleaned up the wok and plates. The conversation with Moose must have taken a lot out of Father because he abruptly announced he was closing the studio two hours early. I was only two jobs short of getting the twenty dollars. Father paid me ten. I tried to sound grateful, but I was really disappointed. I'd tried hard to get the work done but he cut the time short and I'm pretty sure neither one of us had our hearts in our work that afternoon anyway.

As he glanced at the clock on his work table, I heard him proclaim, *"For God so loved the world that he gave his only Son, that whosoever believes in him shall not perish but have eternal life!"*

I thought to myself, that's John 3:16. I remember Father telling me that verse when I saw someone at a golf tournament on television holding up a sign that had nothing on it but 'John 3:16'. I looked at the clock. Its hands set at 3:16, and at that moment I watched the minute hand tick to 3:17. How many times had Father quoted from the Bible based on what he saw on a clock? The enigma grew more complex each day. He was a savior; he was a tyrant. Ranting and raging one minute, comforting and soothing the next. Could I ever understand him? Could I ever please him? If I could help Moose, maybe I could win more of my father's affection.

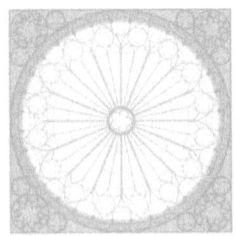

CHAPTER SIX

FATHER WAS SOMBER as we drove home. I could tell he was deeply disturbed about Moose. I rode along in subdued silence, wanting so much to ask him about Jennifer's bones—wondering why anyone would do such a thing—biting my tongue for fear of upsetting him.

Nothing is ever simple. When we pulled up to the house we saw Mom standing in the yard holding a hatchet, her housecoat drenched in sweat. We both stared at her and I heard Father mutter, "What in tarnations?" I was thinking pretty much the same thing. He pulled the car into the garage and I followed him to Mom.

Mom began her explanation, "Dorothy killed them all! Every last one of them is dead! I took care of the problem on my own!"

I looked up at Father, who glanced down at me then back at Mom. "You killed *who* or *what*, Dorothy?" I didn't want to know. While I was a little frightened, I was also hoping none of our neighbors were watching as I tried to shrink back farther behind my father's masculine frame.

Mom grabbed Father's hand, still clutching the bloody hatchet, and pulled him towards the big trash dumpster by the garage.

"I was carrying out trash, you know tomorrow is trash day, and I was looking straight ahead, not down. Suddenly there was a tickling sensation on my legs. I looked down and there were dozens of snakes squirming and crawling around my legs! Maybe a hundred!

"I got the hatchet out of the garage." Mom's eyes glittered and she smacked her lips nervously. "I killed them! I killed them!" She began showing Father, the bloody axe still in her hands, how she did it, making 'whack, whack' sounds with her mouth.

Father reached out to stop her arm from swinging so close to us and asked in an unusually calm voice, "Dorothy, baby, where are those snakes now?"

Mom stopped her demonstration, wiped the sweat from her face and said, "Come here. Dorothy will show you. I've cleaned up the mess—not to worry. Not to worry."

We moved closer to the trash dumpster as she ceremoniously flung open the lid. Father and I looked in at the same time. We were assaulted by the disgusting smell and sight of hundreds of chunks of bloody snake parts piled upon the trash. I thought I was going to throw up. They had been snakes on a migration across our yard and I felt a stab of sympathy for their loss even though I hate snakes.

I heard Father's deep voice soulfully reciting, *"The great dragon was hurled down—that ancient serpent called the devil, who leads the world astray."*

He reached out and patted Mom's shoulder, as if to say 'That's my girl,' but what he said was, "Dorothy, why don't you get cleaned up and make me a snack? I'm going inside to watch a little television."

That was that. Another surreal day at the Grants'. Father continued on into the house. I figured that meant it was time for him to regroup with a little TV and Scotch. What was going to ground *me*? Despite her obesity and casual attire that made her look like a sleepwalker, I'd never been embarrassed by my mom before. How many people looked at our family and thought we might all be a little crazy?

I had time before dinner to consult my friends in the attic about Moose's situation. I resolutely put Mom's bizarre actions out of my mind. Somehow it felt less threatening now to focus on Moose's problems than to worry about her. I thought I knew how to help Moose. I didn't have a clue how to help my mom.

I remember when I began the attic cleansing rituals to help Father control his anger. This was about the time he started the capricious mood swings that kept me in constant turmoil, feeling the pain of his frenzied ranting. What was almost worse was that he seemed oblivious to the effect his inconsistencies had on either my mother or me.

Snug and safe in my secret space, surrounded by my five companions, my secluded protectors, I could escape the chaos below. The ceremony gave me a sense of control and I believed it worked, if only temporarily. And that someday it would offer permanent hope.

I rested my hands on the Ouija board, looking for answers with Kelly, Terry, Gene, Stacey, and Jesse staring down around me, my guardian angels. As I told them about Moose, they were as shocked as I that he could even be suspected of such a heinous act. They were all asking questions at once; questions I had asked myself; questions with no answers. Placing my hands on the plastic indicator, I concentrated on the question, 'Who killed Rachel?' while praying silently that the Ouija spirits would not begin their answer by pointing to the letter 'M'. My hands trembled as the indicator began to move. My impeccably dressed associates crowded around in anticipation, the incense smoke swirling about us.

The board revealed one letter at a time. "C-L-O-S-E." What was that supposed to mean? Close? Who's close?

Jesse stuttered with his inner voice, "M-m-maybe the k-k-killer is c-close, Bree."

I turned my eyes toward Jesse. "I'm scared to death that the killer is stalking me! Are you saying that's a distinct possibility?"

"It was just my f-f-first thought. It could be M-m-moose, too, you know. He's always been c-c-c-close to you."

"No, it can't be! I just know it can't be Moose! Besides, he's got an alibi! I heard him tell Father he was with his girlfriend."

Terry spoke with his inner voice next, his clipped British accent softened by concern. "This murderer…could it perhaps be someone else you know? Someone of whom you haven't yet thought?"

"Like who, though, Terry? Somebody in the neighborhood I've missed?"

Stacey added, "Yeah, and think about this: How do you know Moose's girlfriend isn't just covering for him?"

I thought about it. "I guess I don't know. It's a hunch. I believe Moose is too gentle to kill anyone. Besides, what does 'close' mean, anyway? It could mean close the door, lock the windows—that kind of thing."

"Let's analyze," Gene interjected, "'Close' could mean the person is in close proximity to you."

"Or," Terry added, "could it perhaps imply someone else close to the killer, such as Moose? I've got it! Perhaps Hines is close to solving the murder! Or—"

My head felt like it was going to explode. "Stop! God! This is too much!"

Terry went on with affection, "Dear girl, 'Close' does not have to be a scary word. Perhaps it means you have people who care close to you."

Kelly spoke, "Bree, honey, just keep your little ole eyes and ears open. You'll figure it out, sugar pie. We all believe in you."

"Well, I'm glad somebody has faith in me, because I sure don't!"

That night as I lay in bed I could hear Father at the piano. The distant music calmed me momentarily, but my eyes were glued on the window across from my bed. The Ouija board implied I was on the right track. I decided 'Close' must mean the killer was somewhere between me and the school. Did I know the killer? Did he know me? Was he out there watching me, maybe even right now? I thought I could feel him near me... but who was he? Close? Close to what? Or to who? Eventually I slept.

When I was in the fourth grade, our teacher, my teacher, Mr. Burton, played two films on volcanos as part of the science curriculum. One was in color, one in black and white. Both showed violent, fiery eruptions and molten lava first seeping, then flowing, from fissures in the earth. Lava coursed through the streets of picturesque mountain villages setting trees and bushes on fire.

In our encyclopedia at home there were pictures of the destruction at Pompeii, its people captured in immortality by the ash from Mt. Vesuvius. Even though it was geologically improbable that our town of Englewood sat atop a fault line, for months after the films I had dreams of a volcano erupting from our backyard.

Now, even though our house did not have a basement, I was experiencing nightmares of water seeping into that non-existent basement.

I am cautiously climbing my way down spongy, rotted steps into a dank cellar. As my eyes adjust to the dark and the silence, I see tiny streams of water seeping through the hairline cracks and as I watch the cracks widen until...

I awoke with my lungs burning in effort under a crushing weight. Breathe, I told myself, breathe. Slowly I felt my body release its tension and the fear subsided.

I lay completely still in my bed and listened to the quiet sounds of our sleeping house. The arms of a Russian Olive bush scratched at the window screen. Attic joists creaked in the cooling dark of the night. Somewhere a muffled siren wailed its warning. And my mind ceased its senseless panicked imaginings as I turned my radio on quietly. Queen's *Bohemian Rhapsody* was playing and I smiled while drifting back to sleep, lost in random thoughts, the nightmare fading in memory.

"You have so many talents you know," he mused looking up from his reading. I noticed it wasn't the new book I bought for him but I pretended not to care.

He was silent for a minute and added, "No one else appreciates your talents, but I do."

I promised myself I would forget that horrible night. It is what is best for everyone. But sometimes late at night it occurs to me I could have stopped him, before it was too late. I say I am afraid of him but in truth, I think I could have stopped him… if I had really wanted to.

"You're worrying again. I can tell. Remember, there's still more work to be done. Loose ends we'll have to tie up." He was looking directly at me. "This isn't over—not by a long shot. Besides, now you're involved, whether you want to be or not. There's nothing you can do about it."

CHAPTER SEVEN

WHEN YOU LIVE in a part of the country that celebrates four distinct seasons, summer is a three-month period that must have as much sunshine squeezed from it as possible. The best way I knew to do this was with water, a few friends and lots of time outdoors. During the summer, the public pool was my perfect place to relax and after completing my spy route, I knew I'd need to do something relaxing.

So, the following morning I told my mom I was going swimming. Next, I called my friend Lori to see if she was going up to the pool. I didn't like going places by myself where there might be a crowd of kids my age. Most of the time I preferred to be alone—I'd rather sit in my room and read my set of encyclopedias. I didn't think I really needed other people. Many of the kids tried so hard to be popular and I thought it was a joke.

I hated myself when I worried about being popular and then I worried some more.

I liked Lori, although I was not sure why. After being around her I always walked away feeling insecure about myself. Aunt Sharon said no one should hang around people who make them feel bad about themselves. She said when you have an interaction with someone, you should walk away feeling better about yourself, not worse, and that truly gracious people know how to make others feel that way.

I didn't really have a lot of choices when it came to friends. Some of the girls in my class thought I was weird, I guess because I was the only girl in the gifted program, which had only been around for two years and was part of some college research grant. Some of the other girls I didn't necessarily want to be friends with, because either I didn't have anything in common with them, or I thought they were weird. Obviously none of this was going to make me more popular. Lori was pretty smart; at least we had that in common.

I didn't know why she wasn't in the gifted program, except that our teacher said the guidelines for acceptance were really tough. Only six students from the entire school district were in the program, five boys and me. Fortunately, since the program was housed at the school in my neighborhood, I still ran into the other kids throughout the day. Lori told me she was tested and that she only missed qualifying by one point, and that I only got in because my father was a famous artist. I never knew if that was true or not. Lori often hurt my feelings, but I wasn't so sure if it was because she wasn't gracious or because I brought it on myself.

Lori said she'd meet me at the pool at 1:00. She was anxious to discuss Rachel's murder but I put her off. I wanted to get as much information as I could, but I didn't trust her enough to share what I had learned from Moose.

My spy route had been a total bust that morning. I had decided to focus on the people between me and the school but I was having trouble getting anyone to take me seriously. People either wouldn't answer their door or when they did answer, they told me they didn't know anything. I needed them to at least answer their door so I could inspect their colors. Being a detective was more difficult than I expected.

After my route, I changed into my swimsuit, grabbed a towel, Coppertone, and my transistor radio and went out to the garage to get my bike.

Our city pool was nestled in a park with lots of trees shading the playground and within shouting distance of a couple of ball diamonds. The pool was divided into three sections. I had long outgrown the kiddy pool, besides I knew the little kids peed in it. The main pool was where we would swim, if we actually ever did get in the water. The third area, the diving area, is where we spent most of our time laying out, watching the boys show off.

The pool was crowded, and I had to wait in line behind a bunch of obnoxious little kids before I could get in. I paid with a dollar bill, knowing I would get a quarter as change, *hoping* it would be a Bicentennial quarter. My Bicentennial coin collection had grown. Nine Washington quarters, three Kennedy half dollars and one Ike dollar. Father said I was wasting my time, that they would never be worth anything, but I liked collecting things and anyway I knew my Bicentennial coins would always be worth something because—well, they're money. The only buyer's remorse I felt was towards my Pet Rock collection. Even I had to admit, $3.95 for a rock seemed like a lot.

I received my change, only a plain quarter, no luck. I went through the locker room, where the attendants expected us to rinse off before entering the pool area, but none of us actually did. Wasn't that the point of chlorine? Lori was easy to find; she was the one with a crowd around her. She gestured dramatically, dominating the poolside talk about Rachel Carter. I stood back and listened, waiting for Lori to notice me. Lori was expounding on the fact that school was canceled "just because of a murder" when she finally noticed me standing toward the back of the circle.

"Hey, Bree! Tell us if you think they had a right to cancel the last day of school!"

All the kids turned their eyes on me. I felt awkward and skinny in my two-piece. Boys told me I was too tall and too skinny, like I didn't already know. I thought I'd never have a boyfriend and sometimes I didn't care. Sometimes I cared a lot. Relatives said I was cute, and that I looked like a young Natalie Wood. Supposedly, I'd grow into my large doe-like eyes and full mouth, losing my waif-like appearance. I figured moms, aunts and grandmas were supposed to make such encouraging assurances. I'd never heard of anyone going back to their grandma and accusing them of making false promises, but it seemed entirely possible in my case.

Lori looked great as usual; even kids who hated her self-centered ways admired her looks, especially her hair, which looked like a Wella Balsam shampoo ad. Sure, I could have stolen the limelight away from her just by mentioning that I'd seen the body. It was tempting and I could imagine the looks on everyone's faces as they gave me their full attention, but it would be a cheap thrill and I knew it.

"Well," I hesitated, "my guess is they had to secure the area in order to conduct the investigation. Kids running around could disturb evidence."

The others nodded in agreement, so I continued, "It's like the Kent State shootings a few years ago, they couldn't very well continue classes there, they had to reenact the student protests and do a thorough investigation..." now I was getting blank stares. How could they not know about the Kent State shootings? Father had lectured me at length about the Vietnam War protests and the trouble the radicals caused.

Kristen's eyes changed from a blank stare to twinkling merriment. "I know who killed that girl!" I gasped as she continued, "Albinos. Escaped albinos from the Albino Farm. Everyone knows that place is haunted!"

I was half irritated and half embarrassed. Kristen was outrageous, but I had almost believed she knew something, some clue, not just stupid gossip from old Englewood legends. Wasn't anyone else taking the murder seriously?

Lori tossed her long blonde hair over her shoulders and shrugged nonchalantly, "So, what's with canceling school? Like, I mean, I got a new Bobbie Brooks outfit to wear to the picnic. And I got my hair frosted, too!"

Most days, Lori's shallowness amused me, but I could hardly take her attitude that afternoon. "You know, Lori, I guess Rachel Carter won't be getting her hair frosted ever again. And I guarantee you that she's had her last day of school *and* her last picnic, unless you count lying in the dirt on the playground a picnic." I turned to walk away, tears burning just below my eyes. I hadn't known Rachel. Her death had nothing to do with me—not really. Besides, my initial reaction had been just like

Lori's, disappointment over the last day of school being cancelled. But I had seen Rachel, or at least Rachel's body and that made us blood sisters in a way.

As I walked off I heard Lori confide to the group, "Bree can be just oh so perfect. She thinks she's superior just because she's in the gifted program. Her dad's artsy-fartsy and her mom's just plain fartsy."

Lori's cute remarks got giggles at my expense. I went to the other side of the pool and planted my skinny butt right into the middle of my beach towel. I considered leaving but decided it would be more healing to my spirit to soak up some of the sun and work on a deep golden tan. Being in the sun was therapeutic and always made me feel better but Lori's comments still burned me up.

Mom was once very pretty; I'd seen pictures of her at Grandma and Grandpa's house. Now she was at least a hundred pounds overweight, and it was more difficult to see the woman she once had been. Mom was quite a bit younger than Father. This didn't bother me particularly, because I thought my father was still a handsome man.

How they had become a couple fueled my imagination. On a rural stretch of two-lane blacktop, my parents met when my mom ran away from home. My father picked her up when she was hitchhiking, something they told me I was never to do. Father said he couldn't resist picking her up. He said she looked like an angel in her white gauze blouse and long wavy black hair. In my mind I can almost visualize the Maxfield Parrish-ness of that moment. I wondered where I'd be when love found me.

When Father spotted her on the shoulder of that winding road, Mom really didn't know where she was headed. I don't know what she was running from or running toward. Two strangers side by side, riding to unknown destinies. Father said he was on his way to fight in Vietnam, Mom said she would wait for him. He married her that week so that she could live on the base, not knowing that he had also left her pregnant.

Just as I finished rubbing Coppertone Oil on my arms, Lori came up and sat beside me. Linking her arms around her knees, she stared at the concrete. She was surrounded by a muddy brown glow. Sometimes I thought she probably had more flat colors because she was so shallow. "I'm sorry I snapped at you over there. I guess I can see your point." Pensively, she glanced around the pool. "I suppose I was just thinking about me again. Imagine that!" she added with a self-deprecating smile. She could be both charming and aggravating within the space of minutes.

"Maybe I'm just not up to talking about the murder. It depresses me."

"Everything depresses you, Bree. You need to lighten up. Rachel Carter's murder is the most exciting thing that ever happened in this hick town. Oh my God, just think—the killer might be somebody we know!"

I was really listening to Lori now, interested in that final thought. Could she read my mind? "Do you really think it could be someone we know?"

"Sure, it could be anyone. I mean, my parents won't even let me ride my bike or walk anywhere by myself until they catch the killer. And, God—the school is like right by your house! The killer might actually live in your neighborhood! Besides, you're always talking about the psychos that live on your street. Well, one of those crack pots could be the killer. I can't even believe your parents let you ride your bike up here." Lori sighed. "Your parents are so cool."

Two minutes ago I had heard Lori say my parents were way less than cool. I couldn't tell if she meant this last remark as a dig so I let it go. The important thing was that if Lori thought the killer could live near me, then maybe I wasn't paranoid after all. "Lori, I told you the people on my street are quirky, not psychos. There's a difference, you know." Looking at Lori, I saw a flicker of color in her shadow, I rubbed my eyes thinking the sun must be playing tricks with my vision.

Before I could think too much about it, Lori's gaze drifted past me as two boys I didn't recognize came over and sat on the concrete in front of us in their wet swimsuits. "Hey Lori, what's up? Who's your friend?"

The boy speaking was not as cute as the other boy staring at Lori, neither of their colors impressed me much, but he was still a fox. Dark curls and nice body—and at least he looked about as tall as me, so my height wouldn't scare him away. I figured they were a year or two older than Lori and me.

"Eric, this is Bree. Bree, this is Eric and his friend Benny." Benny tore his gaze from Lori long enough to give me a once over and a smile, but he only nodded. I felt my flat chest being scrutinized and wanted to pull my beach towel over my body and hide.

"Hello, Bree," Eric said. "Cool name."

"Thanks." So maybe Eric was decent. "And thanks for not making fun of it. People usually say it's weird. Or they ask why my parents gave me such a strange name, a question for which I have no answer."

"I'd never make fun of someone's name. That's mean. I'm cool with different names."

At that very moment I thought I was falling in love. A guy who was not a jerk! Saved at last, saved at last! Changing the subject, I quickly asked, "So, what school do you go to?"

"Benny and I go to Riley. We'll be eighth graders next year."

"Oh! That's where Lori and I will go next year. Cool!"

"Where do you live?" Eric spread out on the end of my towel resting his head on his hand.

I wasn't sure how much to tell him, but we were practically classmates. "Oh, you know the house. It's the one that looks like a space ship landed in Englewood, you know the one with the weird shape."

Eric's face lit up, "The one with all the stained glass windows! Eric actually looked impressed. "I've heard of your dad. He's supposed to be really talented."

Thanks to Father's Bible cursing, I was aware of how 1 Corinthians 13:12 summed up my view of his work, "Now we see through a glass darkly; then we shall see face to face." Like when the stained glass panels my father created rested on the work table in his studio, the windows appeared murky and dark; hiding the beauty and harmony of his skill. Once finally installed, though, Father's creations sprang to life with the radiance of sunlight—his artistry infused with magic. I saw it as a good omen that Eric had respect for Father's work.

Eric and I talked for a while, comparing schools, talking about our favorite records and which TV family we'd rather live with, *The Partridge Family* or *The Brady Bunch*. Then Benny interrupted, "How about the four of us go out tonight? We could meet at the movies."

Oh God, he was putting Eric on the spot. I felt my face turn bright red as Eric looked me right in the eye and said, "I think that's a great idea. How 'bout it?"

Before I could answer, Lori piped up, "Super! Let's do it, Bree! My mom will drive us, and your mom can pick us up."

Geez, was this really happening? "I... I'm not sure I can go until I ask my parents..." Lori had been hanging out with boys since the beginning of sixth grade and assumed my "cool" parents would say I could go, but she didn't know how hard it was going to be for me to ask my father—and neither did I. Up until now, I had not been provided with any opportunities. I tried to imagine his reaction to me having a date. I was clueless.

"Oh, please. Your parents are so easy, Bree. They won't care—you know it!"

"Yeah, you're probably right. OK, let's just do it." I could feel my heart thumping at the thought of my first date. Eric was looking cuter by the minute, and so charming, too. As it was, I forgot to remember the murder. I forgot to remember the murderer. I forgot to remember I still had to get permission to go. The gods were smiling on me and it was easy to forget.

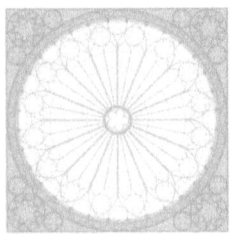

CHAPTER EIGHT

WHEN I GOT home from the pool I found my mom in the kitchen opening her latest delivery from the Sears catalog, apparently another macramé set. Father, sitting in his favorite chair with a glass of Scotch, was listening to his record, *One Flew Over the Cuckoo's Nest*. He beckoned me over. "Breezy, come listen to this part with me."

I climbed into the chair beside him, he put his arm around me and kissed the top of my head. "This is so beautiful." He was referring to the song, *Bus Ride to Paradise*.

When the R-rated movie *One Flew Over the Cuckoo's Nest* came out last year, Father went to see it twice. I thought that was weird. He also owned the book, which he said was much better than the movie. Father had tried to explain how the movie holds a very important political message about society. He said the "east/west" polarity in the story supposedly, represents the opposite philosophies of a person's relationship to society. It seemed important to him that I understand this, so I pretended I did.

He seemed relaxed and in a good mood, so I overcame my trepidation and blurted, "Father, Lori and I met a couple of friends at the pool today…they're boys—Benny and Eric. And anyway, they want us to meet them at the movies tonight. Can I go? We'll be going to the same school next year. They seemed really nice." Gee. That wasn't so hard.

Father looked at me as if seeing me for the first time. I had handled the whole situation wrong. I sounded stupid. I knew he would say no. What had I been thinking? I should have asked Mom first.

"Well, let me think." He really seemed to be considering my request. I waited. It was an eternity before he answered. "Yes, you may go, but I want you to remember one thing and only one thing."

I should have felt relieved. Why did I feel like I was going to be embarrassed? "What is that one thing, Father?"

He put my chin in his hand and said in a low voice, "All boys are jerks. Remember that, young lady. I'm only letting you go so that you'll learn that now. Sooner rather than later, Breezy."

Was he joking? Sometimes he kidded me in strange ways. "But Father," I said through a pinched and painful mouth, "you were a boy!"

"And I was a jerk. If that boy tries anything fresh, like trying to put his arm around you, you change seats, understand? *Flee from sexual immorality. All other sins a man commits are outside his body, but he who sins sexually, sins against his own body!*"

He wasn't joking. There was nothing funny about it. I hadn't even had my first date yet and I felt like I had done something wrong, something dirty. I started to say I would never do anything like that, but maybe I was learning not to argue with my father. "Yes, Father, I understand." But I didn't understand. I had been looking forward to tonight, now I wanted to hide.

He kissed the top of my head again and said, "That's my sweet girl."

Confused I crawled out of the chair. Eric was not a jerk. Father was wrong about that.

I wanted to see the evening paper and any further reports about the murder or Moose; I didn't ask my parents where it was because I didn't want to have to explain why I wanted it. I casually looked around the living room but didn't see it. I walked through the kitchen and didn't see it there, either.

I had an idea. "Mom, I thought I might look up the movie schedule in the paper. *The Bad News Bears* is still playing. Lori and I got asked out on a double date for tonight. Father said I could go."

Mom gave me a big smile and hug. "That's wonderful, Bree! I'm so happy for you! Your first date! Oh, my dear, I think you're growing up too fast."

"Can you pick us up at the theater? Lori's mom is taking us, O.K.?"

"Of course, honey. That's no problem at all."

"So, the newspaper? Where could it be?"

Mom thought for a second and said, "You know, I believe we didn't get a paper today."

I felt my stomach tighten. "We always get a paper! How can we not have a paper today? The day I need it!"

Mom went back to cutting the vegetables. "Call the theaters for their schedule..."

I was getting a panicky feeling inside. Why didn't we have a paper? Was someone trying to keep me from seeing it? I smelled a conspiracy. I ignored my mom's comment and asked, "Have we ever not gotten a paper before? Why do you think this happened…today of all days?"

I heard my mom sigh. "There are lots of reasons one might not get a paper, the most obvious would be that the paper boy accidentally skipped us on his route."

I thought that could be possible but not probable. I went to my room and called Aunt Sharon to ask her if she had today's newspaper. After some reluctance, she read the article about Rachel Carter to me over the phone. Unfortunately, I couldn't tell her what I learned from eavesdropping on Moose and Father because I was afraid she'd tell my mom what I did.

The article reported the same basic information that had been in the news. In addition, however, it alluded to the ritualistic arrangement of the body. I wondered what that meant. I didn't remember seeing an arrangement of any kind. It looked like your basic TV murder to me—except it was real. I told Aunt Sharon this. The article promised more information after the autopsy reports were received. The word autopsy made me shudder involuntarily.

I thought knowing what was in the newspaper would make me feel better, but it didn't. Fortunately there was still no mention of Moose so maybe the police had come to their senses. Still there were too many unanswered questions. Too many unknowns. I needed more information and felt I would go crazy without those answers, that vital information.

At dinner that night in the Octagon, I could hardly eat in anticipation of my first date. It had taken me two hours to get ready; choosing the perfect outfit required several phone calls to Lori and more outfit changes than I normally completed in a week. I decided on my new sundress, meant for the picnic, thinking it made my breasts look bigger, and sandals that I thought made me look shorter. I added two squirts of Love's Baby Soft. I wasn't allowed to wear make-up except lip balm, so I reviewed my collection of Lip Smackers, choosing the Dr. Pepper flavor because it made my lips look red. The result was that I felt like I looked okay, maybe, barely, better than usual anyway.

I felt Father staring at me throughout dinner. "All dolled up, hmmm. This boy better be worth it." He wasn't smiling as he said this. I didn't reply, averting my gaze, staring down through the glass table. I wanted so much to feel pretty, but now I didn't.

Glancing at my Mickey Mouse watch I saw it was about time for Lori's mom to be at my house, so I rushed through dinner and went to my room to watch out the window for my ride. Lori's mom also didn't have to work. She used to spend a lot of her day hanging around our elementary school as a P.T.A. Mom. She was always dressed up with lots of jewelry even if she was only up at school to run dittos. I didn't think junior high teachers would want her hanging around, so I wasn't sure how she'd fill her days next year.

My stomach was so nervous and upset, I was afraid I was going to be sick. I stood at my window playing with my Etch A Sketch, trying to concentrate on the random lines. At last I saw Lori and her mom pull up in the driveway.

I ran out the front door yelling good-bye to Mom and yelling a reminder for her to pick us up at nine. I stopped short at the passenger side of the car and stood, perplexed by Mrs. King's choice of vehicles. It was a two-seater Porsche 914. Cool car, but hardly practical.

"Lori, uh… where am I supposed to sit?"

Mrs. King looked confused, like she realized for the first time that her car only holds two people. "Oh gosh, Bree, ummm, I guess you and Lori will have to share a seat. Just squeeze in, sweetie!"

Typical. My expectations and reality, always out of step.

"I'm bored," he grumbled. "I can't stand just waiting." He was pacing back and forth and making me nervous with his pent up frustrations. "Let's play a game, a pretend game. Cops and robbers or something. " He feigned slapping himself in the side of the head. "I know. We'll be spies. We can take turns tying each other up and torturing each other."

Agitated as he was, I could tell that he was relishing the possibilities of his fantasy. His moods had become capricious and he was getting more difficult to control. Calmly I suggested we go for a drive and relax.

Even as he acquiesced he turned to me and said, "Maybe we should try again with another girl. The last girl was a poor choice; what we saw with her was wrong. We will look at the next girl more closely and make sure she has something special about her that makes her worthy."

This is not what I meant to stir up with him. What am I going to do? How can I live with this knowledge, am I not as guilty as the murderer? I watched and I did nothing. What is going to become of me? What is going to become of him? Maybe if he stopped talking about it I could pretend it never happened…

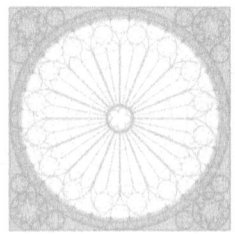

CHAPTER NINE

EXPECTATIONS ARE CHANCY. "Going with a guy" was something many girls my age actually got to do; for me, it had only been a concept. If you were going with a guy, then he was hands-off to your friends. That boy was someone you could write about in your notebook with lots of little hearts. Somebody you could talk to on the phone, and hang out with—if your parents were cool. But there was also the less obvious benefit: the self-esteem that came with knowing the opposite sex found you attractive. These were my expectations, but like I said they were chancy.

Lori and I jumped out of the car at the front of the theater, grateful to stretch our legs. The boys were already waiting for us. They looked different in clothes other than swimsuits, but I guess we did too. I definitely felt more secure in a sundress than I did in a swimsuit. Eric walked over to me, "You look nice, Bree."

"Thanks, so do you." Benny already had his arm around Lori. I thought if Eric put his arm around me I might actually throw up all over my brand new sundress.

Benny and Lori approached us and Benny said, "Come on, let's start this date!"

Eric and I followed them past the front doors of the theater and around the corner to the back of the building. Why were we going back here? I had led my parents to believe we were going to see *The Bad News Bears* because they were very strict about what I saw and only recently allowed me to see PG movies. The last movie I had seen with them was the comedy *Murder by Death*. Lori and I had talked about sneaking into an R-rated movie. We thought it would be more interesting than seeing some lame movie about kids playing baseball.

Maybe we would sneak in through the back exit to avoid having to pay. I wasn't sure I felt good about this idea, but I didn't want to seem like a nerd either, so I kept my mouth shut.

The boys guided us to the alley behind the theater, stopping near some dumpsters. Benny spoke first, "Lori and I'll stay here. Eric, you and Bree go over to that ledge. Dig it?" He cocked his head in the direction of a concrete wall behind the dumpsters.

I finally couldn't stand it anymore. "What's this all about?" I demanded.

Eric took my hand and said, "Trust me." He pulled me up on the ledge and put one arm around my neck and the other on my knee. As he began to kiss me I felt his hand move up my leg. I pulled away, blinking back tears. This was not how I imagined my first date. I was little scared and a lot mad. Was Father always right?

"I thought you were taking us on a date—to the movies! This is just a make-out session!"

Eric threw up his hands in defense. "Hey, don't cry. We can just talk if you want, at first, you know." I couldn't believe I was crying. I couldn't believe I had walked into such a mess. I was stupid and naïve and knew they should lock me up somewhere because Bree Grant didn't stand a chance in the real world.

"No, I don't know… I just want to go home!" I ran back to Lori, but Benny was already sprawled on top of her, making out. "Lori, let's go, please. This is not a date! They're just using us!"

Lori reluctantly pulled away from Benny and sounded perturbed when she spoke, "I'm not leaving, Bree. You can go to the movies alone, if that's what you really want. Good Lord, you can be so immature sometimes." With this, she went back to kissing Benny. I looked back at Eric, who was still sitting on the ledge looking surprised and rejected. Even though it was dark, his shadow flickered with colors, colors that confused me, Eric's shadow was full of calming pastels. Regardless, I decided Father was right. All boys were jerks. The thought made me sick to my stomach. Aunt Sharon had told me make plans but be able to adapt. Control was the goal—"the ability to manage". I was getting a big fat "F" in life's lessons.

I walked back to the front of the theater, I didn't have $2.00 to get into the show. Mom had assured me that Eric would pay since he had asked me out. It would seem in affairs of the heart, I'd best listen to Father. My best movie memory was with him anyway.

Last summer, Father came home from work and asked me if I wanted to go to a drive-in movie that night. He already knew what my answer would be, but what I didn't know was that I was about to see my first PG movie.

"Breezy, you're entering sixth grade and I think you are old enough to see *Jaws*."

My heart did somersaults. Several of my friends had been allowed to see PG movies before. I felt like a baby, only getting to see G movies. And, *Jaws*! I threw my arms around Father and squeezed him, "Thank you, thank you! I love you!"

He kissed my neck and told me to go help Mom with the popcorn. It may sound odd, but I believed popcorn actually tasted better after being carried in a brown grocery sack to the drive-in than any other time. Even better than Jiffy-Pop on a camping trip. I put quilts in the car and Shasta sodas in the cooler, Shasta Creme, mom's favorite and Black Cherry for Father and me. I was ready.

When we pulled into our parking spot at the drive-in, Mom asked, "Bree, do you want to go up front and play on the playground before the movie?"

I looked at the little kids already there, chasing each other and jumping off the merry-go-round and knew I was too old for such fun. Only recently I had given up sleeping with my stuffed animals, playing in my sandbox and carrying my Snoopy lunchbox. Most of me was glad to put away little kid things, but not all of me. Besides, I was at my first PG movie! We spread the quilts on the hood of the car. Mom had to sit inside, for comfort's sake. But Father and I snuggled on the hood, until the temperature dropped and our butts got sore, then we joined Mom inside the car. That particular night I clung extra close to Father. *Jaws* was much scarier than I thought it would be and I knew I would never swim in an ocean, ever. Yet, clinging to Father, frightened and safe at the same time was still such a good memory. I couldn't help but wish I was back there, on the quilt with Father, feeling protected and young.

I decided to sit on a bench in the front of the theater and wait. Just as I was becoming increasingly depressed watching laughing couples pass through the theater doors, I was distracted by a red car driving by slowly, practically stopping in front of me. The windows were tinted and I could barely make out the driver behind the wheel. It looked like a big man. Was he staring at me?

Then the window came down a bit and I heard a voice say, "Hey, you. Come over here, I want to talk to you."

"NO WAY!" I shouted a bit too loudly.

The voice again, "You need to back off!" The red car sped off leaving me fretting and pondering his warning. Did he really know me? Did I just come in contact with the killer? Now I was depressed *and* nervous.

The minutes continued to drag agonizingly by. After about an hour of watching people, and watching for the return of the red car, I saw an elderly couple walk out of the ice cream shop next door. They sat on the bench next to me after asking if I minded. I was grateful for company—and protection. I noticed how the man patted his wife's knee with the familiar ease of long and true friendship. It occurred to me that I rarely saw my parents touch. I wondered why this couple was different, why they seemed so comfortable together, so secure and so much at peace.

Finally Lori came around the corner. I didn't see the boys. She looked a little worse for the wear. I felt embarrassed for myself and for her. I didn't even feel like talking to her.

"I'm sorry about all that. I guess I'm just surprised you cared so much about whether we went to some lame movie or not."

I sat with my arms folded across my chest, not wanting to tell Lori my stupid fantasies of meeting the right boy and having real dates. "I'm not mad at you, Lori, just disappointed with this whole thing."

"I didn't do anything, you know. All we did was kiss and touch a little; it really wasn't that big a deal. Why are you so uptight about a guy touching you? Eric is a fox. I don't understand why you got so worked up."

I knew Lori was trying to make peace. "Maybe I'm just not meant to have a boyfriend, if boys don't like me for who I am."

"Bree, they're intimidated by you! You're taller and smarter than most of them. You should do like me, dumb yourself down. You come across too much like a know-it-all."

I glared at her. "Look, here comes my mom. Just act normal and don't say anything strange that would freak her out!"

Mom pulled up in her Ford LTD, cigarette in one hand and a cup of coffee in the other. Both hands busy juggling, Mom resorted to steering with her knees, cigarette ash dropping continually into her lap. Mom asked if we had fun and if the movie was good but didn't really seem to expect any answers, only saying what she thought was required. She seemed quiet, and I wondered if she'd fought with Father while I was gone. Mostly I was just grateful she didn't ask us what the movie was about.

When I got home I went straight to my room and began to write in my diary, something I did almost every night.

In minutes I was asleep, pen and diary on my chest, dried tears on my cheeks with final thoughts of the man in the red car who seemed to either want to warn me or take me as the next victim.

I woke from a horrible dream in which I was being chased by a group of boys up at the woods behind my school. When they caught me, they tried to slip their hands under my clothes. When I looked at them, every one of them had Eric's face. The woods suddenly turned into the inside of a movie theater, and water began seeping from the walls. I looked down at my feet and saw I was standing in murky water. I lifted my foot and noticed I was wearing a shoe I had never seen before. Looking up again, I saw the water beginning to rush out of the walls faster and everywhere I turned there were new patches of a plaster seeping a dark and mysterious water.

I kicked off the covers, drenched in sweat and looked at the clock by my bed; only 3:00 a.m. I moved my diary and pen to the nightstand. My heart was hammering in my chest and I felt vulnerable in the dark. I kept looking out the windows, worried that someone or something might be out there. I heard faint whimpering. It sounded like it was coming from somewhere in the house. God, I hated this. Did I go check out the noise or close my eyes tight and hope whatever it was would go away? The noise continued. It kind of sounded like an animal was hurt. I slipped on my house shoes and tiptoed to the door, recalling the saying, 'curiosity killed the cat'. It definitely sounded like it was coming from the living room. I eased around the corner and edged along the wall.

Stopping at the corner of the hallway and the Trapezoid, I cautiously peered around the corner. *The National Anthem* was playing on the television with no sound. In the glow of the screen, I saw Father curled up in his chair, his hands tightly clasping his closed Bible. He looked so sad. I'd never seen him do something like that. I wondered what could be wrong with him. Was he that worried about Moose? I backed away before he could notice me and ran to the safety of my bed. Pulling the covers over my head, I began to sob as the night sounds tormented me from beyond my room. All I could think about was how dumb I felt and how much there was at stake that depended on me being a whole lot smarter.

"If things don't work out it will be your fault. You know that don't you?"

I realized I had been waiting for him to say something like this—had been wondering when he would start to lay the blame at my feet. He always thought he was right, knew more than everyone else and was smarter than me. That last part was true. I had been dumb. I had been dumb and dumber right from the beginning. And scared. I might not have been so stupid if I hadn't been so scared, but he was arrogant and naïve if he thought there weren't risks, very real risks.

"I mean it. There's just too many loose ends. You're weak and if we fail it will be because you're weak."

CHAPTER TEN

I DECIDED TO POSTPONE my investigation the following day. I didn't feel like myself. I needed time to rethink my strategy. I knew I had to move fast, but maybe if I didn't think about it so hard, the clues would become clearer. I'd seen that ploy work in the late-night movies I watched with Father. Yes, that's good. Just step back a little, so you can see the obvious. I wanted to go up to the pool again and maybe hang out with Lori if she still wasn't mad. I went into the bathroom to shower. I was hot and sticky from night sweats and the humid June air.

I pulled down my pajama bottoms and saw red—real red blood on my thighs. I felt myself falling to the floor with the color exploding inside my head—red! Red! Blood! Red blood everywhere! I saw a flash of bloody snake parts in the trash can, images of Jennifer's casket, but most of all I saw Rachel Carter's body, streaked with blood, like mine. Right before everything went black I felt myself crash against the door, into the full-length hanging mirror. In the background I heard pounding, far away, and my mom's voice. Then I felt her soft arms around me, holding me tight, her nicotine breath warm on my ear, whispering, "It's OK, honey, you're OK. Calm down, Mom is here."

I buried my face in her ample chest. "I'm dying, just like Rachel!" was all I could choke out.

"You're not dying, honey. It's just your period, that's all. You're OK.

I looked up at Mom, suddenly feeling childish and stupid. My reaction had been so violent and crazy. What was wrong with me?

"Oh. Well, yes. I just saw all that blood and then everything started spinning," I sobbed. "Why did you have to kill all those snakes? Why did someone kill Rachel? Why?"

"I killed the snakes to protect you. They might have attacked you next. I did it for you. Everything I do is for you…or for your Father. My job is to be strong and do what needs to be done. That's my job as a woman."

She looked at me like she was trying to make up her mind about something. "I think you're obsessed with this murder. I know how you worry. You can't go on eaten up with these obsessions. Mom's going to set up a doctor's appointment for you."

"I don't need a doctor! How embarrassing! It's just my period. I just got scared, that's all. I'm going to take a shower, and, uh… clean up." I breathed deeply, trying to control my crying. I couldn't stand to see Mom so concerned. "I'm sorry about the mirror." Looking at the fractured, jagged lines zigzagging across the glass, I knew it was goner.

"Take your shower and watch where you step. I'll clean up the broken mirror, let's hope we don't have seven years of bad luck." Although she wasn't smiling, I told myself she must be kidding.

Mom added, "You may want to keep track of your cycle on a calendar, so it doesn't sneak up and surprise you again. And, yes, Mom is calling a doctor." With this last statement, she heaved herself to her feet, pulled her cigarettes from her house-coat pocket, and walked out to get a broom.

I was *not* going to the doctor, and I was *not* obsessed.

After a horrible and emotional start that morning, the day at the pool was perfect. The sun was hot and intense—pure, natural therapy. Lori wasn't at the pool but I saw Pauline and Kristen from school and we laid out together, working on our tans. Laying out at the pool was one of the few social settings in which I felt comfortable—minus the fact that so much of my body was exposed around boys. Listening to my friends while lying in the sun meant I didn't have to talk too much. Eyes closed, relaxed, yet still feeling a part of the crowd. That was my idea of heaven.

Kristen was the wildest of my friends, although she would backhand me for saying just that. Kristen would do anything for attention. While I enjoyed her in small bursts, my other friends always seemed to want her around, calling her "fun" and "entertaining". Sometimes I felt jealous of Kristen, all the attention she got, but then she'd do something so outrageous, reminding me there was a price for demanding center stage.

Kristen passed around a bottle of baby oil mixed with iodine. She said it was better than Coppertone. She had a very con-vincing way of speaking, about anything, so I bit, and slathered some on too. As Kristen went back to her towel I noticed her shadow flickering with different shades of orange. I squinted but the colors remained.

Pauline began to tell me about a falling out with Lori when Kristen jumped in, "She's such a bitch, Bree!" Pauline nodded and went on, "I told her something absolutely private and she swore to secrecy!" Pauline pushed her glasses back up her nose as they began to slide down from the sweat.

"Well, that was your first mistake. I don't know why you would think Lori swearing means she wouldn't tell. If Lori found it in her own best interest to share your secret, that promise would be forgotten just like that." I snapped my fingers to demonstrate the speed of Lori's forgotten promises.

"So what was the secret?"

Pauline looked down at the concrete, "I don't want to say."

"It's not like it's a secret anymore." Kristen shrugged. "Once Lori knows, I mean, forget about it."

Pauline hesitated, "Ok, fine, but I'd appreciate you not saying anything anyway. It's just dumb."

"Alright, alright, but what'd you do?" My imagination was already moving forward with dramatic thoughts.

"Well, see, it wasn't my fault, not entirely, see, um, Kristen and I were at the mall and I took a tester of perfume from Dillard's."

"Why?" I leaned over grabbing her arm, feeling alarm for a crime that I wasn't even a part of.

"I don't know, Kristen did it first," she replied as she pulled away. "It looked so easy... it was bottle of Charlie, and I really wanted it."

"Did you get caught?"

Kristen scoffed, "No, of course not! But it doesn't help that the big mouth bitch is telling everyone."

"If my mom finds out I'm dead," Pauline added

"You were both dumb to steal something. Kristen, you're so impulsive sometimes."

"What's that supposed to mean?" Kristen glared at me but I didn't care.

"You don't think before you act."

"Oh, yeah, well, Lori didn't think before she told the secret so I guess she's impulsive too."

I sighed in exasperation, "It's not exactly the same thing first of all, but also it's not so much that Lori didn't think as Lori didn't care."

"We'll see how much Lori cares when I tell everyone she made out with Mike in the coat closet last year."

Pauline started to giggle. "I didn't know she did that."

Kristen folded her arms across her chest. "Maybe she did, maybe she didn't but I'll say she did. I'll say I saw her one day during recess and everyone will believe me and she'll deserve it."

Mike Martin was the most unpopular kid in 6th grade. My recent encounter with him at the 7-Eleven reminded me of how annoying he could be. Although he got on my nerves, I still felt sorry for him. A couple of years earlier, when we first began the gifted program together, I saw Mike sitting in the corner. He was holding the class globe in his lap while crying. Our teacher tried to calm him as he carried on about the Burundian Genocide and other world events that apparently weighed heavy on his soul.

He was more sensitive the rest of us and that made him different and different didn't fly well with conforming adolescents. It seemed to me Mike didn't even try to fit in. The fact that Kristen would say Lori made out with Mike, a kid with goofy glasses and K-mart clothes, was a unique type of retaliation, she knew how to hit Lori where it really hurt. While I enjoyed the thought of Lori's reaction to such a rumor, I wasn't okay with Mike being thrown under the bus when he didn't do anything.

I threw myself back down on my beach towel. "Oh, that's great, Kristen. My mom says, 'Two wrongs don't make a right.' No one would believe Lori would ever in a million years have anything to do with Mike anyway. I wouldn't waste your time."

But my words were falling on deaf ears. Suddenly I was distracted from my thoughts of moral indignation as Kristen practically yelled in my ear. "Hey, Bree baby, check out Jake on the high dive, what a fox, he just makes me feel tingly all over!

"So, who's your crush Bree? Every girl has to have a summer crush, come on give it up, tell your mommy." I could feel her breath on my cheek, I thought she might kiss me, she'd done that for shock value before.

I turned away and said, "Evel Knievel."

"You are so totally sarcastic, Bree."

That was the thing with Kristen. Her behavior drove boys away, they either found her annoying, scary or both. It was like she didn't care what anybody thought. That was hard for me to understand. I cared so much what everyone thought and tried so hard not to draw attention to myself and yet I was no better off than Kristen.

I turned on my transistor radio and Kristen grabbed it and turned up the sound. *Do the Hustle* was playing and Kristen jumped up and began dancing. That girl could really move. She said her mom had taught her the dance steps to the hustle. The fact people were staring as she danced all over her beach towel only encouraged her. She seemed to draw energy from attention, where as I found it draining.

Once Kristen wore herself out and settled back down we watched more boys jump off the high dive and recounted some of our favorite episodes from elementary school. Basking in the sun, shiny with oil, recalling fun times with my friends was good therapy. Elementary school was over; we were junior high students now! I don't think that had really sunk in with any of us yet. But per usual, the conversation came back around to the murder. Pauline brought up the news that the murder looked "ritualistic."

"Maybe it was like a sacrifice to the Devil?" Kristen suggested.

Pauline added, "Yeah, there really are witches living in Englewood you know. At my church a guy visited our youth group and he said he used to worship the Devil. He said he was able to burn down a house with his mind and they did sacrifices and stuff."

Feeling confused I asked, "Why in the world would someone who worshipped Satan be in your church?"

"Because he's Christian now, he said he figured if the power of the Devil could be real, then so could the power of God."

Kristen rolled over on her back squinting at the sky. "That's really weird. Well, all I know is if Rachel was part of a sacrifice, I still say they better go check out the old Albino Farm."

I looked at her in disbelief. "Oh for the love of God, you've got to be kidding me? You're really saying you believe the legends of the Albino Farm!"

"Sure, my uncle went there with his friends late one night and said they saw a ghost of the old caretaker. You know, there was once a colony of albinos that lived there and the caretaker went crazy and took a hatchet to one of the families, now their ghosts want revenge!"

Pauline sat up with excitement dancing in her eyes. "It's true! I heard the same story, 'cept I heard the albinos were held captive there and there's an albino cemetery there too and that's where the ghosts hang out. Oh! And I heard there's an underground hospital where they used to do experiments on albinos and now the albinos haunt the old farm…and the cemetery I guess."

"This is all ridiculous!" I shook my head in frustration. "Albinos are no different than you or me, they just lack pigment in their skin, they have a congenital absence of pigmentation in their skin and eyes, and hair giving them an interesting look, that's all there is to it. You can't believe stupid legends like that."

Pauline looked down as if her feelings were hurt. "Anyway, I'm just saying they should look into all areas of spooky stuff since the murder was said to look like a ritual and Satan worshippers perform rituals." But then it was Pauline's last comment that really got my attention. "But anyway my dad says the killer is probably someone who drives that street every day because she was kidnapped around the time people get off work and if it was random, then that makes sense."

This motivated me to rouse myself from the hypnotic spell cast by the hot summer sun and dumb conversation. It was time to resume my search for Rachel's killer and I had to complete my spy route before I went to baby-sit for Detective Hines.

On the way home I got the definite feeling that someone was following me again. I tried to convince myself it was just my imagination, like Aunt Sharon said. Each time I turned around there didn't seem to be anyone following, yet I could feel a presence the entire way home. It was the same feeling that came to me so often in the middle of the night.

Cool and cozy in my room, I took out my diary and pencil, reviewing notes from the past few days. My shoulders and back and stomach were really beginning to hurt; I took off my swimsuit only to discover definite sunburn. So much for baby oil and iodine being better than Coppertone. This was just great, I was an idiot. I wallowed in self-pity for a few minutes and then considered my petty problems compared to what Moose was up against. Time to get moving.

The Ouija board had spelled out 'close' and Cameraman was still my main suspect. He was obviously a stalker of sorts and maybe he had a red car or was associated with the killer in some way. I changed into shorts and walked down the sidewalk toward his house, the five o'clock sun burning bright and aggravating my sunburn through my t-shirt. I didn't see him anywhere around, so I decided to move in closer to his house. I was feeling bold and determined in the righteousness of my mission.

I walked through the side yard, craning to hear sounds or see movement through the windows. I stepped up on his deck, stood for a moment and peeked through the sliding glass door. The glare of sunlight on the door left me staring at my own reflection. Heart pounding, I cupped my hands around my face to try and see past the glare. Pressing my face against the glass, I felt the door move against me and I jumped back strangling a scream. Cameraman slid the door open and stood right in front of me. I felt my heart stop. He stared at me. I stared back at him. Slowly my heart resumed beating, like the knocking of an old, misfiring car engine. He spoke first.

"Little girl, I have been watching you watch me for some time now. It needs to stop. Immediately. You are making me nervous. I believe you're probably too small to pose a real threat, but you are disconcerting."

My mouth was dry; it was hard to speak. But I'd come this far—I had to say something. It was now or never. "Why are you watching people with that camera all the time?" I put my hands on my hips, hoping I looked tough, or at least braver than I felt.

He stared at me like he couldn't understand plain English; his permanent frown seemed to intensify. Then it was like a light went on somewhere in his mind. "What we have here is a failure to communicate." He smiled thinly at his own secret joke. "Come here, child. Follow me."

I took a step backward, shaking my head no.

"Fair enough. I'm not sure I trust you, either. If you will stay put, I believe I can answer your question." He turned and walked into the house.

I decided to wait. I was about to get an answer. I needed answers.

A few minutes later, Cameraman came out with three large photo albums. He sat down on a bench and motioned me over. Rubbing wrinkled hands over the albums, caressing them as if they were a treasure trove.

"You are obviously a very curious child and have gone to a modicum of trouble to hear my story." He cocked his eyebrow as if this was a question instead of a statement of fact, but I didn't react. I wasn't playing games and he better know it.

He cleared his throat. "My wife, Joanne, was the love of my life. We had been married 32 wonderful years when we discovered she had breast cancer. The last month was ghastly. Joanne would have been in constant pain if not for the morphine. I spent my days at the hospital, sitting by her side, and just—well, just loving her. It's all I could do.

"I could not imagine living a single day without her. One evening, when she was unusually lucid, I held her hand and told her that when she died, I too would die. I told her I could not bear the thought of a one-dimensional, black and white existence, devoid of her presence.

"She grasped my hand a bit tighter and said, 'John, don't talk like that! Remember our cruise to the Caribbean? How you'd wake me so early each morning so we could watch the sun rise from the ship? Every day is worth living, even if it is only to watch the sun rise in the morning and set each night. Live for me."

John, as I now knew his name, opened the first album. I recognized the view immediately; it was the homes across the street from his own house. The sun was just rising above rooftops, and the sky had that pretty pink glow to it. A little weather rhyme from school popped into my head, 'Red sky in the morning, sailors take warning'. John turned the pages. Photo after photo of the sun setting in front of his house or rising behind the very deck upon which we now sat.

Confused, I pointed out, "These pictures are all virtually the same thing! I don't get it."

He looked at me. "Each photograph you see is my reason for being alive. Each day I celebrate my darling Joanne, our beautiful years together, and the sunrises and sunsets we loved so much. This is my reason for living."

For the first time, I saw John's colors. His color was blue, lots of blue; a shade similar to my mom's. He couldn't be so bad then, could he? Looking down I saw a shadow coming off John, similar to the one I saw coming off Kristen that day at the pool. The colors were more vibrant and different than the one's surrounding his body. I rubbed my eyes and thought about asking my mom if I could see an eye doctor.

Looking back at John, I felt embarrassed for jumping to such erroneous conclusions. I told him I was just messing around the neighborhood and that I was curious why he took pictures all the time. He seemed satisfied with my explanation and invited me to stop by anytime. He said he appreciated the company of another intelligent being. No need to tell him how stupid I had been. How could I have been so wrong? Making such a bad mistake about John raised serious doubts in my mind as to my ability to help Moose, but it intensified my determination to track down Rachel's killer.

Turning toward the street I saw someone straddling their bike across the way. It was Mike from school and he was watching me curiously.

"What are you doing here?" I asked accusingly.

"I was spying. I am an agent for the CIA and they've asked me to keep an eye on one Bree Grant, who they think may be a Russian mole." There was a flicker of amusement at the corners of his mouth and I knew he was teasing me, but I didn't like it. It was too close to the truth. Did he know I was doing spy work of sorts?

He got off his bike and started walking beside me. It felt weird but seemed natural at the same time. "I was on the way to the library and just happened to see you. Is that where you live?"

"No. I was visiting a new friend kind of. I mean, someone I just met who might be a new friend. I live there on the corner," I said pointing toward my house.

"Wow. How architecturally interesting! So that's where Geoff Grant lives. I should have known. The style of the house says so much about incorporating design and building materials with nature. It speaks volumes—in a rather enigmatic way. What a cool place to live!"

I don't know what surprised me more—the fact he liked my house or the fact that he knew who my father was.

"How do you know my dad?"

"Everyone knows your dad, I guess. I met him when he did the windows at our church. Well, my dad's church. My dad is the preacher at First Methodist."

"Oh, yeah, Pastor Martin. I've seen your church, it's next to my dentist."

"That's him. Your dad made a very interesting window for the front entrance. It's a lot of vines. Thorny at the bottom of the window but lots of growth and flowers at the top. Some people in the congregation aren't that thrilled with it, but Dad and I think it says a lot about Christian growth."

I think my mouth may have been hanging open just a little. I didn't know what to say.

"Well, Bree, I will report back to my superiors at headquarters and let them know you are not a threat to national security." With that comment he hopped back on his bike and disappeared around the corner.

I was left feeling a little odd. Somehow running into Mike had knocked me off center, just a little. I rubbed the back of my head and tried to regain focus by scanning my list. I still had time to pay the witch lady a visit. I figured the witch lady was probably in her thirties. She always wore black and she had lots of beads that hung from her windows. I didn't think I had the nerve to go up to her door but at least I could spy on her from a distance. I didn't really believe a woman could be the killer, but I knew I had to keep an open mind.

When I got to her house I noticed her car was gone. Everything looked vacant and dark. I sidled up to the house and parted overgrown prickly holly bushes to take a little peek in the window. There were lots of candles in her bedroom and books scattered everywhere. Could they be books on witchcraft? This invited further investigation. Goosebumps prickled on the back of my neck; there was definitely something here that needed to be looked into, but I was running out of time.

I decided to move on for now. I was anxious to baby-sit and go through the detective's things.

CHAPTER ELEVEN

AT FIVE BEFORE six I walked over to Detective Hines' house and rang the bell. What was that baby's name? Mrs. Hines opened the door, holding the baby and looking very pretty in a red dress.

"You look nice, Mrs. Hines!"

"Well, thank you, Bree. Come in, hon. Here, you can start earning your pay now by taking Gia for me."

So that was her name! I took Gia from Mrs. Hines, the baby's small fingernails digging into my sunburned shoulders. Stifling a squeal I walked into the living room, already scanning the premises for information relevant to the murder.

Gia and I were playing on the floor when Detective and Mrs. Hines came in to give me the final spiel about where the emergency numbers were, and the bottles, and diapers, and jammies. It seemed to go on forever. I thought they were never going to leave.

Finally, they were out the door. I left the baby on the living room floor so I could go through the evening paper that was lying scattered by the recliner. The front page had a story about Rachel, which I read eagerly. The article was mostly about Rachel herself. I learned she was cheerleader at Kennedy Junior High, an honor student, and the oldest of four daughters. Her mom was an English teacher at the high school and her father was an accountant. Wow. The all-American family. After I finished, I folded that section of the paper and put it in my backpack.

Next, I walked through the house until I found Detective Hines' office in a spare bedroom. A large desk took up most of the wall in front of a window. File cabinets, a bookcase and an overstuffed chair crowded the small room. The total effect was cozy and organized. I began looking through his desk. Uh-oh, Gia was crying, darn it. I ran into the living room, where she was lying on the floor, kicking and screaming. I knew the feeling.

I went into the kitchen, remembering that Mrs. Hines had said something about a bottle. I found it on the counter and mixed some formula for the howling little darling. I handed her the bottle. She must have just learned to hold her own bottle because she couldn't hold it herself the last time I babysat. I remember how annoying it was to have to hold her as well the bottle. This time, it was hello easy street. Back to my search in no time, I thought.

Gia took one sip and threw the bottle to the floor. She continued to cry. Sheesh! I picked up the bottle and took it back into the kitchen. OK, so she didn't want her formula. I opened the refrigerator. Coke! I poured me a glass, then dumped some of it into Gia's formula. I walked into the living room and gave her the bottle. She took one sip, smiled up at me as if to say 'thanks, pal', and continued sucking. Yes! We were in business! This baby thing wasn't too tough.

I went back to Detective Hines' study and looked around with a fresh eye. I saw his briefcase lying on the floor. Frayed corners, the leather scratched and worn, its contents spilling over the top—definitely the briefcase of a detective leading a murder investigation. I felt a little guilty going through his things, but I had to help Moose. I needed clues to figure out who the killer was.

I peeked hesitantly into his briefcase, and right there on top was a folder labeled 'Carter, Rachel'. I grabbed the bulk of papers and went back into the living room where I could keep an eye on Gia. I curled up in a chair and opened the file. It felt heavy in my hands.

On top were photographs paper-clipped to the inside front cover. I quickly flipped through the pictures. My heart beat increasing more rapidly at the sight of Rachel's murdered body. The photos looked different than what I remembered from my tree house vantage point. The close up views magnified the reality. Her face especially looked more horrifying. There was a thin line around her neck and the skin was cut and bloody. Her face swollen, and discolored, could not be mistaken for sleep. She was dead forever.

I laid the pictures aside, forcing myself to look back to that morning in the tree house, reliving the sight of her body for the first time. It seemed like eons ago; following my impulsive curiosity, my inflated ego that insisted I could help, not truly comprehending the horrific reality. I picked up the photographs again. This was not the fantasy and illusion of a movie on a screen. Rachel had been real, just like me. Her death was real. She deserved to be avenged.

I was sweating as I looked at the next photo. Rachel's mouth was pried open by some sort of tool for this picture. The photo barely revealed a slender metal piece wedged between her front teeth. Her teeth looked like they might be loose and there was a little dried blood on them. I hadn't seen any mention of this in the newspaper articles. I flipped to the next picture, which showed the close-up of an old coin. I wondered if this was the coin the police were interested in. Obviously, it must be the object I saw in the first photo that had been forced between her front teeth. Why would someone do that?

Under this photo was an enlarged picture that said it was a partial fingerprint taken from the coin. Clipped to this was a picture of a complete fingerprint labeled 'Michael Sullivan'. Oh my God! That was Moose's real name! I compared the two fingerprints. It didn't look like a match to me, but what did I know? This really bothered me. If they had a partial print, then Moose must have done it. Unless someone stole the coin or bought the coin from Moose. I was so confused!

The next photos were repulsive. I wasn't really sure what I was seeing; it appeared to be a close up of her face, which showed many broken blood vessels in her eyes, she looked terrified. God, who was capable of causing such pain? I felt sick to my stomach. I dropped the picture and it fell upside down on the floor. I left it there and flipped to the final pictures.

At first I had no idea what I was looking at. The photo was of a container of stacked bones, the skull laying face up, on top. I figured this must be Jennifer's skeleton. Someone had robbed her grave and then used the remains at the murder scene. That made no sense. If it was Jennifer's bones, why did the killer have Jennifer's bones? What if Jennifer's death had not been an accident? Two dead girls. Was there a serial killer in Englewood?

Another photograph, apparently showed the location of the box upon its discovery under the rocky ledge, to the right of the body. I hadn't noticed it that day in the tree house.

Looking at the photographs, I was overcome with sadness. How were the two girls connected? Jennifer hadn't been murdered—not in the usual sense of the word. A drunken coward driving a car, someone who ran away from the scene of the accident, killed her. At least that's what everyone assumed at the time. Rachel had been deliberately and brutally murdered.

I was nine years old when Jennifer died. I remember Mom had taken the phone call. Moose's girlfriend, Lisa, called to tell us that Jennifer's body had been discovered under some bushes near the curb of the street early that morning by a girl on her way to work. Her mangled body had been left at the side of the street like trash to be picked up and carted off. Everyone assumed the hit and run driver was drunk, but, of course, there was no way to know for sure because there were no witnesses and the driver was never caught.

Jennifer was 17 when she died. She was Moose's only child and he worked really hard to win her back after the divorce and his time in jail. Jennifer was staying with her dad when she was killed. She'd just graduated from high school and was excited to start college. She had a full-ride scholarship to the University of Missouri, where she planned to major in journalism. Luckily for Jennifer, she had looked a lot like her mom, who was gorgeous. No offense to Moose intended, but you could never call him handsome.

They say most accidents happen close to home. That was true for Jennifer. She was walking home from a girlfriend's house around eleven; no one knows what happened after that. Jennifer's funeral was the first time I ever saw my father cry. The church was filled with high school kids—there were actually a lot more teenagers than adults. Jennifer's mom sat with Moose and Lisa. I even saw Moose put his arm around Jennifer's mom. A couple of Jennifer's friends tried to sing a duet, but they began crying halfway through the song and had to stop.

The casket was closed; I'm sure no one wanted to see her after having been hit by a car. Moose and his ex-wife refused to have Jennifer embalmed, they said that was simply additional torture to her already mutilated body. At one point during the funeral, the minister left the pulpit, cradling in his hands a necklace that was removed from Jennifer's neck at the hospital. It had been a gift from Moose on Jennifer's sixteenth birthday. As the minister handed it to him, Moose's sobs echoed throughout the church. Even Father was shaking uncontrollably. Mom cried a little, but mostly she just smacked her lips and shook her head as if she really couldn't believe it.

That was the only funeral I'd ever been to and it still haunted me. Rachel's murder was bringing up a lot of unwanted feelings. I wondered if I could be the next victim, dying some horrible, unspeakable death. I could imagine my parents' grief and unexpectedly thought about how vulnerable they were.

Under all the photographs in the file were lots of papers. The first item to catch my eye was a copy of an old case report from about five years ago. The report was about a sex crime against a 15-year-old girl. I glanced down at a mug shot and saw a vaguely familiar face. Sans the beard, it was Moose. So, this was what he went to jail for. I was shocked that he was not who I thought he was. It didn't seem possible that he was a pervert. How could I have been so far off base? How could Father be friends with somebody like that? It had to be a mistake.

I always figured he got in trouble for fighting or something more minor, but a sex crime? I scanned the report and learned that the sex had been consensual but that the girl's parents had found out about the relationship and pressed charges. Like, who could blame them! A 15-year-old with a 35 year-old man was hard for me to imagine. Yuck!

The report couldn't tell me why Moose would do something like that. I felt like I really didn't know him at all, now. Maybe he was a killer. Who knows what he might be capable of? Maybe he was into devil worship and I didn't even know it. I was more sad than scared. Even though Moose had always been a friend to me, I felt betrayed. Had his colors fooled me? I'd always believed that what I saw were a person's true colors—the truth of who they were. I wondered if I was wrong about this too.

The Moose who was in the police report and the Moose who stopped by Father's studio, and tousled my hair and told stupid jokes, that were more groan than giggles, didn't reconcile in my mind. Was it possible there were two people existing inside one body, one good, one evil? Could someone as gentle and caring as Moose appeared to be around us, also be a demented sexual predator around others? There was so much I didn't know about human nature. There was so much I didn't understand about my ability to see a person's aura. There had been a line in *Little Women* that I hadn't understood when I first read it: "I don't think secrets agree with me. I feel rumpled up in mind since you told me that..." At last I understood. My mind felt like an unmade bed with crumpled thoughts tossed about.

The rest of the file was less interesting. There were statements from the grandmother and Rachel's parents and statements from the boys who found the body. They didn't admit they were going up there to smoke dope, but I knew better. There was also a sworn statement from Moose's girlfriend that said he was with her that night. As I closed the file tears welled up in my eyes. It was all too much. Just then the phone rang. I jumped, dropped the file, and papers slid out and scattered everywhere.

"Shoot." I ran to the phone.

"Hello."

A man's voice on the end asked, "Uh, is this Margaret Wenson?"

I replied, "No, sorry, you have the wrong number."

I heard the other end go click and I knew he'd hung up on me. Now I was getting nervous. The voice on the phone had been deep and husky, probably a big man. I ran to make sure all the doors were locked and checked on Gia. She'd finished her bottle and was playing happily with her toes. It occurred to me that maybe I shouldn't have given a baby Coke. Oh, well. I picked up the files and spilled papers, walked back into Detective Hines' study and placed the file exactly, I hoped, as I'd found it in his briefcase.

Daylight had turned to dusk, but I hesitated to turn on the lights. Which was worse, dark shadows or illuminating my whereabouts? I thought I heard something, a scratchy sound behind me. It sounded like it was coming from outside. I quickly glanced at the window and shut the drapes. As my eyes adjusted, I waited to hear the sound again. Nothing. I left the room quickly and ran into the living room. Gia was still giggling and rolling around.

An unwelcome thought occurred. What if that man on the phone was checking on me? What if there was no Margaret Wenson? I ran to the kitchen, flipped on a small lamp and grabbed the phone book, paging quickly to the 'Ws'. Wenson. My finger ran down the list. There it was, 'Jim and Margaret'. I suppose I should have felt relieved, but I didn't. I felt entirely spooked, pacing around the house like a caged animal in the dark, trying to decide what to do.

I didn't know why the killer would be after me, but if Rachel and I were connected somehow then finding that connection would lead me to the murderer. If someone had been following me and knew where I was, then they probably knew this was where a policeman lived. Surely, they wouldn't try to hurt me while I was in the lead detective's house? If I could just figure out how I was involved in all this. Sure I was investigating the murder, but no one else knew that. How could they know that anyway?

By the time the Hineses got home, I was a nervous wreck. I tried to appear calm, though, as they came in the door. Their date had obviously been a success. Mrs. Hines was laughing and had her arm wrapped around her husband, whose face looked less haggard.

Mr. Hines turned on the lights as Mrs. Hines went quickly to Gia, shocked that she was still up. "Has she been asleep at all, Bree?"

I looked down at Gia who was grinning, flinging her arms in happy circles, looking entirely too bright-eyed for eleven at night. "No, she's been up the whole time."

Detective Hines rubbed his eyes and said, "Great, that's all we need! I haven't slept this week anyway, so I guess Gia can keep me company tonight, huh?"

Mrs. Hines stood up and reached for her purse. She handed me ten bucks and thanked me. As I headed for the door, Detective Hines spoke, "Let me walk you home, Bree. I know it's only a few doors down but I'd feel better."

I was so grateful he offered, but I didn't want to come across like some scared little kid.

"Sure, that would be fine," I replied offhandedly.

I grabbed my bag and walked out front with Detective Hines, feeling safe and protected. It seemed like a lot of my feelings were changing lately. I had always liked walking around the neighborhood at night. Sometimes people forgot to close their drapes and I would catch glimpses of normal people leading normal lives. I guess those days of walking comfortably alone at night had come to an end. So much had changed.

I thought this would be an opportune time to ask him about the murder again. "I'm glad you and Mrs. Hines had a nice evening. I just love your little baby; she's so cute...so how's the murder case coming?"

His voice sounded tired. "Oh, it's slow, of course, like most crimes. This isn't the movies, you know. The clues don't just fall into place, waiting for the brilliant detective to put all the pieces together and solve the crime in a blaze of glory. It's like a lot of cases that leave me sleepless at night. We'll catch him, though."

We stopped at my front door. The inside of my house looked dark through the leaded glass. I guessed my parents had already gone to bed. I started to dig in my bag for my key when the lights came on. I looked up and there was Father's face, looking through the door, the beveled glass causing his features to look broken and distorted.

I turned to Detective Hines and said, "Now we see through a glass darkly, then we shall see face to face."

He looked at me strangely and instantly I regretted quoting Father. "Why did you say that?" he asked.

"I don't know—it's just a scripture that popped into my head!" I laughed nervously as Father opened the door.

"Thanks, Hines, for walking Bree home. It's good to have the law in the neighborhood."

"No problem. She's a special girl." Detective Hines cocked his head, then squared his shoulders as he ambled back home to his wife and daughter.

I wondered if Gia would keep him up, if he would notice anything amiss in his study. I wondered about a lot of things.

A row of dolls watched me punch my pillow and tug on my blankets as I tried to find that perfect nest for sleep. My body was as restless as my mind that night. My thoughts were skipping from tomorrow, to yesterday, to food, to God, ad infinitum. When I finally slept it was only to enter another eerie dream in which I found myself watching water leak from the ceiling above me. In the dream I am deeply troubled by the water trickling all around me, the cracks in the ceiling scare me but I do not know why.

CHAPTER TWELVE

OⱯER THE NEXT week I felt a strange discomfort, both listless and restless. My continued attempts to interview people around the neighborhood brought on more frustration, people just weren't cooperating. My investigation, on reflection, seemed so naïve and childish. Obviously Moose was involved. People, sadly, weren't always what they appeared to be. It was hard for me to accept, but I knew now that even their colors could be misleading. How stupid of me to think I had some special gift for judging people or seeing things other people couldn't see. Some nights later, I wrote in my diary, contemplating everything that had happened:

Why would God allow something like Rachel's murder to happen? Why did Jennifer have to die when she had so much to live for? Why am I alive? Does my life have a purpose? I wish my parents would take me to church. Sometimes I convince Father to take me along to install church windows just for the excuse to be in a sanctuary. I have decided that a person's religion or choice of denomination can't matter so much. I have been in many different places of worship, and regardless of the religion practiced there, I have always felt something special, a peace and security that I yearn for in my everyday life.

The next morning I awoke to find Mom sitting on the side of my bed watching me, a cigarette hanging from her lips. I jumped, knocking my diary off the nightstand. Mom was never, ever up before me. Why was she just sitting there staring at me?

"Hi, Mom. Why are you up so early?"

"Mom's not up early. You slept late. It's 8:30 and you have a doctor's appointment at ten this morning. Thought I'd wake you and give you a chance to shower and have breakfast."

I pulled the covers over my head in response.

We pulled into the parking lot of the Englewood Professional Building. I had been here before, the three story brick building held my pediatrician and my dentist. I figured I wasn't going to see my dentist. And while my pediatrician was a nice lady, I really was not in the mood to be examined. As we walked through the building, Mom stopped at a door that read:

PHILIP BRYAN, PH.D.
ASSOCIATES IN PSYCHOLOGY AND PSYCHIATRY

"Mom! You never said you were taking me to a shrink! How can you do this to me?"

"Honey, I love you and I'm very worried about you. Your Aunt Sharon called the other day and mentioned that you had a lot of questions about that girl who was murdered—questions she couldn't answer. You keep to yourself more and more these days.

"Bree, you seem distracted, to say the least. Then I find you on the bathroom floor howling like you're dying. You're just not yourself lately. I want you to talk to this doctor and be honest about what is going on."

"You want me to talk about what's in my head? Well, how's this for starters? I hate Aunt Sharon! How could she betray me like this? I trusted her!"

"She cares about you. She didn't really say much, other than that you seemed overly upset about the murder. She called to see how you were doing, but you were out and we got to talking. She thought you might benefit from talking to someone. And there are perfectly good doctors who know all about obsessions and things like that."

"I'm not obsessed!"

"Bree, calm down. Don't you want to feel like your old self again? This doctor can help you. He's even published books. He's supposed to be very good. For $65.00 an hour he should be good."

I was shocked. "You're paying sixty-five dollars an hour for me to talk about stuff? What did Father say to that?"

Mom smacked her lips. "Well, your father simply said I could pay for it. Besides, I have some extra money. Your father thinks you're just fine. He says I'm over-reacting."

"At least there's one sane person around here."

The reception area was pretty fancy; I could see why he had to charge so much. There was a huge salt-water aquarium on one wall. Everything looked very expensive. I was the only kid in the waiting room. I picked up a *Tiger Beat* magazine featuring the Bay City Roller's on the cover. At least this doctor had good taste in magazines. Mom was still filling out paperwork when finally we were called. I looked up to see a handsome man in a suit standing at the door. Mom handed over the clipboard as Dr. Bryan introduced himself.

His dark hair was neatly styled and his blue eyes crinkled when he smiled. Immaculately creased dark trousers and a light colored sport coat reminded me that this was the first doctor I had seen who didn't wear a crisp white coat. Dr. Bryan was almost as handsome as Father but that didn't mean I had to like him.

He ushered us back to his office and closed the door quietly. If he thought I was going to talk to him, he was the one who was nuts but I was totally impressed with his office. Lots of black leather and chrome. Then Dr. Bryan spoke, "Please, make yourselves comfortable. Sit anywhere."

Mom was clutching her purse against her chest as if it were a life preserver. She seemed unexpectedly overwhelmed with what was her big fat idea to begin with. I sat on the leather sofa. Mom seemed relieved that I'd made the choice and sat down beside me. Dr. Bryan chose the leather swivel chair across from us.

"So, what brings you in today?" Dr. Bryan looked questioningly from my mom to me. I kept my mouth stubbornly closed.

Mom cleared her throat. "Well, uh, it seems Bree has become obsessed with the murder of that girl they found at the school. Mom thinks she hasn't been acting like herself."

Dr. Bryan's eyebrows furrowed. "In what way has she been different?"

Mom seemed nervous with Dr. Bryan's rapt attention. He was leaning forward with his pen poised and his eyes staring intently into hers. I don't think she'd ever had someone pay such close attention to what she was saying.

"Bree has been talking a lot about the murder. My sister called and mentioned this. Bree's father said she has been watching the news every day to learn more about the dead girl. My biggest concern was when Bree started her period the other morning."

I felt my face go from pink to bright red. God, how embarrassing. Even if I didn't speak, I was going to be exposed.

"I found Bree passed out on the bathroom floor. It seemed she was hallucinating or something, as though she thought she had been hurt."

Dr. Bryan didn't look as if he found any of this especially shocking. "Is there anything else I should know?"

"Not that I can recall at the moment.... No, no, that's about it." I heard her smack her lips.

"Bree, what about you? Is there anything you'd like to say? Why do you think your mom brought you here today?"

I was too embarrassed to speak. I just shook my head mutely in response.

"Usually I like to get a little family history. Perhaps this would be a good time. I see that Bree has no siblings and there is a father at home." Dr. Bryan glanced up at Mom as if to get her agreement that what she'd written did indeed coincide with the truth.

He now turned his intense blue eyes on me. "Bree, how do you do in school? Do you make pretty good grades?"

I might as well go along and get this over with, "Yes, sir. A's mostly."

Mom piped up, sitting a little taller now. "Bree is in the gifted program. She's very bright."

I really wished she wouldn't do that.

Dr. Bryan asked, "Do you like being in the gifted program, Bree?"

What could I say? "Sure, it's something different."

"What about friends? Tell me about your friends."

This was a harder question. I couldn't very well tell him my closest friends lived in my attic. "I have a few friends. Kristen, Pauline….they're friends but we're not that close. Lori is probably my best friend." Did I just say that? I added something closer to the truth. "Lori's OK. I hang out with her, the most, I guess."

He turned back to Mom. "What do you think of Lori, Mrs. Grant?"

"Oh, she's a nice girl, from a fine family. Her father's an attorney, you know."

I doubted that Dr. Bryan did know.

"What can you tell me about Pauline and Kristen, Bree?"

"They're more casual friends. We just hang out at school or the pool for the most part. Sometimes they spend the night. I guess I prefer the company of adults, when I have a choice."

Dr. Bryan made a few notes.

I noticed Mom didn't make any comments about Kristen or Pauline. Kristen seemed to make my mom nervous. Whenever Kristen saw Mom she would run up yelling, "Hey, Mama G!" grabbing Mom around her neck, practically knocking her to the ground. This seemed to leave Mom shell shocked, smoothing her housecoat and searching frantically for her cigarettes.

I heard Dr. Bryan speak. "What does your husband do, Mrs. Grant?"

"Geoff is a stained glass artist. He has a studio downtown. He's very well known." She sat up straighter, with obvious pride and it made me feel better.

Dr. Bryan eyes flickered in recognition. "Ah, yes. Sure, I've been to your husband's studio myself. Mr. Grant made a small window for our home a few years ago. He's a very talented man."

I couldn't help but feel proud, also.

"Mrs. Grant, do you work outside the home?"

Mom appeared restless with this question. She fidgeted in her chair before answering. "I stay home, mostly. Geoff likes the house taken care of; he wants everything ship-shape, you know. He believes someone should be there when Bree comes home from school."

"Well, keeping a house ship-shape can be a full time job, no doubt." Changing the subject, he asked, "How would you describe your relationship with your father, Bree?"

Oh, God. What a hard question. I hadn't expected it from the way the conversation was going. I thought for a few seconds. I loved my father, but he was complicated. So how did I put that into words when it was hard for me to understand and sort through myself?

Mom interjected, "He's a good man, a hard working man. He really loves Bree, you know." I heard her lips smack three times.

I cut her off before she could embarrass me anymore. "My father does work hard, like my mom said, but he still has time to spend with me. We watch TV together and sometimes we play chess. He taught me how to play when I was seven. I help him in the art studio too." I felt like I was rambling so I quickly shut my mouth.

"Yes. Well, you and your father spend some time together. Good, good. Mrs. Grant, if it's OK with you, I would like to talk with Bree alone for the remainder of the session. Bree, is that OK with you?"

I shrugged as Mom hesitated and then rose quickly, grateful to step outside and have a smoke.

"So, Bree, you play chess?"

"Yes, sir."

"It just so happens I have a chess board here in the office. Would you like to play a game while we talk? Maybe we could have a little wager."

I had already spied his marble chess set over in the corner. "Sure, I'll play you. But what's the bet? I'm usually not a gambling kind of girl."

Dr. Bryan smiled. "How about if you win I have to buy you an ice cream sundae from the hospital cafeteria and if I win you get ice cream anyway, just for being a good sport?"

"Hmmm, sounds fair. But don't count on me showing you any mercy. I never showed my father any, which is probably why he doesn't like to play me anymore."

I knew Dr. Bryan had to be pretty smart, but he really didn't know what he was in for. I may not have inherited Father's art abilities but I did inherit his spatial skills. I could tell by Dr. Bryan's first few moves that he was trying to be gentle but I would not be patronized. Besides, if he thought I was crazy, at least I could prove I wasn't stupid. I got him into a hook and I could tell he realized he might want to try a little harder. On his next move, it was apparent that he expected me to take his pawn. When I didn't, he asked, "Why didn't you take my pawn?"

"Because I knew you wanted me to. You were just going to make the sacrifice so you could get my rook."

Dr. Bryan took a deep breath and pulled his chair up closer to the board.

When I play chess, I go on the attack. I cleaned up with Dr. Bryan in a matter of thirty minutes. He took it like a man, but I could tell he was surprised. I was proud of myself for impressing him and promised I wouldn't tell any of the other doctors.

As I had watched Dr. Bryan across the chess board, I noticed he had a gentle color of light around him that reminded me of Detective Hines. Could I trust his colors? I'd been fooled before.

Walking out of his office, it occurred to me we hadn't talked about my problems at all. He told Mom that he lost a bet with me and that on our next visit he owed me ice cream. Mom scheduled my next appointment, but she never asked what bet I won. This whole psychology business wasn't as bad as I thought it would be.

I looked over at my mom's profile as she steered the LTD out of the parking lot and into traffic, trying to light a cigarette at the same time. She had been so uncomfortable in Dr. Bryan's office, especially when he asked her if she worked. "Mom, I know you like staying home and being my mom and everything, but do you ever wish you had a real job?"

"Trust me, Bree, being your mom is a real job." Mom smiled. "Oh, sure. I've often thought if something, God forbid, happened to your father I'd either go back to school or get a job. I was a good student, straight A's before I got married." She flicked ashes off her cigarette. "Your father and I decided that it would just be better...for you, and for him, if I stayed at home and took care of things."

A lot of my friends' mothers didn't have jobs, but I knew I sure wasn't going to ever let a guy keep me from going to school or working. Whether I ever got married or had kids wouldn't change how I felt about being told whether I could or couldn't do something. That life might be enough for my mom but I knew it would never be enough for me. Now I wondered if it was enough for my mom after all.

He was accusing me of over-reacting and I was defending myself— that's how the fight began. Now we sat on opposite sides of the car in cold silence. I thought he was glaring daggers at me, but I continued to stare out the windshield like I didn't notice. Finally he sighed tiredly and touched my shoulder.

"We'll get through this. You'll see."

Maybe, I thought. But if things worked out, when it was over I was going to leave him. It scared me to think about being alone. But it scared me more to think of what would happen if I stayed.

CHAPTER THIRTEEN

USUALLY THE SUMMER months meant freedom. This summer I felt tied down, weighed down and caged by fear, by sorrow, by feelings of dread. I wasn't getting enough sleep, I wasn't getting enough sun and the laughs were few and far between, to say the least. Moping around wasn't the answer. All that had gotten me was a visit with a shrink. Still no arrest. Maybe we'd all jumped to the wrong conclusions.

Father was worried about Moose so I knew we wouldn't be taking any kind of vacation this summer. Most of my friend's parents weren't allowing bike rides or walks unescorted. Kids running out of the house on the spur of the moment yelling back over their shoulder, "going to the library, going to so and so's house, going to the park" was all a thing of the past.

Everyone was complaining about being bored, but I was burdened with too much to do.

When I got home I decided to take back some control and continue my own investigation. Cameraman was not so high up on my list at this point. I knew I'd made some bad assumptions and almost embarrassed myself. I figured I should be able to learn a lot just by asking questions of the person directly. Anyway, isn't that what detectives do? I decided to visit Mrs. Barker. Maybe she'd seen something or could give me a clue, since she was a widow and stayed home a lot. Father said she was a nosy neighbor. Besides, I loved her cats and she almost always offered me cookies.

I walked up to the neat white house and rang the bell. Several cats had already meandered up to the screen door to check out the visitor. Aunt Sharon said guys won't date a woman that has more than three cats. Supposedly, it scares them off. I figured that was why Mrs. Barker was still single. I saw the old woman hobbling to the door, her legs like parentheses as she walked. She smiled as soon as she saw who it was.

"Bree! How sweet of you to stop by! I haven't seen you for months, honey. You must have smelled the cookies I just finished baking." She opened the door and I stepped inside and gave her a hug, squishing myself up against her large droopy bosom.

Mrs. Barker's house had white walls in every room. There wasn't a single picture hanging on any of the walls except in the kitchen, where there was a large wall clock and a picture of Jesus, the one where He's standing at the door knocking. The first time I visited Mrs. Barker, it didn't dawn on me right away why her home seemed so blank, but after looking around for a few minutes I realized what was missing. Not shy around someone so warm and friendly, I'd asked her why she didn't have any pictures. She said she thought a home looked messy with things hanging all over the walls, and besides, nothing should take away from Jesus. I couldn't help but wonder what Mrs. Barker would think of Aunt Sharon's house.

I knelt down and picked up the calico cat, my favorite.

"How are all your sweet little kitties doing these days?" I asked.

"Oh, most of them are just fine. Christopher has had some stomach problems, though."

A devout Catholic, Mrs. Barker named all of her cats after saints. I knew it was not uncommon for her cats to have stomach problems, because she often fixed macaroni and cheese and tuna fish for all of the cats and herself.

"How many cats do you have now?"

Mrs. Barker cocked her head in thought. "To tell you the truth, I haven't counted them lately, but I'm pretty sure I have eleven."

I continued holding Valentine, the calico. It bugged me that the calico's name was Valentine, because I knew calicos were always female. But I didn't tell Mrs. Barker this. "Mrs. Barker, can I ask you something?"

"Of course, Bree. Come on in the kitchen and get a cookie while you're here too."

I followed Mrs. Barker into the kitchen and let her give me two peanut butter cookies. "Mrs. Barker, have you heard about that girl that was murdered up at the school?"

Mrs. Barker's face turned sad. "Yes, oh my, yes. What a tragic story. I had met her grandmother a few times when I filled in for their bridge group. It's so awfully sad. And scary, too!" She shivered at some thought I wasn't privy to.

"I was wondering if you'd seen anything. You know, since you're home a lot."

"Oh, heavenly days. No, I can't say that I saw anything unusual that day. I most certainly would have called the police if I had."

I was feeling frustrated and motivated to push for more information, even if it meant being annoying. "Think harder Mrs. Barker, anything could be useful in solving this horrible crime. Think about your neighbors. When you think of every single person in this neighborhood, who would you say is the most suspicious, you know, the person who seems different than everyone else?"

Mrs. Barker reached out and placed her hand on my shoulder and smiled, "Well dear, I'd have to say your daddy of course." She paused when she saw the confused look on my face and then added, "I mean he's the only one around here that's famous." She bent down and absently petted a tabby that must have weighed 20 pounds. "I didn't know that he had a twin too."

I shook my head in frustration. "No. I mean no, he doesn't. I know he's an only child. Why do you think he has a twin?"

"Well, I don't know how I could be mistaken." She seemed to be trying to remember something so I gave her time. It would be cool if my father had a twin.

"It seems like a couple of years ago I saw someone at your house late one night. It was when Agnes hurt her leg and I had an emergency visit to the vet. I had stopped at the stop sign by your house and thought I saw your dad outside pacing the driveway. He looked upset and I don't usually see him outside by himself late at night so I assumed something bad had happened. I immediately thought of you and your nighttime bike rides.

I was worried but I had my hands full trying to keep Agnes in the pillowcase while I drove. When I looked up again, he was gone. I guessed he had gone inside. I saw him a couple of days later and asked if everything was all right. He looked at me like I was crazy. Maybe I am because I said I saw him in the driveway pacing but he insisted it wasn't him. She smiled as she remembered. "That's right. I just told myself Geoff had a twin and I wasn't really getting senile."

Mrs. Barker's face went back to a look of concern. "Now why are you so interested in this? Did you know the poor girl?"

"No. Just curious, I guess. Since it happened in our neighborhood, it just seems like somebody around here might have seen something."

"Well, I suppose. I would think the police would already know if someone had seen something. Don't you think so, dear?"

"I guess. Thanks for the cookies, Mrs. Barker. I have some things to do but I'll come back real soon." I gently put Valentine on the floor and took my cookies with me.

Walking my bike, so I could eat the cookies, I headed back to my house. My investigation was getting nowhere and I was lost in thought and self-pity when I saw him. Mike had fallen off his bike almost in front of my house with library books strewn across the street. His bike looked undamaged but both knees were bloodied from the asphalt. I ran to his side and insisted on taking him inside for my mom to clean the wounds and put on Band-Aids.

While my mom doctored his knees I gathered our bikes and his books. When I went back in the house Mike was sitting at the kitchen table with a Coke and my mom was nowhere to be seen. He had clean bandages on both knees and didn't look too much the worse for wear. I set the books down on the table.

"I think my tire hit a rock. I wanted to get home and start reading before time to get dinner on. You're so lucky, Bree. Your mom is really nice. I miss that. I mean, a mom, I guess." He was quiet for a moment so I got a glass and poured myself some Coke too. I had no idea where the cookies had ended up when I ran to help Mike. I felt awkward because I knew he didn't have a mom and I wanted to change the subject by asking him about the books he was planning to read but he began talking before I could say anything.

"I was in the 4th grade and fell off the slide and broke my arm."

"Oh yeah, that was you, I remembered how upset everyone had been that day. Some of the girls even cried."

"They called my mom and laid me on the cot in the nurse's office. Time went by and I was starting to get sick to my stomach but my mom still didn't come. No one knew what to do. Just as Mrs. Stanley was about to take me to the hospital herself, dad showed up.

"When he saw me he started crying and saying how sorry he was. I wanted to reassure him that I was going to be all right, but then he told me Mom had been in an accident after she left the house. It wasn't her fault. Just someone who ran a stop sign because they were blinded by sun glare." Mike took a deep breath and was talking fast like he wanted to get the story out with the least amount of effort.

"I knew she wouldn't have been at that stop sign at that time if it hadn't been for me breaking my arm though. I felt so guilty about that for the longest time.

"We have pictures of her around the house but I know she would look a little different now. And it gets harder and harder to recall her image clearly, to remember the sound of her voice, how she smelled. I just wanted you to know how lucky you are to have your mom."

I was so full of emotions. I felt very sorry for Mike. I couldn't imagine what it would be like to lose a parent, but I knew I would never forget how they looked or smelled or felt. I didn't know what to say so all I said was, "I'm sorry."

Mom came back in with a casserole from the freezer and told Mike she was sending it home with him if he could manage it on his bike. He seemed very pleased and smiled and winked at me before he left, whispering, "Told you you're lucky."

I went into my bedroom and shut the door, walked over to the closet and slid the chrome door open and turned on the little lamp inside the closet. I climbed up on my hamper to push the crawl space board out of the way and reached up for the ladder, which I pulled down. Once up in the attic, I switched on the Christmas lights and turned on my record player, which I had rigged with an outlet that plugged into the light socket above me. I smiled at my friends who seemed glad to be brought into the light.

"So are you all in the mood for a little incense?" I tried to avoid referring to my friends by gender terms; it was a sensitive issue.

They all agreed as I chose a piece of black cherry incense, Kelly's favorite. Kelly hated the musty smell of the attic and the incense definitely helped.

I had just added my record player to the attic decor. I put on my *Queen* album and chose *Bohemian Rhapsody*, which seemed suited to today's meeting.

I heard Jesse's inner voice stutter, "B-b-Bree, have you f-f-figured out who the k-k-k-k-killer is?"

I looked at Jesse in his red-sequined dress and answered, "I really don't know. I was hoping all of you could help me think through some of the clues."

Terry responded, "But of course we'll help you, dear heart. Come on now, tell us what you know." Their eyes were intense, their lips parted slightly in eagerness. I knew they were always pleased when I shared news of the outside world with them, even bad news.

"Moose looks guilty. The evidence points to him. But Father believes in Moose. If I can prove him innocent…"

I went through my list. "First of all, I know Rachel was murdered in the evening or early morning on my school playground, up in the woods. No one seems to have seen anything, although it might have still been light out. Second, she was strangled. Third, Jennifer's remains were stolen from her grave sometime the month before and later placed in a box next to Rachel's body. Fourth, I have few suspects but I'm sure not learning too much just poking around the neighborhood."

Stacey asked, "So, Bree. Of all the possibilities, who's the one who could have done the evil deed?"

"If you asked Detective Hines, he'd say Moose. I think the only thing saving Moose is that he has an alibi. I mean, it was his daughter's bones they found next to the body. And Detective Hines has a photo of Moose's partial fingerprint that was possibly on the coin. And Moose does have a bad history."

Terry asked tightly, his British accent even more evident than usual, "Hold on just a bit, old girl. You said Moose is who the detective suspects. And what about you?"

Stacey, who had the best singing voice, was singing along with the music.

"IS THIS THE REAL LIFE?
IS THIS JUST FANTASY?
CAUGHT IN A LANDSLIDE
NO ESCAPE FROM REALITY
OPEN YOUR EYES
LOOK UP TO THE SKIES AND SEE
I'M JUST A POOR BOY, I NEED NO SYMPATHY
BECAUSE I'M EASY COME, EASY GO
A LITTLE HIGH, LITTLE LOW
ANYWAY THE WIND BLOWS, DOESN'T REALLY MATTER TO
ME, TO ME!"

Terry interrupted her solo. "Stacey, ahem! Pay attention to Bree!"

I had to think about Terry's question for a moment. "Well, I don't know. I was wrong about Cameraman, and I still have my doubts that Moose could do such a terrible thing. But Moose isn't who I thought he was. It's all too confusing! I'm not even sure now that Jennifer's death was an accident. Moose was so upset the other day at the studio, but not crazy, and someone would have to be crazy to do that kind of thing, right?"

We all paused, pondering the disparate facts. *Bohemian Rhapsody* played on in the background.

"Wh-wh-why don't you ask the O-o-o-ouija board?" Jesse offered.

I hesitated, although I didn't know why. "Yeah, sure. I can do that." The last time the board had spelled out "close" and that hadn't helped.

I knelt down in front of the board, concentrating, resting my hands very lightly on the message indicator. As I closed my eyes, my heart began to hammer violently, pounding, causing me to lose my breath. This time would I learn who the killer was? The music seemed to be getting louder.

"TOO LATE, MY TIME HAS COME
SENDS SHIVERS DOWN MY SPINE
BODY'S ACHING ALL THE TIME
GOODBYE EVERYBODY - I'VE GOT TO GO
GOTTA LEAVE YOU ALL BEHIND AND FACE THE TRUTH..."

I felt my hands begin to move by a force greater than any I had ever felt before. They stopped and I opened my eyes to the first letter. 'F'.

I looked up from the board to my friends. "What's that supposed to mean? Whose name starts with 'F'?"

"I DON'T WANT TO DIE
I SOMETIMES WISH I'D NEVER BEEN BORN AT ALL..."

Kelly said anxiously, "Keep goin', honey! Y'all need more letters."

I placed my hands back on the indicator and closed my eyes. I could feel my hands moving again, faster this time. The pointer rested on the letter 'A'. Chills began running up and down my spine as the music grew louder in my ears. I could hear my guardians humming.

"I SEE A LITTLE SILHOUETTO OF A MAN
SCARAMOUCH, SCARAMOUCH WILL YOU DO THE FANDANGO
THUNDERBOLT AND LIGHTNING - VERY VERY FRIGHTENING
ME
GALILEO, GALILEO,

GALILEO, GALILEO,
GALILEO—FIGARO ... MAGNIFICO!"

'T'...'H'... E'...

"'THE'? What's 'THE' mean? 'THE' what?" I felt my hands
continue to move. The board was beginning to shake. The attic
was deathly still. I felt a cold wind blow across my body as
my hands came to an abrupt halt. My friends pressed closely
against me. I felt suffocated, like they were stealing my air.

I looked down at the message indicator. It pointed to the
letter 'R'.

I gasped. The air was being sucked right out of my lungs. I
looked wildly around at my friends, each face mirroring shock
and disbelief.

My whole body began to shake. "No! No! There's no way
he could ever hurt anyone! Right, guys? I'm right, aren't I?"
I was crying now. "Please tell me Father didn't kill that girl!"
I looked pleadingly into each of their faces. "It's just a stupid
game! That's right, just a game! Father is good! He's helping
Moose." I shoved the board away with a kick of my foot.

Gene spoke first. "I believe," he began, slowly and precisely,
"that you may be required to look at your father in a different
way. It is entirely possible that you are too close to him, as his
daughter, to truly know what he is capable of."

"Bree, sweetie pie," Kelly added, "I don't think y'all feel like
your daddy murdered anybody, never no mind what that ole
board says."

Jesse said, "That's r-r-right, B-b-Bree. J-j-just w-w-watch
him. L-l-look at him d-d-d-differently and s-s-see what you
d-d-discover."

Terry added, "Bree, dear girl, the word 'Father' doesn't necessarily mean *your* father is the killer. Rather, it may be he is acquainted with, or perhaps knows a bit about the killer. Or could it be the word 'Father' is a clue within itself? Moose was Jennifer's father—splendid! Maybe that's a piece to our puzzle. Maybe it was Rachel's father. What do we know about him?"

Each one had a different comment intended to make me feel better, but I felt claustrophobic. I had come for comfort, but I wanted to be alone. It had been their stupid idea to use the board and I felt resentment and anger. And guilt. They were only trying to help.

I stepped back, wanting to believe Terry. I felt hysteria rise up and engulf me, separating me from my friends. My voice cracked, "But what if he *is* the killer? *What am I supposed to do?*"

Stacey said, "Hey, turn him in to the cops."

"No!" I yelled, "How could I do that to Mom? Who'd take care of her?"

"If your old man is a murderer," Stacey countered, "then he needs to be behind bars. What if he kills somebody again, or hurts you or your mom?"

"My father would never, ever hurt me! Never!" I cried frantically. What would I do if Father was the killer? What if I couldn't save Moose or my father?

"EASY COME EASY GO - WILL YOU LET ME GO
BISMILLAH! NO - WE WILL NOT LET YOU GO - LET HIM
GO
BISMILLAH! WE WILL NOT LET YOU GO - LET HIM GO
BISMILLAH! WE WILL NOT LET YOU GO - LET ME GO
WILL NOT LET YOU GO - LET ME GO (NEVER)
NEVER LET YOU GO - LET ME GO
NEVER LET ME GO ... OOO

SHATTERED COLORS

NO, NO, NO, NO, NO, NO, NO ...
OH MAMA MIA, MAMA MIA, MAMA MIA LET ME GO
BEELZEBUB HAS A DEVIL PUT ASIDE FOR ME
FOR ME
FOR ME"

CHAPTER FOURTEEN

I REALLY DON'T know how long I had been up in the attic when I heard Mom calling me for dinner. I didn't feel like eating, but I needed to get out of there. I didn't want to hurt my friends' feelings and Mom's calls gave me the excuse I needed.

I hurried down to the dining room, wiping away tears, and took my place at the table. How could I even look at Father without betraying my thoughts? I stared down at my chicken and tried to appear preoccupied with my food.

Father asked, "So, how did the doctor's appointment go today?"

I was really hoping Mom would answer that question. I glanced up and saw Father looking directly at me. "I asked you a question, Breezy."

"Yes, sir. I thought the appointment went fine."

"Did that doctor get those bad thoughts out of your head? What's wrong with your face?"

"I was, uh, rubbing some lotion on my face, too hard I think." Quickly changing the subject, I added, "We really didn't get into too much discussion. We spent most of the time playing chess." Immediately I knew I said too much.

Father slammed down his fist. "Chess! My God, we're not paying that quack sixty-five bucks an hour to play games with you!" He turned his angry face on Mom. "Are you aware of this, Dorothy?"

Mom seemed too scared to answer, although I thought she should remind him that she paid for the appointment out of her monthly allowance. But I was to blame; I'm the one that spilled the beans about playing chess with Dr. Bryan.

"Dorothy didn't realize that they played chess, but perhaps it was just to build rapport with Bree. Psychologists probably have to do that, hmmm?"

Father's face was still red but he stopped talking and started eating. I took that as a good sign. I tried to eat but my stomach was in knots. I looked over at Father, remembering the other night when he got so mad at me for looking at him. I knew he'd get mad tonight if I wasn't eating. I started cutting my food into tiny little bites, trying to look busy.

I simply could not picture Father killing Rachel; my mind wouldn't let me even imagine it. Plus it didn't add up. He didn't know her. He had no reason to kill her or anyone else. The Ouija board had to be wrong. Then again, if Terry was on track, if it was trying to tell me something else, I couldn't figure it out. Maybe the board had been referring to Rachel's father. But wouldn't the police have investigated Rachel's family? I couldn't remember what the papers had said about her parents.

I thought my brain would explode. What kind of daughter was I that I could even imagine my father being a murderer? There really was something seriously wrong with me.

Finally, when I couldn't stand the feelings welling up inside me any longer, with a quivering voice I asked, "Father, could you ever kill anything? I mean, like hunting or something?"

He glared at me. "Why would you ask something like that? You know I don't hunt. I have no desire to hunt. I killed a bird with a BB gun when I was twelve and cried like a baby. I vowed on that day that I would never be a hunter!"

Mom smacked her lips. "You were in Vietnam, dear…" He turned his glare on her and she stopped abruptly.

It was going to take a lot of guts, but there was a question I had to ask if I was going to be able to sleep tonight. "Have you *ever* killed anyone, Father?" We never talked about it. Maybe he had been a cook or a medic…like on *M.A.S.H.*

Father jumped up from the table and grabbed me by the hair, knocking me over backwards. "Damnations! Didn't you hear what I just said? I told you I could never kill anything! I cried over the little dead bird! I am not a taker of life! I am a giver of life!" His eyes glazed over as he continued.

"*There is a time for everything, and season for every activity under heaven: a time to be born and a time to die, a time to kill and a time to heal!*"

He stood motionless, my head still locked in his iron grip.

I couldn't see his face but I glimpsed Mom's shocked look and I cried out, "Please, you're hurting me! Please let me go!"

Mom tried to get him to sit back down, saying I didn't mean anything by the question, but I don't think he was listening.

Roughly, he dropped me to the floor. "Go to your room and wait for me on your bed. Now! GO!"

Panicked, I jumped up and ran down the hall to my room. I threw myself on the bed, sobbing uncontrollably, harder than I remember ever crying before. I was mad at myself for questioning him and I was mad at Mom for not protecting me. And I was mad at Father for being the way he was. Why did he say to wait for him? Then, there he was, looming in the doorframe, his brown hair hanging in his eyes, glittering brown eyes dark with fury. I saw his leather belt in his right hand. My heart skipped a beat.

"No! Please don't spank me!" I pleaded. "I'm sorry I questioned you! I'm sorry! I know you could never kill anyone." I had pushed him too far and I was going to regret it. Maybe I even deserved this punishment because my thoughts had been so horrible.

Father strode grimly to the bed and pushed me down. "Turn over."

I did as he said, tears flowing hysterically. He reached down and pulled down my pants, something he'd never done before. I was humiliated beyond endurance. I cried out, "I hate you! I hate you!"

The first slap of the belt made me scream. By the third lash, I couldn't scream because I was choking on my own tears.

As he left, he paused in the doorway. "Don't you ever, ever suggest I could kill anyone again."

With that, he vanished. Time seemed to expand as I lay there crying. Faintly I heard Father say, "Dorothy, don't you dare go in there! She has to learn not to question me!" I hated him, I hated my own father.

I tried to make myself small, to disappear, to dissolve into nothingness. However, the pain and anger kept me in the here and now. I got up and looked at my butt in the mirror. The skin was welted and a few of the marks were open just enough to really sting. Father had given me the belt before, but this was the worst. I couldn't put my underwear back on, so I just slipped under the covers and cried until I honestly had no tears left. How could he treat me that way?

I remember Mom telling me that he still had bad memories from the war. Mom's comment made me think he must have killed people in Vietnam. Could he have killed someone else? What would have evoked such a violent reaction? Should I do something? Should I tell somebody? No way. Other people already thought I was weird. Probably thought our whole family was strange. I couldn't tell anyone. It would be too embarrassing.

At that moment I hated him, but knew I couldn't live with myself if I got my own father in trouble. What if they sent him to jail? Mom couldn't take care of herself. She desperately needed him. What would happen if I told Dr. Bryan or Detective Hines how he treated Mom and me at times? The truth was I needed him too, although at the moment I was consumed by anger, feeling like no one really loved me. He hadn't always been like this. I knew he loved me. When I was younger we had talked about anything and everything. This just wasn't my father anymore. I still caught glimpses of who he used to be but I also knew something had changed. I just didn't know if it was him or me.

Fearing what might happen if someone found out about his temper, and clinging to the hope that my suspicions about Father were wrong, I lay there pondering what the Ouija board meant by spelling out 'FATHER'. Suddenly, a thought occurred to me and I felt great relief, what if the board really spelled out 'Farther' and I had missed the 'R'? The more I thought about it, the more I remembered how the indicator had moved so very fast, there might have been an 'R' and I had missed it. Maybe it was like that I Spy game where you are told you're getting warmer or colder as you try to guess what object the person is thinking of. Maybe the board was only giving me directions. With this new hopeful thought, I eventually fell into a restless sleep.

That night I dreamed I was back in the tree house at the school. I saw a man bent over Rachel's body. He had his hands around her neck and he was sucking the breath out of the girl with his mouth. I lost my footing and pitched forward, falling from the tree house. As I screamed, the man turned and I saw his face. It was Father. He saw me falling and ran forward to catch me in midair.

I awoke bathed in sweat, my heart pounding wildly. Mom was sitting on the other side of my room, holding her coffee and cigarette. The morning light filtered through my bedroom window. I rubbed the sleep from my eyes, trying to shake off the malevolence I felt.

"Your father hurt you last night." It was a statement, not a question.

I sat up in my bed, trying to erase the dream from my mind. "No, Mom, he didn't hurt me. It doesn't hurt now, anyway." I don't know why I lied.

Mom puffed on her cigarette, staring at me. "He loves you, you know."

"I know."

"You shouldn't question him. Your father hates that more than anything."

Mom looked like a frightened little bird, sad and vulnerable. "I'm sorry, Mom. I'll be more careful." I wanted to make her feel better. I couldn't stand to see her so concerned about me. I don't know which scared me more, Mom's weakness or Father's temper. I knew my mom was capable of strength, I'd seen it on several occasions, but only when my father wasn't around.

"Why is he so sensitive about hurting an animal?"

Mom pondered this for a moment. She may have been timid but she wasn't stupid. She had to have often wondered to herself why he reacted to things the way he did.

"Your father can't stand to ever be wrong, or do anything wrong. His father was very critical of him. So now, he is especially sensitive to the concept of breaking a rule or hurting someone. Your father has bad memories of Vietnam. And now there's new research that shows all that Agent Orange our military sprayed over the jungles was actually very poisonous. Your father was sprayed and sometimes I wonder if that affected him. He came back from Vietnam changed, but I guess a lot of people did. He says his memories are too terrible to talk about. I think he had to do some horrible things."

She took a long puff off her cigarette and continued, "Remember the time your father found that hurt opossum in the ditch? Most people wouldn't have touched it. But your father brought it into the kitchen and bandaged it up and fed it for a week with an eye dropper, until it was all well.

"Sometimes, though, his temper gets the best of him. Mom knows he feels terrible about last night."

I wanted to believe her last comment. "How do you know?"

"Your father had a very restless night. Lots of bad dreams. He left before the sun came up. He probably went to work early since he couldn't sleep."

I was glad he had a bad night. We had that in common at least.

"Mom, who do you think killed that girl? Do you really think Moose could have done it?" I couldn't remember the last time we had talked this much. It felt reassuring.

Mom sighed, "Bree, you need to let it go, that's what the police and lawyers are for, it will all sort itself out." She stood to leave. "You have an appointment today with Dr. Bryan. It's at one o'clock."

"She's going to some psycho shrink," he said watching for my reaction. "She needs a warning to keep her mouth shut and stop asking so many questions. Curiosity killed the cat you know." He was smirking now and I knew we were all on dangerous ground.

"I wouldn't worry about it," I answered trying to sound casual. "What harm can it do?"

"Do you ever think about it? Going to a psychiatrist? Laying on a couch? Trying to explain?"

I was trying to keep my face from showing the fear I felt. I had thought about talking to someone so many times. But I knew they wouldn't believe me. They'd lock me up and throw away the key.

I tried on a calm smile. "Like I said. Don't worry about it."

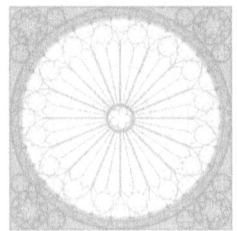

CHAPTER FIFTEEN

I FELT VERY much in need of therapy, so I didn't complain this time. Resting on my pillow, I thought about how to spend the morning. No way could I take another day suspecting my own father of murder. The only way to make the pain go away was to find the real killer and anyway I really believed the board could have said 'Farther'. But did that mean I needed to explore farther from my neighborhood or had I gone too far out already?

I decided to explore the block, one more time. Somewhere out there was a man, or maybe a woman, who knew something about Rachel Carter's murder. Maybe they didn't even know that what they knew was important. I dressed in loose shorts and a T-shirt and grabbed a chocolate Pop-Tart.

I started walking around the neighborhood, looking for something, but I didn't know what. I paused at Mr. Kohler's house. Could he have seen anything that night? I reluctantly rang the bell, feeling guilty for making a man in a wheelchair answer the door.

After a few minutes, I heard the click of several deadbolt locks. He cracked the door; a chain was still latched at his eye level. "What do you want?" He sounded crabby. I'd never spoken to him before. Now I could see why.

"Uh, Mr. Kohler?"

"How do you know my name?" He looked really annoyed.

"My parents have mentioned you. I'm Bree Grant." I pointed across the street in the general direction of my house and saw a flicker of acknowledgement around his eyes, but he didn't smile. "I was just wondering if you had maybe noticed anything suspicious around the neighborhood. I see you looking out your sliding glass door a lot. And—"

"Why! Is there something going on that I should know about? Come a bit closer. Tell me what you know, little girl!" He leaned forward in his wheelchair, waiting for my reply.

"No, I mean, I don't know. I was—I was referring to the murder of Rachel Carter."

Mr. Kohler snorted a mirthless laugh. "And you think I could have something to do with it. Oh yeah, right! I could have rolled over her with my wheelchair, you bet! What a hoot—now *scram*!" and with that he slammed the door. I heard all three dead bolts being locked into place and figured that was the end of that.

I walked on toward the brick house and stood in front of it thinking. I didn't know who lived there but I figured I should talk to them. The problem was they never seemed to be home.

I walked up to the front door and rang the bell. No answer. The curtains were all closed up so tight, there was no looking in.

Frustrated, I continued my walk up the street contemplating my next move. As I was going around the corner, I saw Mrs. Hines pushing Gia in her stroller. "Mrs. Hines! Hey, it's me, Bree. I baby-sat for you the other night!"

"Oh, yes…hello, Bree." She kept walking.

I ran to catch up with her. "I thought I could baby-sit for you again some time." I was actually thinking how it was the only place in this neighborhood where I was learning anything useful.

"We'll see. Maybe I'll call you sometime. Thank-you." She briskly walked right past me, her shadow flickering with color. I rubbed my eyes with my fists.

I wondered what that was all about, but I knew, I had blown it. She seemed less than thrilled with the job I did the other night. Maybe she'd figured out that I had inadvertently induced a soda pop high in her daughter or gone through her husband's things. There went that source of income and information. I was a lousy baby-sitter, a lousy detective and an annoyance to my neighbors. I had a mission and no one was taking me seriously.

As I pondered my next move, I noticed a car driving too slowly behind me. Was it the one from the other day? It looked the same, but I wasn't sure. My heart raced. Why wasn't the driver passing me? Was I over-reacting? I picked up the pace and started running. The car picked up speed and swerved dangerously close to me. I felt panic set in, was it trying to hit me like Jennifer was hit? Impulsively, I cut across the nearest lawn. The car sounded like it had stopped. I ran without looking back and dove into the nearest clump of bushes. I stayed there, hidden and trembling, until my heart found a more reasonable beat. I knew I eventually had to reveal myself, but what if the car was waiting for me? Aunt Sharon would say I was being an anxious child. Mom would say I was obsessing. My instincts told me there was an unknown danger pursuing me. I trusted my instincts, at the same time hoping I was wrong.

I warily crawled out of the bushes, trying to get my bearings.

Oh, God. The witch lady, standing on her back porch, was staring right at me. Cripes! I used the witch lady's bushes as a refuge! Was I nuts? I quickly stood up and dusted myself off, trying to decide if this was an opportunity for deep probing questions or the most opportune time to bolt. She spoke before I came to a conclusion.

"You can't hide from the truth." She turned her back to me as if our conversation had been terminated before it had begun. I was scared, but she wasn't scary looking. She was kind of pretty in a flower-child, hippy kind of way.

"Wait," I yelled, my voice more forceful than I felt.

She stopped, her back still toward me, then slowly turned, revealing a face much prettier than I expected. Her clothes were full and flowing. She wore ropes of colored beads and mood rings on nearly every finger.

I took a few steps closer and asked, "Do you know anything about Rachel Carter's murder?"

"Why," her voice was velvety, "would you ask such a question?"

She looked at me so directly, I wanted to turn away, but somehow this didn't seem like the kind of person with whom I could be vague. "Because I've been thinking a lot about the murder and I want to help solve it. It's important to me."

As an after-thought I added, "By the way, I'm Bree Grant from the down the street." Somehow I had the feeling she already knew that. She still held me suspended with her gaze, but I didn't feel threatened.

I thought she might ask why I was interested in the murder, but she didn't. She stepped toward me, staring intently in my direction. "Come closer, child, and let me see you." In fear, I stepped back several feet and with that, she turned and went into her house. I almost swayed from the sudden abandonment.

Why had she turned away so abruptly? I had felt uncomfortable in her intense gaze, but now I missed her. I almost went to knock on her door, but I didn't know what I would say.

I decided to run home to get my bike and ride over to Aunt Sharon's house, maybe she'd fix us black olive and cream cheese sandwiches. I wasn't mad at her anymore for talking to Mom about me. I guess I really knew all along that she cared and that she would never say any more about our private conversations than she felt was absolutely necessary.

It took no time at all to grab my bike and I didn't see any point in telling Mom where I was going. She probably wouldn't stop me, but why take the chance. I was pedaling down my aunt's street in less time than it took to justify my taking off without giving Mom a head's up. As soon as I neared the door, Aunt Sharon threw it open, scaring me out of my wits.

"Bree, come in here right now! Your dad's been arrested! Your mom is looking all over for you!"

My stomach twisted; I felt light-headed. I couldn't breathe. My chest was so tight it hurt. Was I having a heart attack? So this was how it all ended, huh? I had kept all the secrets and still my so-called life was over. My father was a murderer. I wasn't paranoid after all. I sat down—actually I collapsed—right there on the porch. I couldn't even cry; I must have been in total shock. I was so numb it didn't seem like anything mattered anymore.

"So, he did it, didn't he?" It was all I could say.

"You knew he was going to do this?" She was watching me closely. I could see how concerned she was.

"Of course I didn't know… I just worried he *had* done it." The tears were on their way; I could feel them behind my eyes. What would happen to my mom and me? Things did still matter to me. I wasn't as numb as I would have liked. The fear hurt.

"Why on earth would Geoff be so pig-headed that he couldn't just leave that window be?"

Far away, like the faint sound of thunder rumbling beyond the horizon, I perceived an inkling of hope. Aunt Sharon's words didn't fit with the concept of 'Bree, your life is over.' A fog began to lift from my brain. "Huh?"

"You may have suspected it, but Dorothy is beside herself with worry! She had no idea your dad would really drive out to Greenview to try and take that window back from St. Michael's. She's gone to bail him out. We're just hoping the priest won't press charges. I'm so mad at your dad I could just shake him. That was a dumb and crazy thing to do!"

It was becoming clearer now; relief washed over me. "You mean Father tried to steal the Catholic church's window?"

"Yeah, that's what I am saying. He wanted to redo it or something. He tried to break into the church in the middle of the night with an extension ladder and a bag of tools. A neighbor saw him up on the ladder, in the dark, and thought it looked suspicious. Duh! So she called the parish priest—woke him up, in fact—to ask if he was having any work done on the church at four in the morning. Apparently the answer was no, because Father O'Malley called the police."

"I can't believe my father would do that!" Yeah, but just minutes ago I believed he could commit murder. I began to giggle hysterically.

"O.K., fine. I'm glad you're amused, but Dorothy isn't. She was really shaken. I don't know what Geoff was thinking, but it sure wasn't how this would affect Dorothy…or you."

I could tell Aunt Sharon was really angry and I felt guilty that I felt so much relief. Another time maybe I would have been embarrassed, but now I was just so glad Father was a thief and not a murderer.

"Your mom said she wants you to keep your doctor's appointment, though. Maybe you should head home. She should be back before too long. It was just about an hour ago that she called and said she was on her way to the police station. If she doesn't get back in time, call me and I'll take you."

On my way home I ruminated over how it felt to believe, even for a minute, that my father had been arrested for murder. The feelings were overwhelming. I had literally felt the ground fall out from under me. I turned my bike onto 32nd Street and noticed a red car turning right behind me. I felt a familiar wave of panic well up in my chest. I pedaled harder, looking back over my shoulder, but with the glare of the sun I couldn't see the driver. There were no streets for me to turn onto to get away. Rashly, I turned my bike sharply, right in front of the car, making a U-turn in the middle of the street. I heard brakes squeal and the horn blared, freaking me out even more.

A big male voice shouted, "You're going to end up dead!"

I kept pedaling, now headed in the wrong direction, not looking back, his threat echoing in my head over and over like a jackhammer. I was pretty sure it was the same car and voice from the theater. By the time I rode around the block, my heartbeat had begun to return to normal. My fear had nearly gotten me killed, or saved my life.

Mom was waiting for me at home. I didn't see Father. "Where have you been?" It was rare that she sounded so exasperated and I was truly sorry I had made her morning worse than it was already.

"I was out exploring the neighborhood, just checking things out. Then I stopped by Aunt Sharon's, and she told me about Father. Is he OK?"

"Hmmm, well, Dorothy thinks so. Father O'Malley seems to be an understanding person. He said he won't press charges, but he wants your father to stay completely away from the church, unless he is attending Sunday mass."

"So we might go to that church sometime?" I asked hopefully.

"Heavens no! Your father would never step foot in that church again, with what's happened! And the way he feels about that window…"

Mom seemed distracted. "Oh, I need my cigarettes." Her search for nicotine kept me from asking further questions. I watched her dig under the bags of chips and Little Debbie Snack Cakes for the missing carton. I sighed in annoyance as I was starting to become bothered that she cared so much for her cigarettes.

While not a lot was said about smoking at the time, I was aware of the Surgeon General's warning on my mother's cigarette packs which read, "Cigarettes may be hazardous to your health." The 70's had brought campaigns raising awareness of problems I never knew existed. A Native American (Indian to me at the time) caused me to feel guilt for littering. Smokey the Bear let me know I could burn down an entire forest if I wasn't careful. These messages all had an impact on me. I didn't want the Indian to cry and I didn't want Bambi's mother to burn to death, and I didn't want my mom to be dependent on something that was apparently hazardous to her health.

I had made several attempts to get her to stop smoking. When I was nine I hid all her cigarettes, but this tactic was short-lived once my father got involved. When I was ten I tried writing up a contract, swearing I would not back talk for as long as she didn't smoke. I broke the contract within 24 hours and she happily went right back to smoking.

I also tried a heartfelt letter that I presented to her on my birthday, pleading for her to stop so she wouldn't die and leave me. This approach seemed to work for several weeks, until one day I opened the closed bathroom door and saw her on her knees, leaning over the tub. My mom was desperately puffing on a cigarette, next to the running water, in hopes of masking the smoke. She didn't see me so I quietly walked away, deflated and sad.

The first time she resumed lighting up in front of me, I caught her watching me nervously out of the corner of her eye, waiting for my reaction. But I didn't say a word. By this point I figured people were going to do what people wanted to do, and campaigns, pleading, and warnings weren't going to stop them.

Mom fumbled through another kitchen drawer until she found a pack of Camels. "All right now, we'd better get you to the doctor's. Mom will get a cup of coffee so we can leave."

The drive to Dr. Bryan's office was mercifully quiet; I needed the time to think. Just how much was I willing to tell him? What could I tell him? Mom interrupted the silence to say that she would appreciate it if I didn't tell Dr. Bryan about Father's arrest. She said it would be embarrassing, and I agreed. I felt this was all pointless if there was nothing safe to discuss. I would keep my secrets at all costs.

Minutes after we arrived, Dr. Bryan stepped into the waiting room and reminded me that he owed me some ice cream. He didn't have to remind me. I hadn't eaten lunch; no time with Father's arrest and all. He led the way out of the office, giving Mom a casual hello and nod of the head.

The hospital cafeteria was connected to Dr. Bryan's building via a long tunnel. Dr. Bryan made polite conversation while I made my sundae at the ice cream machine. I didn't want to make one too big, because he might think I was a pig. When I saw the one he made for himself I instantly regretted that decision.

Dr. Bryan looked from my sundae to his and said, "You know, Bree, I think you can do better than that."

I was hungry, but my stomach felt queasy. Maybe it would help to eat. I added another big scoop of chocolate ice cream and smothered it in marshmallow topping, adding a handful of maraschino cherries for good measure. We carried our sundaes back up to his office. Once inside, I chose to sit on the sofa. He sat in his same desk chair. As we ate our ice cream, I was getting tense and nervous at the prospect of discussing anything personal.

Dr. Bryan broke the silence. "Bree, your mom thinks you're worrying too much about the murder of Rachel Carter. Do you believe your mom's feelings are correct?"

I wondered why we couldn't just sit in silence. "I think about the murder, yes. In fact I've been thinking about it a lot, but I don't mean to worry Mom."

"That's thoughtful of you. Why are you concerned about your mom?"

"I just don't like to upset her... she is..." I floundered for the right words. "She is fragile."

Dr. Bryan looked perplexed. "Fragile in what way?"

"I don't know exactly. She just always seems...well, I don't know for sure..." I wasn't sure I wanted to pursue this. I felt disloyal talking about Mom. Besides, there were too many secrets. What would Dr. Bryan think of her killing all those snakes?

"Go on."

"Nervous, I suppose. She seems nervous all the time, and I guess I know what that feels like."

Dr. Bryan leaned back in his chair. "Why do you think your mom might be nervous?"

"I don't know." I wanted him to stop asking questions about my mom.

"Tell me what it feels like to be nervous."

OK. It was now or never. I could make this a safe confession. No secrets, just the facts. "I worry all the time, and I get scared really easily." Dr. Bryan looked interested, so I kept going,

"I have a recurring dream of water leaking in through the ceiling and walls. I know that doesn't sound very scary but somehow in the dream it is very scary. I guess I don't know why I'm dreaming that when we've never had a leak, that I know of." I thought for a second, "And anyway water shouldn't be scary."

Dr. Bryan looked thoughtful. "Bree, a lot of times dreams don't mean anything. Think of your brain as full of stored information from all the years it's been storing information. It's like your brain is full of filing cabinets and they randomly open up while you sleep and a random pieces of paper from many different files mix together in your head to form one dream. You can see how people can dream some pretty unusual things.

"However, there are dreams that do have meaning. Certainly a recurring dream is worth evaluating."

"So, what do you think it means?"

"When something in a dream springs a leak or takes on water this suggests that feelings kept inside for some time are now seeping into your consciousness. It could be that something you have successfully put out of your mind may now be elbowing its way to the front, requiring attention."

"You mean there is something I know that I don't know I know?" Somehow this thought seemed very troubling to me. I began to chew on my bottom lip.

Dr. Bryan seemed to notice my concern and added, "On the plus side, your psyche would not be pushing this issue into consciousness if it were not time to work it through. You are, in more ways than one, ready to deal with it. Something we could try is hypnosis…"

I interrupted him midsentence, "Oh, cool! I saw that on Scooby Doo! An evil clown hypnotized Daphne and made her think she could ride a unicycle in a circus! I'd love to be hypnotized!"

Dr. Bryan smiled and said, "Yes, cartoons can make hypnotism look like magic, but in reality it can't do that. Hypnosis is normal and natural. You'd be in a safe, relaxed state in which you are fully aware, in full control but more capable of deeply focusing on thoughts. You may not know it, but you have been hypnotized many times before. Have you ever been daydreaming, reading a book or watching a TV program and did not know your mom or friend had been talking to you?"

I nodded. I often felt that way.

"You were likely hypnotized and didn't know it. When you're in hypnosis you can think of it as using parts of your brain that are powerful—but rarely used. Hypnosis helps some kids build better study habits, develop more self-confidence, understand dreams, and become less fearful of things that most people do not fear, like elevators or roller coasters."

"That sounds like it could really help me. At night, it's the worst. I wake up, and my room is dark, and my first thought is that there's something out there, something bad…"

"Like a person, or more of a monster-type thing?"

"I know there's no such things as monsters, but it doesn't really feel like the presence of a person. It's hard to explain. It's like I just wake up with this bad feeling, and my heart's really pounding and everything feels…threatening."

"What about during the day? Do you have these feelings then?"

"Sometimes. Lately it's been more often."

"Since the murder?"

"Yes."

Dr. Bryan thought for a moment. "Can you give me some examples of times during the day that you have felt the type of heart-pounding-feeling you described?"

"When I think about the murder, which is all the time, it seems. And when I think someone is following me. Ummm, when I'm in a room and I think someone is watching me, and…." I hesitated.

"Go on."

"And when my father gets upset."

"What happens when your father gets upset?"

"He yells a lot and sometimes…uh, well….ummm, some-times, sometimes…." my voice faltered. I didn't want to talk about this. How was I going to cover?

"Sometimes what?"

"Sometimes, not very often, just sometimes…he spanks me."

"How does he spank you?"

"With a belt." My head was down. Wasn't confession sup-posed to be good for the soul? I hadn't intended to say anything about my father's temper. What if Dr. Bryan told Father what I said? What if he reported it to someone?

"Enough to leave a mark?"

"Oh, no." I answered a little too quickly, trying to ignore my sore bottom. I didn't want to talk about this.

"During the school year, did you have many worries?"

Thank God. Dr. Bryan was asking questions about some-thing else, something safe. "I worried about my grades, friends, boys—or a lack thereof." I tried a little smile.

"What made you worry about grades? Your mom said you were a straight A student."

"I worried that I might make a B and that my parents would be disappointed in me." I hoped that was okay to say. "They know I'm capable of more than a B, and I know I shouldn't make a B, but still…it could happen. Just like death can hap-pen…to children. It shouldn't—but it does and it scares me how unsure life is. I wish I had a good written plan of how my life's going to go, even the bad stuff. I think it would be a lot easier to handle, you know?"

"I can understand those feelings. Lots of times it feels as though life would be easier if we knew what was going to occur in advance. Tell me, the blood you saw, when you had your period? Was that the first time you remember being upset by the sight of blood?"

I was still embarrassed Mom told him about that. I didn't want to tell him that I had seen Rachel's body and the blood on her face or my mom's bloody snake rampage. "Yes, sir."

"Sometimes when a person goes through an anxious time they can become fixated on one thing, and that thing becomes the source of their anxiety. For example, a child whose parents are going through a difficult divorce may become very anxious. The child may cross a bridge while riding in a car and become terrified of falling off the bridge and drowning. See how his anxiety about the divorce has spilled over into another area? Then, what can develop is a fear of bridges that may, indeed, last the rest of his life. Many phobias and fears start this way."

He made sense. I had gotten really upset, seeing the blood on Rachel. Then the same feeling overwhelmed me when I saw the blood on my own body.

"What can I do?"

"Let me ask you something. When you have these worries or feelings of panic, do you have someone you can talk to?"

"My Aunt Sharon. I talk to her all the time. Anytime I get upset, actually, I ride my bike straight to her house." An image of my friends in the attic came to mind, but I didn't see how they had anything to do with this.

"That's good that you can talk to your aunt. We all need someone safe to talk to."

"Dr. Bryan, I do have a question…"

"Yes?"

"Well, I'm not a little kid and I don't play with dolls or anything, but if sometimes a person…like me…talked to let's say a doll or something, would that mean they're crazy?"

Dr. Bryan didn't laugh as I feared but explained, "When someone, and it doesn't have to be a child, is experiencing high levels of anxiety in their external world, they may develop an imaginary internal world.

"The person does this to alleviate their anxiety, it doesn't mean they're crazy. Is there something else you want to tell me, such as how you are coping right now with your anxiety?"

"Oh, it's not me who does anything like that, I saw something like that in a movie about a man who talked to a big imaginary rabbit, and I was just wondering if he was crazy…" Whew, I thought I covered that well.

"*Harvey* is the name of that movie."

"Yeah, that was it!"

"Bree, I once had a young girl who used her dollhouse to cope with her parent's divorce."

"How did she do that?"

"She talked to the dolls, and she said they talked back to her and explained why the daddy doll, which was actually a G.I. Joe, had to live in the Barbie camper out back behind the dollhouse."

I laughed, "That's really funny."

"Cute, yes, but also therapeutic for the child."

"What ever happened to her?"

"Well, she's a teenager now and no longer plays with the dollhouse. She's doing very well. The imaginary play helped her through a tough time but as she healed, she was able to move on. When control goes up, anxiety goes down. Remember that.

"I believe there are several areas in which I can help you deal with your anxiety as well."

Help me? Someone could help me 'move on'? I didn't have to be so weird? I suddenly felt a weight being lifted off my shoulders. "How? When?"

Dr. Bryan smiled. "First, I need to speak to your parents. You have a problem with anxiety, which means you worry a lot. Anxiety can be treated with medication, but there are other strategies as well."

"Will I have to take medicine?"

"I need to speak with your parents before we make any decisions. Rest assured, you can learn to soothe yourself. I have some techniques for you to use."

"I don't mind taking medication too. I mean, if it would help. I want to feel normal." I felt tears coming, and told myself not to cry.

"Bree, let's go talk to your mom and schedule an appointment when your dad can be here too."

Father? Here? Right. I was sure Father would be pleased as punch to come in and chat with the man he called a quack. Besides, I had told Dr. Bryan about Father spanking me. I wished I could remember exactly what I had said. How much I had told.

Dr. Bryan stood and opened the door. Mom was asleep in the waiting room, a magazine on her lap. She jumped when I gave her arm a little nudge. She was exhausted, I'm sure, from dealing with Father's arrest, and having to bail him out of jail and from worrying about me. "Mom, Dr. Bryan wants to talk to you."

"Oh, my goodness, Dorothy must have dozed off. Yes, Doctor?"

"Mrs. Grant, I would like to speak with both you and your husband at the next appointment."

Mom nervously clasped and unclasped her hands. "Is everything all right?"

"No disasters," Dr. Bryan smiled. He lowered his voice, as if we were in a conspiracy together. "Bree and I talked about her worrying. She knows now that she can change and stop worrying so much. When do you think your husband could come in?"

"I don't know. I could ask him." She looked like she had as many doubts and reservations about Father coming in, as I did.

"Why don't you chat with him, and then call the office to set up an appointment. This week would be best."

Mom picked up her handbag as she nodded. I held out my hand and Dr. Bryan looked a bit surprised as he shook it. "Thank you," I said, "you're a good doctor." And I meant it.

CHAPTER SIXTEEN

I HAD THREE things on my mind. First, I was a little worried about being hypnotized. I wanted Dr. Bryan's help but there were things I didn't want to talk about. For now, Dr. Bryan acted like I was a normal kid with normal problems that he could help.

I didn't know how he would feel about my attic séances or the flickering lights I was seeing, not to mention the auras. I was pretty sure he would see a strait jacket in my immediate future.

Second, I was very worried about Father coming to see Dr. Bryan. There are some people who should just never be in the same room together, like putting Wiley Coyote and Roadrunner in a cage together and telling them to talk things out. Oh, and let's throw in a box of Acme explosives just to make it interesting.

The third thing on my mind was wanting to know more about anxiety. On the drive home I asked Mom what she knew about anxiety. "Bree, I don't like to see you worrying about things, especially when you can't do anything about them. I took you to a psychologist because you were so worried and now you're worried about being worried. Most of what people worry about never comes to pass, anyway, it's just borrowing trouble. None of us have any control over the future. You have to take one day as it comes. Do what needs to be done at that moment."

"But sometimes I hear people say something like, "I'm really anxious for my birthday," and it doesn't seem right – unless they were actually afraid of getting older. So, what is anxiety, exactly?" I wanted to know.

She lit a cigarette and concentrated on the traffic. "I guess you could look up the definition in the dictionary. For the most part, it's feeling nervous or fearful but something good can also still cause anxiety, like going on a big trip or starting a new job."

Aunt Sharon. That's who I should talk to. She's a psychology professor—she should know all about anxiety. So I said, "Mom, when we get home I think I'd like to go for a bike ride. I might stop by Aunt Sharon's."

She didn't even ask why; she rarely did anymore. I hoped it didn't hurt her feelings that I spent so much time at her sister's house. She never hinted that it did. Maybe she was glad that someone else could share the burden of raising me.

As I wheeled my bike out of the garage, I noticed the newspaper lying in the driveway. I walked my bike to the end of the driveway, intending to throw the paper up to the door. As I picked it up, I saw a familiar image. Quickly, heart racing, I pulled the rubber band off from around the newspaper. Moose's picture stared back at me from below the headline:

'Director of Rehab Center Arrested for Murder'.

I was sick with disappointment but also relieved. While I was blown away that Moose had been arrested, I was also reassured that the murderer had been captured. Once again, though, Moose had proven not to be the person I thought he was. It didn't feel right but the relief was welcome. I sat down beside my bike, in the middle of the driveway, and read the article.

Englewood—Founder and Director of the Jennifer Sullivan Drug and Alcohol Center, Michael Sullivan, was taken into custody late yesterday on charges related to the murder of 13-year-old Rachel Carter.

Carter's body was found on the playground of Brighton Elementary School. The girl was reported missing by her grandmother when she failed to return from a walk. Carter's parents said their daughter routinely spent a week night with her grandmother.

Police estimate the time of death at between 6 and 7 p.m. The two boys who found the body said there was "a box of bones" next to the body "with a skull on top." Englewood Police Chief Ryan Hood acknowledged that the grave of Sullivan's daughter had been disturbed. Forensic tests identified the bones found at the scene of Carter's death as the remains of Jennifer Sullivan, who died as a result of a hit-and-run accident three years ago.

In 1971, Sullivan was charged with having sexual relations with a minor but charges were dropped after letters written between Sullivan and the girl were obtained by authorities, proving the relationship had been consensual. Police refused to discuss evidence against Sullivan in the murder of Rachel Carter.

The article didn't mention Satan worship or the coin for that matter; evidently the police must not have wanted to release information about the coin. I knew from watching *Police Woman* that sometimes the police withheld information that only the killer would know in order to weed out the psychos and wannabes.

Moose did collect coins, although he sounded so sincere when he told Father he had no idea what coin they were talking about when the police searched his home and office. Come to think of it, Moose didn't describe the coin. He didn't say that the police described it either. Detective Hines was the only person I knew who was aware of what the coin looked like. Of course, I knew too. I thought it better not to say anything if it was supposed to be a secret. I figured I could go to jail for letting that information out. Maybe the police would consider that tampering with evidence. I began to chew on my thumbnail. I kept staring at the article, trying to make sense of it.

Aunt Sharon! I'd forgotten that was why I was out there in the first place. I rolled the newspaper as smoothly as I could, slipped the rubber band back around the middle, and tossed it up next to the door for my parents to discover the sad news for themselves.

I knew my father would be devastated, even if he put forth a stoic face. Moose was his best friend and they had an incredible bond. I had yet in life to find a true friend—the kind of friend who you know will be there for you come what may. I was too young to understand the bond between my father and Moose but I had seen them together enough to know their relationship was unique. Where others would disappear when trouble arose, I knew my father would be there for Moose.

I rode as fast as I could, hoping Aunt Sharon was home. If she wasn't, I didn't know what I was going to do. Maybe camp out on her front doorstep and wait for her as long as I had to.

Dropping my bike in Aunt Sharon's yard, after seeing her car in the driveway, I ran up to the door and started knocking a little too hard. I heard Aunt Sharon undoing the latch.

"Bree, what's wrong!" She didn't say 'this time', but I heard it just the same.

"Moose was arrested for Rachel Carter's murder!" I blurted out the news in a single breath almost choking on the words.

Aunt Sharon grabbed my arm and pulled me inside. "Are you sure?"

I took a deep breath and said, "It's on the front page of the paper."

Aunt Sharon looked out her front window. "Run next door and grab the neighbor's paper. I'll put it back later. They never pick it up until after work, anyway."

I ran outside, scooped up the paper and ran back, feeling like a thief. Aunt Sharon took the paper from me and pulled off the rubber band. She sat on the sofa and read the article to herself. After a few minutes she laid the paper down and sighed. "Well, I guess that's it."

I was shocked. "What do you mean, 'that's it'? This doesn't mean Moose did it!" But I wanted it to be Moose. At least, part of me did. If it was Moose and he was arrested, then it was safe. We were safe.

Aunt Sharon leaned forward. "What other proof do you need? If the police arrested him, they must feel they have pretty good evidence. I know it's hard for you to accept that Moose could do something like this. But you know about his jail time and his drinking problems, right?"

"Yes and do you know about what he did to that girl a few a years ago?"

"Well, sure I do, love. It was in the papers. And of course, your mom and I talked about it. I didn't know *you* knew about it. A lot of research is being done in regards to what happens to soldiers in wartime. I don't mean their physical injuries, but what they suffer emotionally. Maybe someday we'll be able to diagnose and treat those wounds that we can't see.

"Sometimes that kind of pain can lead to depression and depression leads to trying to ease the pain with drugs or alcohol. Then the drugs and alcohol lead us to do things we wouldn't ordinarily do—and we become more depressed because we don't like ourselves. Moose was one of those young men who come back from war, but find they left something of themselves over there.

"None of us would have expected anything like this from him. It is sad and confusing. Moose made a lot of mistakes during that time but I never saw him as a bad guy. Vietnam took a toll on him, like it did a lot of guys. None of this excuses his behavior but it may help explain it."

I was actually feeling relief. For one thing, this meant my ridiculous fears about my father were unfounded. Secondly, it helped to know that Aunt Sharon was having just as hard a time grasping the news as I was—and she was a professor of psychology. Moose felt like an older brother or an uncle to me. I had always found him comforting to be around, until his daughter died, then I felt awkward, but certainly never had I ever been afraid of him.

"Aunt Sharon? You know how Father saved Moose's life in the Vietnam War?"

"Yes, what about it, hon?"

"I'm thinking Father shouldn't have saved his life."

"Oh, Bree, honey. Are you thinking that Rachel would still be alive if Moose had died in the war?"

"Yeah, and a lot of other people wouldn't have been hurt, like how about that 15-year-old girl that he uh…uh, you know…" I stammered. "And also Aunt Sharon, why did he dig up his daughter's bones and put them beside Rachel's body?"

"I was wondering about that, too, frankly. Maybe he was trying to make a statement about Jennifer's death. Bringing attention to the fact that it was never avenged, I don't know. He must be a sick man, love. I doubt his thinking is based on logic."

"Do you think he could be involved in witchcraft and that he was performing a sacrifice? If so, maybe others are involved?"

Sharon looked confused. "I haven't heard any mention of that motive. Seems a bit far-fetched. Not that this whole murder isn't strange though…"

"Sharon, everything scares me lately. Even though Moose was arrested, I'm still scared."

She looked at me with concern and patted my knee. "Tell me more."

And so I told her about my visit to Dr. Bryan. "He thinks I have a problem with anxiety, do you know much about anxiety? You're the one who first told me you noticed I worry too much."

"Well, it's not my specialty, I teach more general psych, but I know it can be treated relatively easily with medication and some behavioral therapy."

"What's behavioral therapy mean?" I wanted to know.

"It's like teaching you to control your thoughts. Your brain tricks you and makes you think things are a bigger deal than they really are. I'm sure Dr. Bryan will explain more after he talks to your parents. I've heard him at conferences. You're lucky. He's good."

I didn't like the thought of my brain tricking me and I wasn't sure I believed Aunt Sharon. Dr. Bryan seemed to think my leaking water dreams were caused by something my brain was hiding, a thought or memory that was ready to come out. I found that difficult to believe. How could I have thoughts I didn't think about? Or memories I couldn't remember? This made very little sense to me. I was smart, everyone said so, therefore, my brain knew exactly what was going on.

I excused myself, having had enough therapy for one day. I left Aunt Sharon's planning on stopping for a Slurpee and then heading out to look for the supposed old albino farm, in hopes of putting that theory to rest.

The color of a person's skin didn't make them any worse or any better than anyone else. I knew the stories were a mix of gossip and ghost stories made up by teenagers trying to scare little kids, but the idea of making people live secluded from everyone else just because they were different made me mad. I was different. I knew it. Most of us don't want to be known that way, that completely. But obviously I didn't know people that completely. I had been wrong about Moose. Or was I?

The area of the old farm was isolated and secluded. Some-one could hide there for months probably. If you were someone with a plan to abduct and murder young girls, there wouldn't be a more perfect place to hide. And maybe, just maybe, if I made a discovery at the old farm, I could prove Moose's innocence.

As I rode towards the 7-Eleven I saw a sign I hadn't noticed before:

'CHURCH OF THE LORD—FREE WILL BAPTIST!
BICENTENNIAL BRUSH ARBOR REVIVAL ALL WEEKEND!
COME WORSHIP WITH US IN GOD'S COUNTRY!'

I slowed my bike to a stop, trying to remember what a Brush Arbor might be. I rode on after memorizing the directions on the sign, knowing I would be traveling farther than allowed but figuring it would be in route to the old albino farm. I took the main drag out of Englewood and followed the two-lane old Route 66 west until the suburbs changed to manicured five-acre sites and then finally yielded to small farms scattered along rolling hills.

I rode my Schwinn onto a gravel road lined with blackberries, barbed wire and poison ivy. Stopping at a steep embankment, I saw cars and pickup trucks parked all the way down into the valley below. At the base of the grass parking lot were about a dozen make-shift shacks and tents with little campfires crackling in front of them. They must have been for cooking; it was at least 90 degrees outside. Beyond the campsite I saw a creek that had attracted quite a few kids. They had their pant legs rolled up and looked like they were trying to catch something under the water; tadpoles probably.

I wondered where to go? All the people looked like they knew what they were doing. A group of people were gathered around what looked like a little table. Beyond them, I could see the canopy of the Brush Arbor, where it would all happen. All what, though, was still a mystery. The canopy seemed to be erected on eight-foot poles with lots of brush, sticks and leaves giving shade to the area below. Hence the name 'Brush Arbor', I figured.

I sauntered nonchalantly down to the bottom of the hill and saw several folding tables covered with items for sale. Trying to blend in, I spotted a table spread with little leather wallets with pictures of Jesus tooled into the leather. A man with a gray beard and suspenders sat behind the table. A handwritten sign said the wallet was blessed and would never run out of money. The sign also said it was for sale for five dollars. Another table had Bibles for two dollars. I really wanted one of those Bibles.

I heard a bell chime, and everyone started into the Brush Arbor to get a seat. I kind of wanted to join them, knowing it would be a little cooler in the shade of the branches and leaves. That seemed like a commitment I wasn't ready for so I leaned against a tree where I could still watch and hear what was going on.

A few bugs flew in lazy circles above my head. I noticed some of the people fanned themselves with cheap cardboard advertising fans. Some were shifting their weight from cheek to cheek in an effort to find that one accommodating position of forgiveness on the hard wooden seats.

Once everyone was seated, a group of men with guitars proceeded up the aisle, playing as they walked to the front. I didn't know the song but most everyone else seemed to, something about how it only takes a spark to get a fire going. This, of course, made me think they were sitting under a pretty good target with all the dry branches overhead. I sure hoped God liked what he heard; I didn't want a lightning bolt to hit that thing.

I looked around at the congregation during the song. They were all ages. Maybe the older people outnumbered the rest, but there were young families, too. I thought it would feel very good to be sitting between my parents in a church service, very safe and comforting. Some of the women had their eyes closed and lifted their hands as they swayed to the music. Everyone looked peaceful.

As the song ended, a man in a rumpled seersucker suit stepped up to the front, holding a worn Bible in his left hand. He introduced himself as Preacher Bob. He stood in silence at the front of the crowd, his ruddy face damp with sweat. He asked the congregation to bow their heads and pray, which I too did obediently. Preacher Bob blessed the word he was about to deliver and he blessed the place in which we were gathered and he praised the Lord for the opportunity to speak to this fine group. Then he began what could have been his thousandth sermon, but for me it was the first. I hung on his every word.

"We gather to today to celebrate our country's 200th birthday and to offer appreciation for all of God's blessings. And folks, our greatest blessing is to live in a country that allows us freedom of religion! Yet, our country needs more religion! There are other countries that have so much less freedom but give religion so much more value. I see a positive change in America, this last year that gives me hope, and I'm sure you see it too. Patriotism, my friends.

"Amen!" I heard several voices shout, as one elderly man stood and waved a small flag over his head.

"America is standing united with their red, white, and blue and it is a beautiful sight. Now, Paul addressed in his first letter to the Corinthians the problems with divisions and immorality in the church. He wrote, 'By the authority of our Lord Jesus Christ I appeal to all of you, my friends, to agree in what you say, so that there will be no divisions among you. Be completely united with only one thought and purpose!' This year America is united, but were they united during the Vietnam War? Will they be united tomorrow?"

I saw many of the worshippers shake their heads no, while others looked down in shame. It made me think of Father again. I remembered other references to the divisions that occurred because of Vietnam. Maybe I needed to ask him about it. Or maybe I needed to do a little research.

"Does it take a celebration for us to band together and stand by old glory? I hope not, but I'm beginning to wonder. Jesus seems to get most of our attention when there is something to celebrate. Such as, His birthday or His resurrection and even then we can't seem to do that right—bringing reindeer and rabbits into the mix!"

The congregation chuckled.

"As we gather together in the bounty of God's nature today, let us remember our ancestors who began the Thanksgiving tradition. A reminder—a celebration—of God's plentiful harvest and His blessings of the land. Feel God's glory and presence all around you as we celebrate this great country's birthday. Is that enough to give you reason to celebrate year after year? Is that reason enough to love your country and your Lord after the party is over? I hope so."

Preacher Bob read more from the Bible. His voice sounded a lot different than Father's voice, when he quoted the

Scripture. Then a man named Brother Dick took the pulpit. Brother Dick told us how Preacher Bob's Plymouth was on its last leg, and how Pastor Bob couldn't make his house calls much anymore.

Brother Dick implored, "My brothers and sisters in Christ Jesus, we must help this great man of God get a car. If you feel in your heart that God has spoken to you today, and if you want to prove that Jesus lives in your heart, help us buy this car for our devout Preacher Bob, loving servant of God."

A woman in the audience stood up and shouted, "I give fifty dollars to help Preacher Bob! God has spoken to my heart!"

She walked swiftly to the front and placed a wad of bills in the offering plate. One by one, others walked up and added their contributions.

I felt so much love passing through the crowd. No one here could be involved in a murder. No one here could possibly be having outrageous thoughts that their father could be a killer. God could give me peace. He loved me. He wanted to help me. It was so easy—all I had to do was let Him into my heart.

Preacher Bob asked for sinners to now come down front, and he would blast the devil from their souls. Men, women, and children left their seats behind, ready to take part in whatever Preacher Bob had in store for them. I wondered how children could be sinners. I didn't think I was a sinner, yet. But I had to admit, I had felt the devil living in my heart this past month. I bet it was the devil that made me worry all the time and not trust my own father.

Pastor Bob held his hand above each person's head. He would then push the air in front of them—and without him even touching them, they would fall to the ground. Some jerked and writhed and twitched. I couldn't take my eyes off of this man of magic, this man of God. I wanted to feel the power, too. I wanted to be cleansed. Cleansed of my anxieties, my suspicious thoughts, my fears, my uncertainties. Oh, how I wanted to follow the crowd down to the altar; how I wanted Pastor Bob to touch me with that power.

Once all the sinners were purified, Preacher Bob said he would do baptisms and foot washings down at the creek.

As everyone stood to leave, I ran back to my bike, not wanting anyone in the congregation to notice or question me, surely they would see I didn't belong.

I nearly jumped out of my skin, but there stood a grinning Mike, his own bike leaning against his hips.

"This is ridiculous Mike. You are following me!" I was embarrassed at being caught here in the trees and angry that he would think it was okay to follow me.

"Bree, I am not following you. I thought I would check out the brush arbor for the experience. I like visiting other churches and hearing someone besides my dad. I just happened to see you up here. Seriously, I am not following you. But I am curious what you thought of the sermon."

I could tell he was sincere and I kind of felt like talking anyway. "The preacher mentioned the Vietnam war. I was thinking my dad and his best friend were there. So were a lot of the winos that come into his studio. I think they were all damaged in some way by the war and I keep wondering why God would allow wars to happen…"

"*War, huh, yeah. What is it good for, absolutely nothing, uh-huh. War, huh, yeah, what is it good for, absolutely nothing,*" Mike sang in a pretty good imitation of the song and I smiled in spite of my concerns.

"That's exactly what I'm talking about. What's it good for?

"Well, there was a lot of opposition to the Vietnam War in particular because our imperialistic government forced young men into service with an immoral draft process. Your dad didn't want to go. No one wanted to go."

I had forgotten how often Mike expressed his political views in class, making the rest of us groan inwardly at his worries about how the world was going to ruination and damnation. I decided to change the subject. "Well, I have something I need to do so see ya. Oh, and nice seeing you again," I added out of politeness.

"Bree, what's really bothering you?"

Who knows what key unlocks the closed heart? He sounded just like Aunt Sharon. So Mike was a total nerd, but a nice nerd and the words spilled out of me. "The murder, Mike. The murder bothers me. You once accused me of being a spy but I am a detective investigating a murder."

Mike looked a little confused. "But they caught the murderer—that Sullivan guy. There's nothing to investigate."

"Moose didn't do it!" I was almost shouting. "I've known him my whole life. He couldn't hurt a fly." I couldn't stop myself from talking now. "A girl was killed on our school grounds. I didn't know her but I do know that Rachel and I are tied together in some way. I don't know how but when I find out who killed her, who really killed her, then I'll understand how we're connected."

"Transference. It's called transference when you make that kind of association. If you didn't know her you can't be connected to her.

"Anyway, I did know Rachel. Well, a little. She came to our youth group a few times with one of her friends, although she was Catholic. She was really nice. She volunteered on some projects Dad and I were involved in too. Kind of shy but you could tell she really cared about doing good, or whatever you want to call it."

I told Mike about my plan to check out the albino farm and I thought he was going to laugh but he said, "As illogical as you're being, I feel it is my Christian duty to accompany you." He said it so formally that I was the one who almost laughed, but I considered his offer and decided I liked the idea of having someone go with me.

I had a general idea of where the albino farm was supposed to be, it was still quite a ways out and over an old steel bridge. We rode while making mental notes so we could find our way back. Once we found the bridge it was just a matter of time before we came upon an overgrown rock wall Kristen had told me about. The wall was meant to keep people out but it couldn't keep out someone with my climbing abilities. We left our bike in the weeds and I hoisted myself up over the wall, I was taller than Mike so I grabbed his forearm and helped him over.

Up on the hill we could see an abandoned old white farm house. As we began hiking up the ridge, making our way through the wild flowers, we came across a small stone building. Spray painted across the side read the words, "Evil Awaits". I began to feel anxiety building inside me, the place looked abandoned and the windows were broken out. I took a deep breath, walked up and looked in one of the openings.

I called Mike over. "Hey, check this out. There's beer cans and burnt pieces of wood. Could it be burnt offerings? Could Kristen and Pauline be right about sacrifices and satanic rituals?"

Mike looked in and shrugged. "Looks like someone's been partying up here."

Just as I was pondering this idea I heard a terrifying explosion—a gunshot—causing me to jump right out of my skin as bits of concrete exploded close to me. Mike knocked me to the ground and landed on top of me. I felt my heart racing faster than it ever had, a jack rabbit kicking in my chest just as Mike rolled off me apologizing, his face bright red. I jerked around trying to see where the shot had hit. I saw a hole in the side wall and crawled over to see a bullet stuck in the concrete. I reached up and touched it with my finger. It was still hot to the touch.

"Was someone shooting at *us*?" I whispered to Mike.

Mike told me not to move so we crouched down and waited, my heart pounding in my ears. I don't know how long we waited but my thighs were really beginning to burn from being crouched for so long.

Once my heart rate slowed, I told him we should make a run for it. We shimmied over the wall, and jumped onto our bikes. I was expecting to feel a bullet penetrate my back at any moment. I rode faster than the wind, or at least I hoped faster than a speeding bullet, while trying to convince myself that the gunshot was only a hunter taking aim at a deer and not at me. Mike kept pace and we didn't talk while we rode with our legs pumping the pedals at warp speed.

Then as I was working on convincing myself that all the legends of the albino farm had to be just made-up stories, I suddenly noticed the sun was beginning to set and I was still an awful long way from home. My legs felt sore and I knew I would pay for my trip tomorrow.

Riding back, we were less sure of the directions. I was worried we were going to get lost and I would be in big trouble with Father for being so late. Already working on an alibi that involved Aunt Sharon, familiar land appeared before me and I breathed a sigh of relief. We approached Mike's neighborhood first and I told him good-night. "Thanks for going with me. I'm sorry my idea almost got you killed."

"Not me, you, that bullet barely missed you." His face flushed, maybe because he remembered falling on top of me.

"Do you think it was a hunter or isn't it possible someone was trying to kill us. I think someone was trying to kill *me* anyway."

"Nah, it was a hunter. But I don't know if it's okay to hunt that close to the road. I doubt it. I'm going to tell my dad—"

"No! You can't do that! Oh, please promise you won't tell. My father will kill me if he finds out I rode that far out, please don't tell..." I was begging now.

"But that hunter could hurt someone and if I don't tell, that's like lying and I'll feel guilty."

"Oh, good grief, can't you just like go to confession or something."

"That's for Catholics, I'm Methodist."

"Please, just this once, can you please not tell?"

"Well...okay, sure. I don't want to get you trouble."

With a sigh of relief I turned my bike around and rode home to face my parents.

"I have found a girl," he announced breathlessly as soon as he entered the room. He poured a drink and gulped it down before continuing. "She will achieve our goals. This time our plan will most definitely work."

Why did he keep using the word 'our'? Too excited to sit, he was pacing back and forth. I wished he would pour another drink, maybe one for both of us. We could sit and discuss this calmly. Anything to give me more time to plan. I desperately wanted out of this madness.

Smiling as benignly as I could under the circumstances, I said, "Great, but perhaps we shouldn't rush this time, the importance is in the planning. You've always said that plans are nothing but planning is everything."

At first I thought he was annoyed that I had rained on his parade, but the flattery of repeating his own words worked its customary charm and he smiled back at me. "Good point, you're right and I'm glad to see you're finally starting to play an active role in thinking this through." He laughed and grabbed me by the shoulders. "The two of us together can achieve anything!" Then he hugged me tight. His strength was always a surprise.

I prayed silently, hoping I had just bought more time...for all of us.

CHAPTER SEVENTEEN

I WAS TIRED, sweaty and hungry. On wobbly legs, and with a pounding heart, I wandered through the house, looking for my parents. They were sitting in the study going over mom's checkbook and I knew enough not to bother them when they discussed finances. However, I assumed they had noticed how late it was and I was hoping I wouldn't be in trouble for being out so long. I couldn't make out what they were saying, but I figured they'd heard about Moose by now.

"Hey, I'm home."

My parents abruptly ended their conversation. Father asked, "How long have you been home?"

"Oh, I've been here a while." Relief washed over me that they didn't seem aware I had just walked in. "But I haven't eat yet," I hinted.

Father ignored the insinuation. "I'm helping your mother balance her checkbook, this is not for the faint of heart. Do you know about Moose?"

"That he was arrested? I saw the newspaper. Do you really think he did it? Can you help him, Father?"

"So many questions, so many questions…I have only one answer: let God's will be done!"

OK. Hmmm. That made no sense to me. I let it go, for now. I wondered if he thought it was God's will for Rachel to die, or Jennifer. I was frustrated but too exhausted to feel any real anger.

Mom spoke, "Father said he will go with us to see Dr. Bryan tomorrow."

Father scowled and made a little grunting sound as she said this, as though he'd been coerced. I wanted to talk about Moose, but my parents remained aloof and more focused on the checkbook than on me.

Without looking up from the calculator, Father spoke, "Bree, you can go in to work with me tomorrow. Of course, we'll have to leave early to pick up your mom here, so we can all go see that doctor together. There's plenty for you to do at the studio, before your appointment, like sweeping up the lead dust and changing Van Gogh's litter box. And you need to wash the stained glass windows. The dirt filters the light—I have to have more light. The sun's not as bright anymore."

I needed money as usual, too many Slurpees. Maybe I would have a better opportunity to discuss Moose's guilt or innocence with my father while we were alone at the studio. I agreed and headed for the kitchen to scrounge for food. My parents weren't going to continue their discussion in front of me. I decided on a bologna sandwich and was heading for my bedroom, when I heard Father's voice, "Dorothy, I hope you see I am only trying to help you, you're an intelligent woman and should be capable of following a budget. I'm very generous with you, you want for nothing."

Mom spoke, "I know, I know, I don't know what's wrong with me; I guess I just love the thrill of a package in the mail..."

I had heard enough, me and my bologna sandwich had other things to do.

I updated my confidants up in the attic. I told them about the Brush Arbor and Moose's arrest, but not about the gunshot at the albino farm, thinking about the gunshot made me think of Mike and thinking about Mike felt disconcerting. Then, later that night I got on my knees beside my bed and said a formal prayer for the first time in my life. I asked God to be with Moose, and if he was innocent, to set him free. I asked God to help me with my anxiety and let me feel normal. I prayed for my friends and my family. I had hoped praying would give me some feeling of control but it didn't.

After several hours of sleep I awoke to hear classical music and I knew my father was sharing my night disturbances. I could recognize most classical pieces by ear; I'd heard them so many times in that house. The piano fell silent, the Bach fugue stopped. Soon I heard Father return to his bedroom and as the echoes of his music faded, I found myself watching the curtained windows, heart pounding, worrying that someone was out there. Someone watching from the camouflage of shadows, the way I watched Father.

The harder I stared, the more convinced I was someone was crouched in the corner of my room. I stared hard, willing my eyes to adjust to the darkness. Should I pretend to sleep and hope whomever or whatever it was would go away or should

I make a run for my parents' bedroom, hoping I make it in time? But I knew I was getting older, too old for fleeing to my parents' bed at two a.m.

At some point, I convinced myself the thing crouching in the corner was just my dirty clothes, carelessly tossed over my chair, their untamed shapes a threat in the darkness. Why did my imagination torture me so? I did not know. I wondered, what phantom did my father see that roused him from sleep so many nights?

Eventually I fell into a deep sleep only to be awoken by my face being forcibly smashed into my pillow. I struggled but my head was pushed tighter against the pillow making it hard to breathe. Heart pounding like a caught rabbit, I kicked with both legs but they were twisted under the covers.

Then I heard a muffled voice, "Take this as a warning. You need to mind your own business."

I felt the pressure loosen and I quickly lifted my head and took several deep breaths. Then I began to scream.

My parents came bounding into my bedroom, looking extremely startled and disheveled. Father grabbed me by the shoulders. "What's wrong?"

"Someone was in my room!" I choked out between sobs.

"Oh, Breezy, you just had a bad dream."

"No! It wasn't a bad dream! Someone tried to suffocate me with my pillow and I couldn't move and it was hard to breath and they threatened me and told me to mind my business!" I began to sob and hiccup.

Mom glanced warily around the room. "There doesn't appear to be anyone here now."

Father sat down beside me and began to stroke my hair. "No bad guys are here, Breezy. It was just a bad nightmare." Here I'll show you. Father stood and went over to closet and opened the door. "See? No one there in your little playhouse."

"It's not a playhouse! And there was someone here!" I hiccupped again.

"Don't shout at me. I'm only trying to help." He got down on his knees and looked under my bed, "Nothing here either."

Mom walked over to the curtains and pulled them back, "Geoff, look, the window's open."

"See!" I yelled, "Someone did break in!" My heart felt like it was going to beat right out of my chest.

Mom sighed, "No, Bree honey, you left it open. Remember? Earlier you had it open while you were cleaning your room. I remember because you were playing your records so loud I could still hear your music when I walked outside to get the mail."

I considered what she said. "OK, so maybe I left it open but that just proves a bad guy was able to crawl in the window." I felt so stupid for leaving the window open. How could I be so careless?

Father said, "I'll go take a look outside, but I doubt I see anything." He left the room.

"Take your gun!" I yelled out after him.

Mom sat next to me and I put my head on her lap. I was still shaking. Mom said, "Remember that time you took scissors and cut your pillow open in the middle of the night?"

"I was only seven."

"Even so, you convinced yourself in the middle of the night that someone had sewn a dead rat into your pillow. You cut it open only to find the down feathers had become clumped into a hard funny shape."

I hiccupped. "I made quite a mess, didn't I?"

Mom squeezed me. "I thought I'd be cleaning up feathers for years."

Suddenly we heard a loud "Boo!" and we both screamed. Father stuck his head through the curtains and laughed. Mom hurled a throw pillow at him. "That's not funny, Geoff! You really scared me!" Now she knew a bit of what I felt.

Father came back into the house, walked over, shut my window, and locked it, pulling the curtains tightly shut. "There you go. Safe and secure."

How he could say that so light-heartedly? I knew what happened was real. It wasn't a dream. Now I was even more concerned the gunshot was meant for me. While my heart rate was slowly returning back to normal, my stomach was hurting really bad. Fortunately, Mom felt sorry for me and stayed in my bed for the rest of the night, curled up against me. And even though I was now a 7th grader, I didn't mind a bit.

The next morning I decided to resume my investigation. I believed what happened in my room was not a dream and the fact I was threatened implied Moose *was* wrongly accused and the bad guy knew I was onto him. If Moose was wrongly accused, I wanted to be the one to save him. I knew with all my heart the whole truth still was not known. The sun was just coming up and I figured I could do some reflective walking before Father was ready to leave for work. I was headed down the street, deep in thought, when I saw John on his back deck with his camera. I smiled to myself, almost able to laugh at my own foolishness just weeks before. Walking towards his back deck, he noticed me, smiled and waved me over.

"Good morning, Bree. Come join me and I'll show you what I'm looking at."

Stepping up on the deck I came up beside him. "I'm out trying to get a little exercise." I thought I should explain so John didn't think I was up to my old tricks.

John ignored my defensive comment. "Look through the lens of this camera and tell me what you see."

I took the camera from him and viewed the sun rising over the house behind him. "I see a really beautiful sunrise, with lots of pink in it."

"Do you know what causes the pink in the sky?"

"Isn't it from the humidity and the dust particles in the air?"

John smiled. I could tell he was impressed. "That's right, not very romantic is it? It's dust that makes that pretty color."

"Yeah, and I just remembered, in school they taught us a rhyme, I think in third grade, 'red sky in the morning, sailor's take warning, red sky at night, sailor's delight.' Have you heard that one before?"

"Yes, I like it. And it's logical. If you have a red sky, or pink as the case may be, then the humidity would indicate a chance of rain."

"What does the dust indicate?"

"Pollution."

We both laughed. I liked John, he seemed pretty cool for an older man.

When we finished our picture taking, John invited me to have a seat in his living room while he fixed us a couple of English muffins with blackberry jam. I busied myself by picking up one of this photo albums and flipping through the pages. All of his photos were so organized with the date, type of film and camera settings listed by each photo. I realized I was looking at the album from this summer and instinctively turned to the date of the murder. His photographs captured the beautiful weather of that very early morning. Then, my eyes did a double-take as I noticed something familiar between two of the houses behind John's, houses that line the street in front of the school. Quickly I pulled the picture out of the album and slid it into my pocket.

John came out seconds later with a tray carrying our breakfast and two glasses of orange juice. I asked him a question I had been pondering while he was making our breakfast. "John, you said you take pictures in memory of your wife and it makes each day worth living. But what do you do on cloudy days?"

John smiled and replied, "It depends. Some clouds make for a rather striking photo opportunity. You can capture the sun's rays filtering through the darkness or the contrast of their darkness against the light. If it's really cloudy and the sun is completely obscured it becomes another story. In the beginning, after Joanne died, I would get down and depressed on those days; feeling I couldn't fulfill my life's mission. Of course, it was easier then for anything to depress me. I knew Joanne wouldn't have wanted me to feel that way. Time is a great healer. I began to realize that just because I couldn't see the sun, didn't mean it wasn't there. I often use that time to work on my albums or to reminisce, count my blessings so to speak. In fact, Bree, you have become one of those blessings."

I know my face registered surprise, but before I could say anything, John continued, "Your visit the other day showed me how wrapped up in my loneliness I've become. I was hiding behind my camera. Sunrises and sunsets will always be special for me, but Joanne loved people. I had become a recluse. To honor her and her life, I've decided to get out more. In fact, today I'm going over to a nursing home and give a free class on photography to some of the elderly who might be interested. It's a start."

I was touched that without meaning to, I had changed someone's life—and probably for the better. If only I could change my life that easily. I decided to ask him the big question. "John, do you believe in God?"

He looked thoughtful and then a small smile lit his face. "How could I not?" He winked at me.

Thanking John for breakfast and wishing him well on his class, I began my walk home. As I passed the all brick house, I saw the garage door open as a red Firebird pulled into the garage. Was that the same car that had been following me? Does the scary man actually live so close to me? Was he in my bedroom last night? Did he shoot at me? I dropped to my knees behind a large maple tree and watched closely, hoping to get a glimpse of the man and inspect his colors but the garage door went down before I could even see his face. I sat in the dewy grass pondering what this could mean. I pulled John's photo out of my pocket. Between two houses a shot of red captured in the early morning light. A car that looked like his Firebird…driving right in front of the school.

Lots of people have red cars. But could this be the murderer leaving the scene of the crime? Or was this the murderer returning to the scene of the crime? The man in the brick house keeps to himself, but then so does John and he's not a killer. I tried to reason with myself as I ran home in a sprint. I needed to sneak into the house before anyone noticed I was gone.

Father seemed like his old self this morning and after he finished his breakfast we left for the studio. The police had roped off Moose's building with yellow crime scene tape. I asked Father why they'd done that.

"I imagine, Breezy, they're looking for evidence—or found some. They've been around for several days, digging through stuff and carting things out."

"Like what?"

"I have no idea. Anything they want, I suppose." He didn't seem to be interested in the details.

At least Father was answering my questions, sort of. You just never knew with him. I figured I'd better not push it, though.

I worked around the studio for several hours. Father gave me two five dollar bills. He still wasn't finished with a church window he'd been working on all day, so I sat at his worktable and played with Van Gogh. He was a sweet little kitty who spent most of his time right on Father's worktable. Father had even made him a cat bed out of stained glass, with a mouse etched in the glass. The little mouse looked like it was hiding in the corner of Van Gogh's bed. He also put a little pillow and blanket in it and positioned a light over the bed to keep Van Gogh warm at night during the winter. Van Gogh liked to curl up under the light even in the summer.

Just as we were about to head out, a disheveled and pale figure pushed open the door. It was Tom, one of the local characters, he looked like he had the shakes, but he said hello to me before shambling over to where Father was working. Father had an interesting relationship with those guys, the winos that hung out downtown. Sometimes they came in just to visit; sometimes they needed money. Father said the interesting thing about the winos was that they usually paid him back, out of their next welfare check. I wondered what this one wanted, money or conversation?

"Well, hello Tom. How are you doing today, champ?'

"Good, Geoff, good. I've been staying out of trouble, for once."

"Pull up a chair and visit, if you want. I need to finish soldering this window, and then I need to take Bree to a doctor's appointment. But I've got a few minutes."

"Naw, I won't keep ya. I'm just hangin'…lookin' for some fun." Tom snorted a laugh. "It's a shame about Moose. None of the guys thinks he did it. There's no way and we all agree. We Vietnam vets stick together, right?"

Father agreed with a nod but cut Tom off before he could continue the talk of Moose. He told him we had to leave and shooed Tom out of the studio. As Tom opened the door he turned and mentioned, "They're havin' that chili cook off down at the Square, It smells so good but I'm outta cash."

Father looked up from his work but didn't offer any money. I stepped out on the front sidewalk with Tom and as he turned to walk off I reached into my pocket, pulled out one of my fives and put into his hand.

"Aw kid, you don't have to do that, I can't pay you back this month."

"I want to Tom, really, go enjoy some chili, I get homemade good cookin' all the time at home." I smiled hoping he could see I was sincere.

"Ok, thanks kid, you're a good egg, just like your dad."

I hesitated but then added before Tom could walk away, "Tom, what did you mean when you said, 'vets stick together?'"

Tom smiled and put his hand on my shoulder. "Kid, it's like we're brothers 'cause we've been through somethin' no one else can understand. Anyways, Moose needs us right now and we're gonna be there for him. Moose told me right before his arrest that the cops had it all wrong but your dad was going to be his savior. See? It's like I said, Geoff's a good egg and a brother to Moose. If anyone can help, it'll be your dad 'cause he's got the money, the rest of us don't." Tom looked down at the cash I'd given him and shrugged. "Well, off to get some chili, thanks again, kid."

I walked back into the studio as Father was scooping up Van Gogh. He gave him a kiss on the top of his furry head. Van Gogh pawed at my father's face and meowed. Father gently nestled him into his little bed, and we drove home to get Mom for my appointment. I was excited about getting help from Dr. Bryan.

The minute we stepped into Dr. Bryan's waiting room, Father's mood turned temperamental. He made me nervous when he was like this. I hoped we wouldn't have to wait long. Father refused to sit and began pacing. Not a good sign.

"Why do doctors always make you wait? They think they're so much more important than us peons, with all their degrees and fancy offices. I suppose that makes their time more valuable than my time," he complained. "Of course, I can charge as much an hour as I want, so I guess that makes *my* time just as valuable as this quack's, huh! My creations endure for generations. Dumb shrinks just stir the pot, and luck and time do the rest—right? Am I right? Huh, huh?" He was looking at me. What was I supposed to say?

Finally, Dr. Bryan entered the waiting room. "I am *so* sorry. I had an emergency situation on the phone."

He held out his hand to Father. "Mr. Grant?"

Father snorted and shook Dr. Bryan's hand. "Yeah."

"Hello, Mrs. Grant," he nodded to Mom. "Let's go into my office. Bree, can you wait out here for a few minutes? I'd like to talk with your parents just now."

I nodded, unhappy about being left out of the initial discussion. Once the three of them had walked back into Dr. Bryan's office, I sat down and stared at the fish. I'd heard fish were supposed to be relaxing. I didn't feel too relaxed. I noticed that Dr. Bryan's secretary seemed engrossed in a serious phone conversation, something about insurance. A woman sat in the corner, reading a magazine. I casually walked over to the waiting room door. Nobody seemed to notice, so I went through to Dr. Bryan's private office. I stood by the door, as if I was about to go in. Thankfully, the corridor was deserted. I could hear voices through the door; I gently pressed my ear against it.

"…if it's not the murder, it will be something else. Children with anxiety disorders always find something to be anxious about. When school starts this fall, it may be grades, or boys, or any number of things. Children who are highly intelligent are more aware of the problems in the world but don't have the emotional skills to deal with their own deep thoughts."

I heard Father's voice. "So, what's the problem? A little worrying is good for a kid. It keeps them in line."

"Of course; everyone worries to some extent. But I'm talking about persistent worry; worry that affects your daughter's everyday life."

My father's voice again. "What *is* your point?"

"My point is, Mr. Grant, that Bree suffers from an anxiety disorder. She needs counseling and an evaluation for medication.

"She's also having some recurring dreams with images and I'm interested in trying hypnosis with her." I heard Dr. Bryan pause and then silence before he went on.

"I don't know if you're familiar with hypnosis but it's a naturally occurring state of focused relaxation. Hypnosis allows someone to use more of their mind so they can change their thoughts, feelings, and behaviors and, in turn, improve their life. Many adults have used hypnosis to lose weight, stop smoking, or manage stress."

I heard a loud thunk, as if something fell over, and then I heard Father yell, *"Humble yourselves, therefore, under God's mighty hand, that he may lift you up in due time. Cast all your anxiety on Him!"*

Uh oh. Father lost his temper again. I knew I should back away from the door, because he might charge through it any minute, but I couldn't make myself leave.

Again, Dr. Bryan's calm and soothing voice. "1 Peter 5:5. I see you know your scripture, Mr. Grant. How about Isaiah 41:10? 'So do not fear, for I am with you; do not be dismayed, for I am your God. I will strengthen you and help you, I will uphold you with my righteous right hand.'"

Father was actually quiet for a moment. I'd never heard anyone throw scripture back at him before. Then, his thundering voice again. "My daughter is not mentally ill. If you ever go near her again, I will sue you for every penny you ever thought you could earn. I will own you and your family! You got that?"

Still the calm voice, "I'm sorry you feel that way, Mr. Grant. Perhaps you'd better leave now."

I took that as my cue. Dreading the thought of facing any of them, I scurried back to the waiting room and threw myself into a chair. Within seconds, Father stormed out, Mom trailing passively behind Father's shadow which was flickering with stains of dark red. Dr. Bryan gave me a weak smile and said he was sorry as Father grabbed my arm and pulled me out of the office.

CHAPTER EIGHTEEN

I WAS DEVASTATED; Father just ripped away all hope of ever feeling normal. Back home, in the privacy of my room, I called Dr. Bryan's office. His secretary, Sherry, answered. I told her it was an emergency.

Within seconds, Dr. Bryan was on the phone. "Bree, I'm really sorry about what happened today. Tell me what's going on."

"I need you to help me. I can ride my bike to your office, and I have some money, and…"

I could hear the sadness in Dr. Bryan's voice. "I'm sorry, Bree. I can't see you without your parents' written consent. It's the law, dear, and you're a minor."

I felt tears roll down my cheeks. My voice choked, "I need help. Please, please, I'm begging you, help me."

Dr. Bryan sighed. "Bree, I can't see you. There is no way around it right now. But you're a smart girl, and you may be able to help yourself. Do you have a library card?"

"Yes, sir."

"Do you feel comfortable doing research and using a card catalog?"

"Yeah, we do it all the time at school."

"Why don't you try going to the library and looking up anxiety. You may learn some tips and methods that could help you. In fact, there are excerpts from a book I wrote about anxiety, they have it at the library, under my name. It's the best I can do, Bree. I'm truly sorry."

I felt like the rug had been pulled out from under me. That feeling of suffocation pressed down on my chest. But, Dr. Bryan was right. I was not helpless. He said when control goes up, anxiety goes down. It was time to take control.

I hopped on my bike and headed straight for the library. Well, I did stop for a Slurpee on the way. I hoped Dr. Bryan was right, that I really could find plenty of information by way of the library. Sure enough, a quick search of the card catalog led to many options. I looked under 'Anxiety in Children' and that narrowed down the search considerably. I found a book with a check list for childhood anxiety. Could I answer 'yes' to any of the following questions:

Constant thoughts and fears about safety of self and parents— yes, definitely.

Refusing to go to school—No, I never thought that was an option.

Frequent stomach aches and other physical complaints—My heart pounds and I get sweaty at weird times, and my stomach gets to churning, but that's not really a stomach ache.

Sleep disturbances—Oh, yes.

Extreme worries about sleeping away from home—I spend the night with friends, but I've always refused to stay away for more than one night.

Overly clingy behavior at home—I don't think so.

Many worries about things before they happen—O.K., a big yes on that one.

I had to admit it did look like I had an anxiety disorder. I looked for information on how to make it go away. I couldn't find any permanent cure but I did read that treatment for children often includes the same treatments used with adults, such as medication (out of the question), therapy (not an option either), and thought control techniques. I didn't know what these were, but I continued my research, hoping to learn more.

The more I read, the more determined I became to help myself, in spite of Father. All I had to do was stop the bad thoughts as soon as they entered my head and think about something more positive. And I had to do it *every* time irrational fears came to mind. Surely I could do that. I also learned that it might take ninety days or more before I noticed a difference. Ninety days? I wanted immediate relief. I had read somewhere that the journey of 1,000 miles begins with one step.

I knew Aunt Sharon loved me, and she'd help me any way she could. But as Father always pointed out, she didn't practice psychology, she taught it. Father had made plenty of comments about Aunt Sharon's arm-chair-pop-psychology. He was afraid Aunt Sharon would put ideas into Mom's head. Who knows what ideas he was so concerned about. I'd never considered telling my aunt everything, anyway, for fear she would tell Mom. She was prone to do that. It would be more difficult without Dr. Bryan's help, but he was right, I was smart. And I was determined to be normal. It would be worth a try at least.

I didn't see Mike approach my table until he was right beside me and then, because I was sitting and he was standing, it was his knees I noticed first. The bandages were gone but he had two scabs like the heads and tails of a large coin. It reminded me of the pictures in Detective Hines' file and maybe I frowned because Mike said, "They're not that bad. Your mom did a good job of cleaning them. No infection or they would look a lot worse."

Mike laid his books on the table: *Alistair Cooke's America, All the President's Men,* and *Man's Search for Meaning.* I said, "A little light reading?" forgetting my own books that were spread out before me until it was too late.

"And it looks like you're studying to be a psychologist. Or do you know some crazy people?"

I could feel the beginnings of a blush but I didn't know what to say. Oblivious to my discomfort Mike continued, "I'm pretty sure we're not supposed to refer to people as crazy. How about mentally handicapped, or emotionally stunted, or maybe, human?" He smiled at his own joke.

"If you must know I do feel a little anxious sometimes and I was reading about that and how I might get over it." There, I had said it and the world hadn't imploded and Mike hadn't grabbed his books and made a dash for the doors.

"So what's the big deal? We all worry about things. There's so much to worry about. That's where prayer comes in. We cast our worries at God's feet and let Him take care of them. He's the one in control anyway."

"Do you really, truly believe that, Mike? That God is in charge? Because if he is, he's been asleep lately. Where is he when children are murdered? Where is he when people are falsely accused?" In a matter of minutes I had gone from quiet reflection to anxiety level nine. I felt tears welling in my eyes and there was a familiar lump in my throat. I didn't want Mike or anyone else to see me like this.

Mike moved almost invisibly closer and said in a very soft voice, "Hey, I wouldn't upset you for anything. I didn't know you were hurting." I almost expected him to give me a soothing pat on the back like my mom would. Instead he changed the subject, which was the best thing.

"It's hard to be as smart as we are and as perfect as everyone expects. It'd be easier if we could be compared to, say, a dumber brother or sister.

"Sometimes I wish I had a brother that was all jock and no brains so I could go off to my room and read comic books if I wanted because my dad wouldn't care. Don't you wish you had a sister that was all beauty and no brains so your parents wouldn't expect you to be so perfect, to get all A's, to discover the cure for cancer?"

I smiled because I agreed with him. He had told me about what happened to his mom so I could share some things with him too.

"I think I did almost have a sister, or maybe a brother. I was nine and my mom got sick. Instead of getting up and fixing breakfast, she'd let my dad do it. He seemed to enjoy it and never complained. But one day she got very sick and my Aunt Sharon took care of me while my dad took her to the hospital.

"She came home and lay around in bed for a couple of weeks. Then one day she came out of the bedroom, started cooking and cleaning like normal, but everything was different. She started gaining weight." I sighed and I felt my shoulders drop with the pain of remembering the year everything seemed to change.

"My dad spent more and more evenings at his friend Moose's house and he was drinking more. That was the last time I had a baby-sitter, when Aunt Sharon took care of me while my mom was in the hospital. Now they never go out and leave me alone. Either we all three do something together or we don't do anything at all. Mostly we don't do much." I was surprised I had shared this with Mike since I had never even verbalized it to myself. I didn't even know I knew this.

"Well, Bree, I'm kind of glad you're an only child because I can't imagine the trouble we would be in if there was another Grant girl out there."

While I was still smiling he stood abruptly and took his books to the counter to check out. I had never had a guy for a friend before. I had never had a friend who was smarter than me before. This was going to be interesting.

The next morning I had just finished watching *Bugs Bunny*, and was flicking the knob between the three channels, when I saw Moose's picture on one of the news stations. It was disconcerting to see him on television. The reporter said that Michael Sullivan had been arrested for the murder of Rachel Carter. According to the reporter, somehow, Moose murdering Rachel was believed to be part of a bizarre ritual intended to resurrect his daughter, Jennifer.

A solemn older man reported, "Today the police released more information regarding the arrest of Michael Sullivan, founder and director of the Jennifer Sullivan Drug and Alcohol Treatment Center. Police indicate that Sullivan's friend, Lisa LaPlante, admitted yesterday that she was not with

Sullivan the entire night of the murder. LaPlante told police that she was shielding Sullivan, who, in her words, 'could not possibly be capable of murder'. Police also said that Sullivan's daughter's bones were found at the scene, arranged in a ritualistic fashion, reminiscent of an ancient Vietnamese custom. Sullivan served in the Vietnam War. Dr. William N. Friday, a forensic entomologist, from the University of Arizona, was seen leaving Sullivan's place of work just yesterday. When questioned, police stated that items recovered from Sullivan's office include hundreds of flour beetles, believed to have been specially ordered from a biological testing organization and delivered to a nearby post office. An anonymous source has informed this reporter that the beetles are thought to have been used to clean Sullivan's daughter's bones. This, according to our source, is the first ritualistic step in preparing the remains for a primitive Vietnamese ceremony. Three years after the deceased is buried, so the tradition goes, the bones are exhumed, cleaned and then arranged in an ornate ceramic box. This time-honored Vietnamese custom involves stacking the bones to resemble a human skeleton. Vietnamese gravediggers undergo a one-year apprenticeship to perfect their ability of arranging the bones.

"Rachel Carter's killer was familiar with this practice, as indicated by the arrangement of the bones. Sullivan's daughter's bones were swathed in gold paper, and the eye sockets of the skull were left uncovered. According to Vietnamese belief, this allows the deceased to see loved ones in their new afterlife.

"The bones are believed to have been cleaned over a several week period prior to the murder. *Dermestes Maculatus*, the scientific name of the flour beetle, is sometimes utilized by museums to clean the bones of specimens collected for display or research. The beetle tends to be most active during the summer months, preferring hot and humid weather. The police say additional evidence will be introduced at the trial."

The report mentioned nothing about albino ghosts or Satan worship—not that I was that surprised. I also noticed the coin was still not being mentioned. I remembered the pictures in Detective Hines' file. There had been a close-up picture of both sides of the coin; it looked really old. One side had a picture of Jesus seated on a throne. He was holding a Book of Gospels in one hand and a staff with an orb in the other. The other side of the coin had the Virgin Mary placing a crown on an emperor's head.

My thoughts were consumed with death and religion. How could God let this happen? Maybe what happened in my room was just a dream. It really appeared Moose was guilty. Logic tells me he did it. Why did I feel this had something to do with me? Jennifer and Rachel were dead. I was trying to live a normal life. I hadn't really known either one of them. Why did I feel like I knew more than I did?

Detective Hines had made notes under the photos describing the pictures. He'd also written: *Nomisma—thin, gold coin from about 1000 A.D. Slightly larger than a quarter, but one-third as thick. Price: $500 to $1,000. From the Byzantine Empire—'Romans Christianized'.*

The reporter mentioned none of this. I felt important knowing something no one else knew, even if I was still confused as to the coin's purpose and how it fit into the murder. In fact, I understood so little about the murder. I could understand Moose wanting to bring his daughter back to life. What I couldn't understand was how sincerely distraught he seemed that day in my father's studio. I remembered how he cried talking about how Jennifer's grave had been desecrated.

I didn't feel right running to Aunt Sharon again with all my questions. Besides, there was someone else I could talk to—and trust, for that matter.

I went straight to the attic, seeking my five friends' thoughts on this latest news report.

Kelly spoke first. "Moose is in a heap of trouble now, honey, with no alibi. And his li'l girlfriend—why, I jus' can't believe she lied. Y'all know, she's gonna be charged with that, that… thing," he finished lamely.

"P-p-p-perjury?" Jesse interjected.

"Thank you, sweetheart; that's jus' what I meant."

"You guys—help me understand why Moose did it…if he did it. I just don't get what he was trying to do. How could he justify taking another girl's life and putting her parents through the same agony he went through?"

Terry explained his theory. "In the first place, the bloke is batty. I'm positive we all agree on that point, right?"

Gene interrupted, "It's my hypothesis that Moose learned about or witnessed this ritual while in Vietnam. Then, unfortunately, he created his own demented variation, which involved killing a girl who perhaps reminded him of Jennifer. Rather than cleaning the bones by hand, he procured the special beetles. Moose believed, I feel, that it was necessary to create the same terror in Rachel that his daughter must have felt the night she perished.

"Somewhere in his fanatical mind he must have gotten the idea that as the potent and dynamic life energy drained from Rachel it would infuse Jennifer's remains and some how resurrect her."

Gene made sense. His explanation was chilling; we shared a horror-struck silence.

Kelly spoke up, "Sugar, you are nevah gonna understand entirely what ole Moose did, even if you ask him straight out."

I hadn't thought of that. "Hey, I could ask him."

Kelly went on, "You could ask him, I 'magine, if you ever see him again. When pigs fly."

I felt a wave of sadness. "Gosh, that day at Father's studio might have been the last time I'll ever see Moose." I couldn't tell them how involved I still felt. I had expressed some of my questions, but not all the unsettling anxiety about what those questions really meant.

The child spends too much time thinking and asking questions. I don't want anything to happen to her and if she gets too close, I don't know what he'll do. I don't believe he could ever hurt her but then, I remind myself of what he has already done... I'll need to find a way to take her with me. She won't be able to stay...not with him. Leaving will be the riskiest, most dangerous thing I've ever done. It will be dangerous for him too, everything I do affects him, I can't forget that.

Suddenly I hear the door slam and I jump a bit as he comes into the room. He glares at me. "Why do you look like the cat that swallowed the canary?"

I was afraid he could tell I was getting jitterier day by day. "You scared me when you slammed the door, that's all. I was resting and didn't know you were here."

He stared hard at me as if he was trying to decide something. "Hmmm. Something in your face tells me you're lying. I hate liars. We have to be able to trust each other, especially during these unusually tense times. If you have something to say to me, just say it."

He was trying to make me think I could trust him, that he would be understanding, but I knew better. "I am telling you the truth. I was only resting. You know me, I don't have deep thoughts like you, you do enough deep thinking for the both of us." I smiled, hoping flattery would cause him to back off.

He smirked. "Fair enough. But I advise you to keep your trust in me, it will soon be obvious I have your best interest at heart, regardless of what I have to do."

CHAPTER NINETEEN

A FEW DAYS later, I decided to stop by Aunt Sharon's before dinner, since I hadn't seen her in awhile and I still wanted to tell her about the Brush Arbor.

Since Aunt Sharon didn't teach in the summer she spent a lot of time in the summer going to garage sales, flea markets and auctions looking for old furniture to refurbish. Whenever she found an old icky piece of furniture, she'd always say, "This is something Benjamin Moore can fix."

She was under the carport, happily restoring an old stove, the kind with high legs and warming compartments.

"What's that for? You're not really going to cook on that thing, are you?"

She brushed a comma of hair from her forehead and shook her head, "No, I'm going to put my TV in it."

"You want to cook your TV?"

"Very funny. This is my new entertainment center. What do you think?"

I pondered this idea and smiled. "I think it'll be cool."

Aunt Sharon was using a strong-smelling paint remover to strip off the old white paint. I held my nose.

"What color are you going to paint it?"

"You mean colors, plural, don't you?"

"Of course—how silly of me."

"I was thinking of purple and yellow, perhaps with a touch of red."

"That's interesting." Aunt Sharon's color palettes were never boring.

I told Aunt Sharon about the Brush Arbor Revival. She listened and smiled, laying down her paint brush, "You crave religion, Bree, and I run from it. Sometimes it's all about wanting what we don't have. Your mom and I were raised with a lot of hell and damnation lectures from our father. He said we had to go to church for 'fire insurance'. I never felt that was a good enough reason. Now I pretty much only see a sanctuary when it's full of Easter lilies or poinsettias."

I thought about this. "Even though I've never been to a regular church service, I bet I've been in more churches than anybody you know. Father takes me with him lots of times when he installs windows, so I get to explore and hang out in the church or synagogue or cathedral or whatever."

Sharon asked, "Of the three, which do you like best?"

Hard question. "I can't really say. I mean, some are prettier, that's for sure. Some of them are very traditional and other ones are more sleek and contemporary. I guess, in my mind, though, they all have one thing in common."

"What's that?"

"All of them give me a feeling that I don't get anywhere else. It's like I feel peace, and a quietness touches my heart, just for that small space of time. Then Father says it's time to leave. I want more, but I have to leave."

"Bree, love, I had no idea you felt so passionately about religion. Are you glad you went to this Brush Arbor? I'm interested to know if you felt that peace you're seeking, considering you weren't technically in a place of worship."

I hadn't thought of that. "I can't say I felt it any less. It's hard to compare because it was the first church service I've ever witnessed, unless you count that jumpy guy on TV Sunday mornings…" I thought about how fortunate Father must feel to be able to create beauty that led to worship. No wonder he was never satisfied, creating the perfect window was a worthy goal.

A red car drove slowly past the house, catching my attention. It turned at the end of street and drove by once more. Was it following me? My heart began a familiar, agitated thump when a truck pulled up behind Aunt Sharon's Spitfire.

"Who's that?" I asked.

"Oh, that must be Paul. He's a new guy I'm seeing. He's a little early. I'm cooking dinner for him tonight. It's kind of a get-to-know-each-other thing, or I'd invite you to stay."

"How'd you meet him? What's he like? Is he better than Buck?"

"Blah! Don't mention that man's name, you'll irritate my ulcer."

"Sorry!"

"To answer your question, I work with Paul, he called out of the blue and anyway, he used to be a clown for the Shriner's."

"Well, that's…so very sweet."

"I think that shows the kind of guy he is…shhh! Here he comes!"

Paul waved at us and grinned. I watched him saunter up the driveway. He wore cowboy boots, and the big silver buckle on his belt glinted in the sun. I had to admit he was pretty nice looking. He kind of reminded me of Terry—except for the clothes, of course—blonde, handsome, self-assured. I hoped he would treat Aunt Sharon well. She deserved it.

"Howdy, Miss Sharon. Look at you, painting your heart out. Who's your friend?"

Aunt Sharon stood, wiping her hands off with a rag. "Paul, this is Bree, my niece. Bree, this is Paul, he teaches in the education department at the college."

I shook Paul's hand and made small talk, excusing myself as soon as possible.

On my way home, I thought about Paul and wondered what kind of guy he was. I liked his bright colors. He seemed kind of country but nice enough. More genuine than Buck. Would Paul demand a lot of Aunt Sharon's time, would she still have time for me? What if they got married? How would that change things? Would she have a kid and like it better than me? Something else to feel anxious about.

I couldn't help but wonder how far Aunt Sharon went with her boyfriends. In my naïve mind I figured they made out but I couldn't bear the thought of her having sex with any of them. I had never known one of her boyfriends to stay over and I knew I would be mortified to stop by early some morning and find one sitting at her kitchen table, in his underwear, eating her food.

I knew all about sex from my friend Kristen. I knew what went where and how it all worked but what I didn't understand was why someone would want to do such a thing, unless they wanted to make a baby. That thought bothered me the most, thinking that Sharon might want a baby.

Reflecting on this new problem, I turned onto my street. Oh no! A red car drove slowly by my house, slow enough to read the address. Was that the same car I saw at Aunt Sharon's? Is that my neighbor? If Moose wasn't really guilty then the killer was still out there. The car drove on, and I was left to wonder if it held the bones of a dead girl as the driver looked for a victim.

Father was in a good mood at dinner that night, especially considering his best friend was going to prison for murder. Father was acting animated, agitated somehow, babbling about minor events in his day. The colors around him were glowing as they vibrated, which was something new.

"My dear family, don't worry about Moose. Jail is not a place I recommend for anyone, especially myself." He grinned widely at Mom and me, his fingers drumming insistently on the table. I continued to eat my meatloaf.

"Now I know my sweet girls are concerned about Moose, but there's no need to fret. Yours truly has provided our dear Mr. Sullivan the best attorney money can buy. I told Moose I'm paying for everything. Yes indeed! Not to worry, our Moose will go free! He's no murderer!"

I put down my fork, feeling a little sick to my stomach, as Mom gushed on about how wonderful and generous Father was. I wanted to ask if we really wanted Moose to go free if he was guilty, or even mentally ill.

Father seemed overly confident to me, considering the evidence against Moose. I would have loved to challenge him on this but I didn't want the belt again; it wasn't worth it. Then came that same dizzy, heart-pounding feeling that I was learning to recognize as an anxiety attack. I really didn't want to finish my dinner, but I knew I'd be in trouble if I didn't. I tried to concentrate on the moment and not on the what-ifs.

Father continued his tirade against the judicial system. I decided to try some of my new relaxation techniques I read at the library. I tried to remember what I had learned: breathe deeply, stop my thoughts of worry, substitute more pleasant thoughts. I tried to imagine myself in my attic, talking to my friends, the comforting sounds of *Bohemian Rhapsody* playing in the background.

"SO YOU THINK YOU CAN STONE ME AND SPIT IN MY EYE
SO YOU THINK YOU CAN LOVE ME AND LEAVE ME TO DIE
OH BABY - CAN'T DO THIS TO ME BABY
JUST GOTTA GET OUT - JUST GOTTA GET RIGHT OUTTA
HERE
OOH YEAH, OOH YEAH
NOTHING REALLY MATTERS
ANYONE CAN SEE
NOTHING REALLY MATTERS - NOTHING REALLY MATTERS
TO ME..."

Father was saying my name as I blinked back to the present. "Huh?"

"We're losing you, Bree. You're not smoking pot, are you?"

He looked serious. "No! Of course not! I was just daydreaming."

"Uh-huh. Right. You know, you're an odd child."

I nodded but at the same time I was thinking about how I could raise my control to lower my anxiety. Father jabbered on, hardly touching his dinner. Now he was berating the Democrats and all the problems they caused President Ford. When at last he seemed to run out of steam, I cleared my throat and said, "I was wondering..." Mom and Father were both looking at me. "I was thinking we could go to church at some point."

Father's forkful of potatoes stopped in midair. "Oh, no. Don't even think about it, missy. Those folks will put outrageous ideas in your head, worse than that Dr. Psycho boy. First, it's church on Sunday, then they're judging us by Baptist standards."

I felt a sinking feeling in my stomach. It hadn't really occurred to me that my parents wouldn't *let* me go to church. I knew I was feeling the onset of more anxiety; I recognized the signs now. I tried to calm myself, reassuring myself that I could still pray and have a relationship with God, in spite of my father.

With a sudden urge to stand up for myself, I blurted, "But how can you quote scripture at the drop of a hat and create monuments to honor God, yet still deny your only child the simple privilege of going to church? You're a paradox. No wonder I'm not normal!" I stopped my diatribe as soon as I noticed my father's shocked expression. I looked over at my mom who was staring at her plate while smacking her lips and mumbling. It felt really good to speak my mind for a change.

Father stood up from the table touching his belt. "Is this what you want, Bree? Is the belt the only way I can get through to you? YOU DO NOT DISRESPECT YOUR FATHER! As far as *you're* concerned I AM YOUR GOD!"

Feeling panicked and scared, I began apologizing profusely and explaining how I didn't really want to go to church anyway. The more I repeated back his own thoughts to him the more calm he seemed to become. Father finally sat back down and resumed eating but I noticed he kept one eye on me the rest of the meal.

That night, I spent hours trying to control my thoughts. It wasn't working too well. I wanted to stop worrying but I was afraid to stop. I was convinced I'd be blindsided if I released my mind from its protective mode of thinking. I kept running the what-ifs over and over in my mind. And if there was something buried deep in my memory, I wanted to pull up the memory so the leaking water dreams would stop but try as I might I couldn't figure out what it could be.

I could hear Father playing Bach's *Fugue in D Minor* on the piano in the living room. The music wasn't comforting tonight. I kept thinking my same old worrisome thoughts: was there something outside my window ready to hurt me if I wasn't on guard? Would Moose go free and hurt another girl? Was there a kidnapper in a red car following me around the neighborhood? Did the kidnapper actually live in my neighborhood? Something bad could happen to Mom; Father could die and there would be no one to take care of us; and on and on. I needed to worry, didn't I? It was how I protected myself. It was how I protected us.

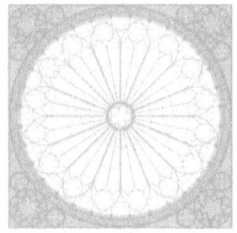

CHAPTER TWENTY

THE EARLY MORNING of the Fourth of July brought anticipation and excitement as the Bicentennial came to a head, after years of planning and promotions on every commercial product from soup to nuts. From the license plate on our car, to stamps, candy wrappers and soda bottles—patriotic logos were stamped supplying me with many collectables. But the climax of all this cultivation for our town and many others would be today's parade. Father's studio, being in the downtown, gave us a perfect viewing location. Father and I headed to the studio in the old Pontiac. He didn't have much work for me, but he was desperate to finish a window for a synagogue in St. Louis. I gave him wide berth as I played with Van Gogh, waited on customers, and counted the minutes till parade time.

The parade began around 2:00, Mom said she had things to get ready for the picnic and declined the early eight a.m. ride to the studio. We agreed to pick her up after the parade, when the roads were open again.

I watched from the front curb as the crowds gathered. Most of the throng were dressed in red, white and blue and waving flags above their heads. Children, dogs and people of all ages flaunted their collective patriotism. Leading the parade was our high school band playing, *Get Into America,* the official Bicentennial theme song. I saw several kids I knew and wished briefly that I had learned to play an instrument. Next came fire trucks, cars of Shriner's, Campfire Girls on their decorated bikes, floats of heroes—from Molly Pitcher to Ronald McDonald. My favorite part of the parade was the Revolutionary War reenactment. Father watched most of the parade with me, but during the reenactment he became agitated and went back inside his studio. I followed him in, although I didn't want to miss any of the parade. "Father, what's wrong?"

"It's this country, their attitude!" His colors were vibrating again. "Where was all this support when I fought in Vietnam? Why now? Why support people they don't even remember, never met, or even gave a thought to? I resent their pathetic patriotism because it will be gone by next summer, because it's shallow, it's all about an excuse to party, no reflection on the sacrifices made by the soldiers, the soldiers that gave *them* freedom!"

I remembered the sermon I had heard at the Brush Arbor and felt I could sort of understand what Father was saying, what he might be feeling. "I can see your point, it is all about a party for a lot of people and I admit I have been caught up in all the items I've been collecting, especially my Bicentennial coins. I forget how thousands of men did give their lives so that we could live without Great Britain's control, not be exploited, and go on to create one of the only countries in the world today that is based on a constitutional republic—which guarantees certain rights for its citizens—but avoids the tyranny of the majority found in a democracy." Father looked at me strangely but didn't stop me so I continued, "Thank you for reminding me of that and for bringing me here today. I will try, I really mean it, to remain patriotic after this year."

I reached out for his hand and he grabbed me, hugging me tight. "Thank you, Breezy, I believe you almost understand… and at least you were listening. Sometimes I think you know me better than anyone."

I was embarrassed, so I didn't respond. Father went back to his work table and I followed him, feeling he needed my attention, besides, the parade was dying down. I locked the doors, in order to avoid post-parade crowds from wandering in, Father didn't do well with idle gawkers and their questions.

Standing beside him at the work table I watched him work. Muscles flexing in his forearms as he applied pressure to the glasscutter. Long fingers masterfully wrapping each individual piece of colored glass with copper foil. The smell of solder as he melted it and smoothed it between the edges. Ever so slowly, it came together like a puzzle in which the pieces seemed to fall naturally into place.

When the panel was finally finished, I asked Father what he'd hidden in this window. He told me to find it myself. I searched the window for several minutes but couldn't find anything. Father never liked to show me what he'd hidden; he always made me discover it for myself—or not at all. It was a game to him. I just didn't see whatever it was he had secreted in that window. Sometimes the thing was so subtle that no one would ever see it, which was what he always hoped to achieve.

"OK. I give up—show me."

"Keep looking." I could tell he was enjoying this.

"Please, show me!" I pleaded. His lack of response told me I was on my own. It was good training for a future investigator and I usually enjoyed the game. I thought that most of the time I could look straight into the heart of a situation, seeing what others missed. The time spent searching for my father's quirky signature designs helped me look at the whole world as though it was a puzzle to solve. I had heard Father say once, "God is in the details." I remember that quote because when Father said it, he seemed so sincere and I was left wondering if he truly believed in a God.

The window incorporated a contemporary geometric design and I squinted my eyes to see if any part of the design stood apart. Sure enough, one line of solder seemed inconsistent with the rest of the motif. My finger moved over the smooth silver edge from the top, down, a twist, then up again.

"I found it, but I still don't get it." That was fair. I didn't have to understand his symbols.

"The Exodus. This line of solder represents the route of the Exodus, in which Moses led the Israelites out of Egypt. See? This point right here at the bottom would be Mt. Sinai."

I didn't quite see, but nodded anyway.

"*The Lord said to Moses, 'When a man wrongs another, that person is guilty and must make full restitution for his wrong!'*"

Well, there was nothing really I could add to that. "Are you ready to go, Father?"

"Umm, yes, just about. Let me move this window over to the wall so I can get the crate ready for delivery tomorrow morning." I stepped back out of his way as he lifted the heavy window up from the worktable, the veins and sinews of his arms stretched and pulsed. He had carried it cautiously for a few steps, when Van Gogh jumped down from the table and landed right in front of Father's feet. I tried to yell out a warning, but it was too late. Father's foot was in mid-air. He tried to sidestep but tripped and fell forward, the full weight of the window falling on Van Gogh.

I screamed, "Oh, my God! Van Gogh!"

I ran over and dropped to my knees. Father struggled to his knees and joined me, amidst all the shards of glass, next to Van Gogh's crushed body. I saw blood oozing from his mouth. My vision blurred and I almost lost my balance. Bile rose in my throat and I thought I was going to vomit or faint—maybe both.

Father whispered hoarsely, "He's still breathing! Quick, run and get his bed! We'll take him to the vet."

The desperateness in his voice kept me from fainting; I grabbed Van Gogh's stained glass bed. Father was leaning over the lifeless cat, giving him mouth-to-mouth resuscitation, but Van Gogh's body remained limp and unresponsive. Father gently cradled his little pet in his already bloodstained arms, then laid Van Gogh gently in the bed. I could see a wound on Van Gogh's side where he was cut. Blood was running down into the box. I began to cry.

Father tenderly kissed Van Gogh's head and turned to me, tears running down his face. Father's hands were cut from the broken glass and his clothes were stained with blood. Small flecks of shattered colors dotted his hair and skin. *"And I saw the dead, great and small, they were judged with what they had done in their lives.* This kitty was pure. Van Gogh has done no wrong. He lives again, although now, perhaps he appears dead, his light extinguished, his color diminished."

"Dead?" I sobbed, "He's dead?"

Father pulled me to him and held me in his arms. "Yes, precious one, he's dead—but will live again." Father was quiet for the longest time. I remember thinking it was good that he could just sit quietly and mourn Van Gogh. Then he began to cry, his big body racked with grief. I wasn't sure who was holding whom at this point. We stayed that way for a while, sobbing and swaying to some silent rhythm. At last, Father pulled away, sighing he said, "We must carry on and go get your mom for our Fourth of July celebration."

"How can we go enjoy fireworks when Van Gogh is dead?"

"Because Van Gogh would have wanted us to. Besides, we can bury Van Gogh while we are out in the country. We'll celebrate Van Gogh's life with fireworks. The window—pah! It was junk anyway. I'm glad it's destroyed. The design was deplorable—it was all wrong. I'll do another. One better—more worthy."

It occurred to me that this, obviously, was not the 'perfect window'. I personally didn't care much for it in the first place, but I wondered if I would even know the perfect window when I saw it. I felt queasy about this inexplicable charade. Father had just lost his companion of many years. He was, in fact, partly responsible for Van Gogh's death. Yet after not much time he was willing to go have a good time, a celebration? He had lost several days of labor and probably quite a lot of money when the window was destroyed. He seemed relatively calm. This response from someone who routinely lost it over far more trivial matters worried me.

We spent the next half-hour sweeping up the broken glass. Father had washed and bandaged his hands. The cuts had been small and he had refused my help. He put on a clean shirt he kept in the back room and soon, except for the small mound beneath a blood stained towel, it was as if nothing so grizzly had happened. As time passed, Father seemed more upset about having to redo the Exodus window than he was about the fact that his studio pet was dead. I called Mom while Father was in the back room; I wanted to warn her about Van Gogh. She answered on the second ring.

"Mom, this is Bree."

"Hello, dear. How was the parade? Do you need a jacket for tonight? It's supposed to be a little cool later."

"Mom, you'll have to drive your car here. Father can't come get you right now, I have to tell you something. It's about Van Gogh—he's dead. A window fell on him." I was careful not to say that Father *dropped* a window on him.

Mom was silent for three beats. "Well, that's a shame. Really sad, yes, well I am so sorry for you and your father...do you need a jacket, dear?"

I wasn't really surprised by her response. I figured it was more than she could handle. Even though Mom didn't spend much time at the studio—definitely not enough to be very attached to Van Gogh—you'd think she would at least be more upset for Father or me. Yes, I thought, she is upset and doesn't know how to deal with it.

By the time Mom arrived at the studio, all traces of broken glass and blood were gone. Father told me to climb up in the back of his pick-up truck. He placed Van Gogh and the shovel in the back with me, and my mom up front with himself. I really didn't want to ride back there with Van Gogh's body, but I knew Mom couldn't and Father had been through enough for one day. I kept telling myself that Father's kitty was already in Heaven chasing angelic mice just for fun while trying not to eat them. I tried to picture it like a Saturday morning cartoon, but my eyes kept coming back to that small towel-wrapped mound laying immobile by the shovel.

We drove out to the countryside, finally parked in an out-of-the-way, secluded pasture, the setting sun casting an orangey-pink glow over the dry grassland. Father ceremoniously lifted Van Gogh's bed out of the truck, and I knew he planned to bury the little cat before we began shooting off fireworks.

Without a word, Father began digging a hole. Mom and I waited quietly, not sure how to help. I wanted to protest that it made no sense to bury Van Gogh out here in the middle of nowhere; we'd never be able to visit his grave. Evaluating Father's set and sweaty face changed my mind. Curtly, he called us over, and as Mom set the little stained glass bed in the ground, Father shoveled dirt over Van Gogh's lifeless body. I knew I'd start to cry again. I concentrated on the prisms of light reflecting off Van Gogh's bed, as the dirt began to swathe the little animal.

Father began his eulogy. *"A righteous man cares for the needs of his animal, but the kindest acts of the wicked are cruel. But ask the animals, and they will teach you, or the birds of the air and they will tell you, or let the fish inform you. Which of all these does not know that the hand of the Lord has done this? In His hand is the life of every creature and the breath of mankind."*

Father bowed his head so we did the same. Father closed with a prayer.

"God, take this precious little kitty with his one ear and give him two; grant him life as a perfect creation and bestow on him a new name."

Mom told him it was a beautiful sermon. I was speechless.

As the sky darkened and crickets filled the pasture with their song of summer, we finished our picnic and began our blazing display.

Once Father walked away from Van Gogh's grave, he seemed peaceful. He began lighting his big firework displays as we laid back on the quilts Mom brought, enjoying the show. Father liked being the center of attention and I think he enjoyed the fireworks even more than we did. With multi-colored lights filling the sky above us and flashing in all directions around us, it was easy to feel blessed to live in America and be part of a family, crazy or not.

We didn't get home until after eleven. I was exhausted, too tired to mourn Van Gogh or worry about Moose or myself. I slept better than I had in a long time.

"Nothing is working out the way it was ordained. The way I figure it, it must be your fault." He scowled at me. He seemed unusually irritated.

I glanced up at him, trying not to look too interested for fear of encouraging him. I had always known that his playing the "fault game" would be the most dangerous trap. Did he want me to fall into it? Was he just baiting me? Sometimes I felt like I didn't know him at all.

"Think about it, it's logical, the original plan was perfect until you decided to show up at the woods that night. Since you are obviously the problem, I have to figure out what to do with you, so you don't interfere this time."

I rubbed my face and leaned back with a sick feeling building in my stomach. Here I'd spent the last couple of months worrying about what he might do to others and I forgot to think about protecting myself. All along I thought I had more time. I needed to end this relationship…and soon.

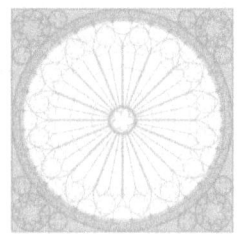

CHAPTER TWENTY-ONE

FEELING MORE RESTED and calm than I had in weeks, I started out on an aimless bike ride the next day, but as I pulled out onto my street I noticed the hippy witch lady working in one of her colorful, overgrown flower beds. I had been so wrong about our neighbor, John; maybe I had been wrong about her too.

I pedaled up to her drive-way, dismounted my bike and laid it in the grass between the curb and sidewalk. I walked into the shade of her yard. I couldn't believe I had made any noise to attract her attention, but she turned and looked right at me. Her straw garden hat shaded her face, but the beads she wore around her neck glimmered in the morning sunlight. She looked as if she had been expecting me, but that was impossible—even I hadn't known I was going there.

"Bree, child, you're early. I haven't finished mulching the parsley."

"Early? Early for what?" I wasn't sure I had heard what she said. Was it a code or some magic words to cast a spell?

"Uh…," I felt like I might be under some spell. The morning shadows seemed heavier and seemed to have more suggestive forms in her garden, but I forged ahead anyway.

She turned back to her garden. I didn't feel like she was being rude or ignoring me; I felt like she was thinking things through before answering. I wondered where that impression was coming from. I watched as she piled shredded bark around the base of her plants and patted the mounds gently and almost tenderly with her bare hands.

"These plants are herbs. This is my kitchen garden. Everyone should have a kitchen garden. I don't know how people can cook without fresh herbs. These plants can turn an ordinary vegetable into food fit for a god." Her back was still turned to me. "Oscar Wilde wrote that mere color, unspoiled by meaning and unallied with definite form, can speak to the soul in a thousand different ways. Did you know all living things have an aura of color; even these plants?" Now she turned around to face me. She was smiling warmly, but my own face must have reflected my surprise.

Her own colors appeared around her like a mist rising from the ground. Colors wavered and blended, shifting in moving ribbons about her feet, twining up her legs and caressing her shoulders. A kaleidoscope of hues synchronized to some unheard music. "My name is Diana," she said and held out her hand.

I shook her hand and without thinking, I blurted, "You can see people's colors too!"

"Let me ask you, whose colors do you think you see?"

"Everyone's."

"Tell me more, child."

I couldn't believe I was confessing. "I see people for who they are, I think, for instance, my mom's aura is shades of blue, soft, gentle, like she is. But I see lots of colors around my father...vibrating intense colors. And lately, just this summer I'm starting to see colors in people's shadows and that has me rather concerned."

Diana smiled. "You have the gift."

"What gift? It doesn't feel like a gift...it feels overwhelming."

"Don't look so discouraged, Bree." Diana placed her hand on my shoulder. She smelled like warm dirt, like earth itself. I hadn't been aware of how good dirt could smell. "You can see auras, not just sense them like many people, but actually see them."

A quick chill ran down my spine, finally I was going to understand what was wrong with me. "What are auras?" I asked.

"An aura is the electromagnetic field that surrounds everything that is alive, basically it's the energy given off by all living things."

I cleared my throat. "Can you see auras like me?" I asked hopefully.

"To an extent, but no, Bree, I do not have the very unique gift of seeing the shadows. Very few can see the colors in shadows. While the human aura is kind of a blueprint of a person's soul, or their potential if you will...the colors in the shadow are what the person will actually become, your gift is a very rare gift indeed. The shadow's colors are something few people have the ability to see and usually develops around puberty. You can see what people are becoming."

Diana tilted her head, the shadow of her hat exposing a secret smile. "You know, I don't always see colors so strongly but I can see colors all around you. Your colors are rich."

I was beginning to feel dizzy. "So what does that mean? I noticed my friend Kristen's shadow has different colors than her typical aura, and then it seemed I started noticing a lot people's shadows were different from their auras...it scared me."

Diana explained, "Seeing the colors of shadows is a very useful gift because like I said, you can see what people are going to become. People change and you can see who they are going to be in the future. Of course some people don't ever change much and their shadow's colors reflect that flatness, the inability to grow as a person."

"So if I like Kristen's shadow, I shouldn't give up on her yet?"

"Perhaps not." Diana laughed.

"OK, because I've been really worried about her!"

Since I was a small child I had relied, or tried to rely on my gift of seeing colors. That ability to discern what people were really like and to protect me from who people really were. "How else can I use this gift?"

"That is what you have to learn, through the lessons."

"What lessons?" I wanted to know.

"The lessons that life gives to you, you will learn through your own experiences how truly strong you are. You are able to...read people...for lack of a better word.

My mind was whirling in fixated, tight circles and my head was starting to hurt. How did I know Diana was telling the truth? How could I know if she even knew what she was talking about? I sensed it was true. It felt right.

I have a question, "I've seen a color that's new to me, it's like a deep red, any idea what that's all about?"

Diana looked perplexed and thoughtful before responding. "Red generally is a color which creates friction, usually associated with anxiety or fear."

I couldn't imagine Father being afraid of much of anything but I didn't want to contradict Diana. I thought of another question. "Why do the colors around my father vibrate?"

Diana started to speak but I could see her stop herself and hesitate. "That's for you to discuss with him."

What was that supposed to mean? "You mean I have to tell him about my gift?" I wasn't so sure I wanted to do that.

"If you want to understand the vibrations you see, that's for him to discuss with you. Learn to trust your own feelings, Bree."

So, I was the one to help me. It didn't feel that frightening. I could trust myself. I could trust Bree Grant. I might make mistakes but I wasn't all alone. I had so many questions, but I didn't feel rushed to have them answered. I knew I had made a new friend and ally.

When I left Diana's I actually felt like a weight had been lifted from my shoulders. Maybe confession is good for the soul— but confusion is not. I had a lot to ponder, and I felt drained. I would think about it later I decided. I rode my bike easy around the neighborhood for a while and then swung by the pool, even though I didn't have my swimsuit, just to check out what was going on.

Lori was surrounded by a group of kids from school. I leaned my bike against the chain link fence and yelled to get her attention.

"Bree!" She acted like she'd actually missed me. She ran over to the fence, several girls following obediently as they had been trained to do. I saw her shadow flickering behind her with shades of the same flat brown that made up her aura.

"Bree, what's up? You comin' in to swim?"

"I don't have my suit. I just thought I'd see what was going on."

"How was your Fourth of July?" Lori continued before I could answer. "My dad took us all to the lake. He has a new 36-foot boat. It is so fast! We had a blast—we got to go see the fireworks from the water. Way cool!"

"Wow, that sounds like fun. We shot off fireworks out in the country. Van Gogh died yesterday. My father dropped a window on him by accident."

"Geez, that's gross. Were you there?"

"Oh, yeah, I saw it all happen. It was sad."

"Did you cry?"

"I cried, and my father cried too. It was sad, Lori. What do you expect?"

"Chill. Hey, I haven't been to the Grant palace for awhile. When are you going to invite me over? Oh—I heard about Moose, by the way. That sucks, huh?"

I didn't want to talk about Moose. "I'll ask my parents if you can come over and spend the night tonight, OK?"

"Very cool. Hey, can I invite Kristen and Pauline, too? They're here at the pool today."

"I thought Kristen and Pauline were mad at you. They said you told their secret."

Lori tossed her hair off her shoulder. "They can't stay mad at me, you know that." She raised an eyebrow and looked as if she expected me to challenge her but then she quickly changed the subject back to the sleepover. "Come on, let's have some fun tonight. Ask your mom but you know she'll say yes, she always says yes. Your mom doesn't know the meaning of the word 'no.'"

Lori was partially right. Mom was well-acquainted with hearing 'no', but not well-acquainted with saying 'no'. She would be relieved that I was doing normal girl stuff again. I hadn't had a slumber party in a long time; it would feel good to have friends come over.

Before they arrived I decided to bring my Ouija board down from the attic. Kristen always wanted to play with it. Of course, none of my girlfriends knew about my secrets in the attic, and I planned to keep it that way. I stopped to visit with my protectors before going back down to my room.

"Hi, guys! I hope you had a good Fourth without me. I missed you!"

Kelly said, "Bree, honey pie, we-all did miss you. Y'all shoulda been here, sugar! Gene and Stacey put on a hilarious show! Some sorta tainted version of *Oh! Calcutta.*"

Stacey looked indignant. "It was *not* tainted! Cripes, Kelly! Like I'm supposed to remember the entire original version? Gimme a break!"

Kelly laughed. "I s'pose not, sweet pea! So, Bree, sugar, how was your Fourth?"

"Not so great, really. I mean it was OK, but Van Gogh died, and I'm still sad about it. Van Gogh was my only pet, even though he belonged more to my father." I didn't bother to say how he had died and I hoped they wouldn't ask. I didn't want to recreate that picture in my mind.

Terry spoke up, "Poor child. Pop over here! Give this old chap a hug. You used to do that when you were small, remember? You'd come up here after a fight with your da', and you'd be crying. I'd always reassure you, but you handle him ever so much better now. You are growing up, sweetie."

"Well, the cleansing rituals help. And, of course, I'm learning to keep my yapper shut! I wish I could stay, Terry, but the girls are coming over to spend the night."

Jesse exclaimed, "Oh, c-c-cool! I love slumber p-p-p-parties!"

"Maybe sometime I'll spend the night with you guys. But I can't tell my friends about you—you know that." I watched for protest.

"I'm borrowing the Ouija board for tonight, but I'll bring it back tomorrow."

Gene sounded serious. "Bree, be careful with that thing. Remember, it is not a game."

I don't know why I didn't tell them about my visit with Diana. It was still so overwhelming. I just wanted to feel like a normal girl having normal friends over to spend a normal night. Wasn't that normal?

I hurried back down to my room to straighten it up, just a little. When I felt like everything was right for my friends, I walked out to the Octagon, only to see a huge stained glass window hanging from the skylight. It was Van Gogh! I knew, because the stained glass cat had only one ear. He built it in one day and it was definitely not his best work. It was really very disconcerting. Father had used green bevels for the eyes, and as I walked through the house I felt those eyes following me. Father was in the Trapezoid reading the Bible and listening to a record. I didn't want to make him mad right before my friends came over, but I was going to be so embarrassed when they saw that window.

"Hi, Father. I don't want to interrupt you," I said tentatively.

He glanced at me, so I kept talking. "Why did you make that huge window of Van Gogh and hang it here. Wouldn't you rather have it at your studio?"

"No, I like it here, in the center of the house." That apparently was that.

Lori arrived first, looking way cute with her hair all feathered back. I was jealous. We went back to my room.

"I have entered the Octagon!"

I corrected her. "It's the Hexagon."

"Whatever. I bet I've been here a hundred times and I never get tired of looking at your house. It is so beyond different!" I assumed that was a backhanded compliment.

"I have to ask," here it came, "what's with the giant cat window?"

"I told you at the pool, Van Gogh died."

"Yeah, and so did my dog last year, but we didn't make some huge monument. Sorry, Bree, but that's just flat out weird. It has a freaky thing goin' on, you know?"

"I know, trust me, I know."

Mom knocked on my bedroom door and opened it. Pauline and Kristen came in.

"Hey, Mom, will you make us a pizza now?"

"Of course, dear. What kind do you want?"

"I want cheese and black olive."

My friends grimaced. "Yuck! How can you eat black olives all the time? That is so gross." Lori stuck out her tongue to show how she really felt.

I ignored her. "So, what kind do the rest of you want?

"Cheese," said Lori.

Pauline shrugged, "I like everything, really."

Kristen asked for pepperoni and Pauline admitted that was her favorite too.

Lori took control right away. "Look, I brought music! Bree, put on my new album, 'Frampton Comes Alive' It's so cool!"

Rats. I forgot to bring my record player down from the attic. Hmmm. What to do? "Sure, I'll get my record player. Umm, can you guys go get some glasses of Coke? I'll put on the album."

Kristen and Pauline shrugged and left, but Lori stayed behind. "They don't need me. They can carry four glasses."

I was annoyed. "Could you go with them anyway? You know your way around the kitchen, at least. I mean, you've been here more."

"Whatever!" Lori said and left, her shadow flickering behind her, a mix of dismal colors.

I hustled up to the attic and grabbed my record player, apologizing to the mannequins that I couldn't stay. Just as I came out of the closet, the girls walked in with the drinks.

"All right! The music is ready!"

Kristen plopped her overnight bag on my bed. "I have a surprise, girlfriends. Come see what I brought."

We all walked over to the bed, I expected to see something like candy, maybe Pop Rocks, but instead Kristen pulled out a bottle of vodka. "Oh, no way!" I said. "My parents will kill us!"

"Don't go bananas. Vodka doesn't make your breath smell like other liquor does. My brother told me, and he got this for us. Your parents will never know. It tastes great in Coke."

"Let me guess. Your brother told you, right?" Lori said with a laugh.

Kristen smiled. "Actually, he did."

I was feeling more than a little nervous. I'd never drank before, but I knew of some kids that had tried it. I didn't want to seem like a total loser, and I felt like I had to regain Lori's respect, which I'd lost at the movie theater. No telling what she had told Kristen and Pauline about that night.

As she grabbed the bottle from Kristen, Lori commanded, "Bring your glasses over here, and I'll give you a shot or two."

We all did as we were told. I have to admit it really didn't change the taste of the Coke too much. It was easy to drink. In retrospect, too easy.

By the time my mom brought the pizza, we were giggling up a storm. Mom just smiled and asked if she could have a couple of slices of my pizza. Sure, I told her. I was willing to share. She looked so happy and I knew it was because we were giggling and acting silly in a way that assured her I was going to be okay.

As we ate pizza and drank vodka and Coke, Kristen brought up Moose. "Lori told us that your dad's best friend is the one who killed that girl. That's so crazy!"

Thank you, Lori. "We don't know he did it for sure. And even if he did, he is crazy—sick, I mean. I hate talking about it; it upsets me. I've known him for years."

Lori interrupted, "Yeah. Well, I heard the girl, Rachel Carter? I heard she was really wild."

"What!" we all yelled out at the same time.

"Yeah," Lori continued, "my brother said his friend went to the same Catholic church as Rachel and he said that she was pretty loose with the boys, if you know what I mean…"

This time I interrupted, "The Catholic church in Greenview, where Father O'Malley is?"

"Yeah, that's the one Eric goes to, I remember the name because he said Father O'Malley had been on Rachel's case really bad, you know, about her reputation and stuff."

I was thinking he must be pretty strict, I didn't know if that was typical for a minister or priest, being as my religious experiences were limited.

Pauline made the point, "You know, no one has ever said Rachel was raped, my parents say she wasn't, as far as they know, so that means Moose didn't go after her because of her reputation, right?"

I remembered what my friends in the attic concluded, Moose was trying to bring his daughter, Jennifer back to life. Rachel's reputation had nothing to do with anything. She was dead, murdered. I took a big gulp of my Coke.

"Will your dad still be friends with him, even though maybe he's a killer?" Pauline asked.

"My father says he'll help Moose get a fair trial. He hired this really high-powered lawyer for him." I didn't tell them that Father was adamant that Moose would go free.

Lori ears perked up. "You guys know my dad's an attorney, but he's a litigator. That's like the toughest kind of lawyer—and the richest. So he couldn't help Moose anyway."

Father said he got the best attorney in the state, but I didn't tell Lori that. In her world, her dad was the best attorney around.

Just as I predicted, Kristen wanted to play with the Ouija board. I set it up, feeling pretty good at this point, warm and kind of fuzzy all at the same time. Usually, I was a little apprehensive using the Ouija board with anybody but the mannequins. The vodka must have made me reckless. I was going with the flow. I could be as normal as my friends.

Kristen suggested, "Why don't we ask the Ouija board if Moose did kill Rachel? Bree seems to have her doubts."

"Oh, I don't know..." I stuttered.

Pauline and Lori thought it was a great idea and gathered around the board. What could it hurt? I placed the message indicator in the middle of the board and said, "OK, I'll ask the question, the rest of you be serious and quiet and rest your finger tips on the indicator too."

Kristen added, "Don't just ask if Moose killed her, 'cause that's a yes or no question. Ask *who* killed Rachel and see if it spells out Moose."

Good idea I thought. Once I felt everyone was calm and focused I spoke, "Who killed Rachel Carter?"

The indicator began to move swiftly as we all looked down to see the words spelled out one letter at a time, "Y-O-U-K-N-O-W".

Lori grabbed the message indicator. "That's stupid of course we know it's Moose. Duh!"

I wasn't so sure that's what it meant but my brain felt too fuzzy to contemplate this. I decided to change the subject immediately. "Let's see how many babies we're all gonna have. Lori, you go first. Come on, you guys put your hands on it too."

We all squeezed in around the board and placed our fingertips on the message indicator. We closed our eyes, and Lori said, "Oh, magic Ouija board..." We all started laughing.

"Stop it, I'm serious!" We tried to concentrate, but it was hard.

"How many babies will I have?" Lori continued.

We all waited as the indicator began to move. We opened our eyes and saw it approach the number two.

"Hey, just what I wanted! But then, I always get what I want, don't I?" Lori tossed her hair, in that way I was growing to hate.

"O.K.," I said, "Let someone else ask the next question."

Pauline asked, "I want to know if my parents are going to get a divorce. They're fighting a lot lately."

"I'm sorry, Pauline." I said.

Again, we all put our fingers on the indicator. Nobody was laughing as the indicator pointed to 'Yes'. Pauline started crying.

"It's just a game," I said, although I wasn't too sure. I remembered Gene's admonition. "I've heard more and more parents are getting a divorce, Pauline, you're not alone."

Lori sounded smug. "Not my parents. They never fight. My parents are like best friends. My dad makes a lot of money and my mom spends it. It's the perfect relationship."

"Lori, please." I said, "That's not helping Pauline feel any better."

Pauline continued to cry. Kristen looked down at her lap and didn't say anything for once, probably because her parents were already divorced. The vodka was making me a little bold and more than a little mouthy.

"I have an idea! Let's ask the Ouija board if Lori's parents are ever going to get a divorce!"

Lori folded her arms across her chest. "Go ahead, see if I care! I already know the answer."

Pauline stopped crying and joined us as we placed our fingers back on the indicator. I asked the question this time. "Will Lori's parents ever get a divorce?"

The pointer's window moved swiftly over the word 'Yes'.

Lori jumped up. "This is so stupid! Everybody knows this game is fake! Right, Pauline?"

"Well…my parents have been fighting a lot."

"That's your parents, chickie, not mine! My parents never fight, I told you!"

I should have agreed with Lori and just dropped it right there, but I couldn't. "Well, from what I've seen it's apparent your dad would rather be at the office than home with his family."

Lori jumped up from the bed. "That's not true, Bree! You're such a brat, and your feet look like skis and I hope you grow up to be fat like your mom!"

Now I was mad. "Well at least my mom has real boobs!"

Lori charged at me and shoved me with both hands. I heard Kristen gasp as I fell to the floor.

As I started to get up, Lori said, "At least my mom doesn't weigh 500 pounds!"

That was it. Nobody insults my mom. I threw myself on top of Lori, shouting, "She weighs 280 pounds, you stupid dork!"

Uninhibited by the vodka, I pulled back my fist and punched her in the mouth.

Pauline and Kristen were both yelling for us to stop when I noticed a little drop of blood form at the corner of Lori's mouth. All of a sudden everything was blurry and I could feel myself gasping for air. All I could see was the blood. I was falling, the color red spinning all around me. I felt myself collapsing, when I heard Pauline's voice,

"Bree, Bree! What's with you?"

I sat up, only to hear Lori yelling, "You freak, you cut my mouth! My father is gonna file a civil suit against you!" She wiped the blood from her mouth with a Kleenex that Kristen handed to her.

"I'm sorry, Lori. I didn't mean to hit you. Really, I *am* sorry. But you shouldn't have insulted my mom." The alcohol was definitely taking hold; I was beginning to feel woozy.

"You insulted me first!"

"I know. I'm sorry about that too." It occurred to me that Lori hadn't apologized for her role in any of this. It felt really good to stand up for myself but now I just wanted it to stop. We had lost control and I was beginning to feel anxious and nauseated. The room was starting to spin and not the good kind of whee-I'm-on-a-merry-go-round kind of spinning but more of a get-me-off-this-ride-I'm-going-to-hurl kind of spinning.

Kristen jumped up. "I'm gonna be sick!"

Before she could make it to the bathroom, she threw up all over Lori's sleeping bag.

Lori was furious. "Great, Kristen, way to go! That's disgusting! You clean it up, you hear me? Geez, that's going to smell! Now I have to get a new sleeping bag, you dummy!"

"If you're going to get a new one, why don't you just throw this one away so Kristen doesn't have to clean it?" I suggested.

Lori tossed her hair. "She needs to clean it, as part of her lesson."

Kristen was sitting on the floor, looking from one of us to the other. She didn't look like she was in good enough shape to clean anything, not even her mouth.

"Blegh! It smells like rotten pizza! Gross! Do something!" Pauline said.

Obviously, I was the one who was going to have to do this. I gingerly picked up Lori's sleeping bag and took it into the bathroom, rinsed it out and hand washed it.

By the time I returned, Kristen was already passed out, and Lori had made herself comfortable and was sleeping in my bed.

In some weird way she reminded me of Goldilocks. I settled down next to Pauline. At least she was still awake.

Pauline spread out her sleeping bag. "Here, I'll share."

I got a quilt off the end of my bed and joined Pauline on the floor. "Thanks. Looks like I lost my bed to Miss Selfish."

"She's pretty self-centered all right, but look at her mom. All Mrs. King ever does is shop and dote on her two stinking kids."

"Yeah. Bree, can I ask you something?"

"Sure."

"What happened a few minutes ago?"

I raised up on my elbow and looked at Pauline. "What do you mean?"

"When you punched Lori, you got kind of weird. You called out for your mom and kind of like passed out or something."

"Pauline, if I tell you, will you swear not to tell anyone?"

"I promise, cross my heart. I told you about Jerry kissing me in the back of the skating rink last year, and you're the only person that I told. You can trust me."

"OK. I do, actually. It's so stupid, but it's like I've got this sudden fear of blood. I know it's totally lame. Please don't tell anybody."

"Blood?"

"Yeah, when I saw it on Lori's lip, it really upset me. It made me all dizzy and lightheaded, and I think I did pass out. Please, Pauline, please don't tell anyone! Promise? If you do, I'll never live it down. And if the boys find out, they'll make a big joke out of it. They'd probably start bringing bloody meat to school and leaving it in my locker."

"That's disgusting. You know you can trust me with your secret. But remind me not to share a locker with you next year."

"Ha ha. Cute." I felt better, sharing secrets.

"Bree?"

"Yeah?"

"I don't think you should be a nurse when you grow up."

I turned over on my side, smiling, thinking this is what it's supposed to feel like to have a girlfriend. Yet, once the lights were out and the room fell quiet, I couldn't stop thinking about what the Ouija board alleged, "You Know". Just what did I know?

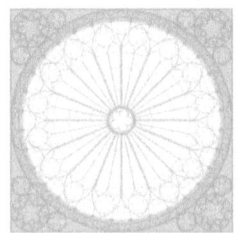

CHAPTER TWENTY-TWO

AS JULY TURNED to August, the languor was almost as palpable as the humidity. July 28th brought my next wave of anxiety as an earthquake with a magnitude of 7.5 rocked China, killing what would later be estimated as 240,000 people. My nights became consumed with worries about an earthquake destroying my town, all of us being crushed to death in our sleep, never knowing. Aunt Sharon reassured me that couldn't happen here but I wasn't sure I believed her. And even if didn't happen to me, there was still the horror of all those killed and many more injured, the pictures were vivid in my mind. I watched the news each day as they dug more victims from the rubble, imagining what it would be like to be trapped, not knowing if they would find you before you took your last breath. It would be dark, maybe wet, and you would probably be in pain. If you had the energy you might try shouting for help, but would anybody hear you?

My time was not all spent in turmoil because I had July to enjoy the Summer Olympics, Nadia Comaneci became my hero, her poster took its place alongside Peter Frampton, and Donny Osmond came down; I was so over him. Finally, ten days went by without a catastrophe or me running to Aunt Sharon for comfort. Ten days of peace. I know, because I counted them.

I didn't worry so much about Moose anymore, either. I knew it could be months before he went to trial. Father continued to say he'd go free. Even though he had hired Moose an attorney, the judge had ordered Moose held without bail. So those late summer days settled into a routine of sorts: Moose confined to jail, fuming against God and fate; Father visiting Moose every afternoon after leaving the studio; Mom puttering in the yard or pouring over the Sears catalog; and me looking forward to Junior High School. The investigation appeared to be over and I had only been able to prove what a poor investigator I was.

I tried and succeeded at being a normal kid for a while. I basked in the lazy hot July days, hanging out, to my surprise, with Lori. We hadn't had a fight since my slumber party. Conversations with my guardians in the attic were becoming less frequent and less needed. I spent fun times with Aunt Sharon and our conversations centered around movies, books, and music. Life was good. But part of me was still waiting—always assessing what I might need to worry about next. Restlessness would suddenly over take me and I would feel like I had forgotten something—something like turning off a burner or locking a door. Try as I might I didn't know what I was forgetting. I just knew the calm couldn't last.

My grandfather's sixtieth birthday was August 3rd. Aunt Sharon and Mom had planned a surprise party in honor of this special milestone. They had giggled like school girls sitting at the kitchen table, Mom chain smoking and Sharon with a phone cupped under her chin while they made lists and reservations. I got to help with the plan and I felt part of a special, secret society. If Grandma were there, we four would have been an invincible force, but both Mom and Aunt Sharon agreed that Grandma would never be able to keep a secret. Besides they wanted to surprise her too.

My mom's parents lived in a neighboring town, about a half hour drive from us. For whatever reason we didn't visit very often, but I always enjoyed going to my grandparents. Sometimes during the summer I would get to stay with them for a few days by myself and also Mom and Aunt Sharon took Grandma to lunch every other week. Father avoided most of the visits by saying he had a deadline at the studio. He seemed to get along with his mother-in-law okay but he said Grandpa Harold was a doomsayer, depressing and annoying to be around. They didn't argue so much as avoid one another. I don't know what Grandpa held against Father, but I could see a tenseness around his mouth on those rare times they did try to converse.

But none of that mattered. This would be a very special family celebration. Best of all, we rented a limousine and all Grandpa Harold knew was that he was supposed to be dressed up and stand with Grandma Mary outside their house at exactly 7 p.m. I was so excited I had butterflies in my stomach. I couldn't wait to see their smiles of surprise.

I wore my fanciest Gunne Sax dress, although it wasn't my favorite. Mom helped me put my hair up in a French twist. I had to admit I felt sophisticated and rather pretty. Mom kept smiling at me and fussing with my hair and pulling on my dress. She couldn't stop touching me and I think I even saw a tear in her eye once but I couldn't imagine what that was about.

I heard Father's voice. "Hurry up, Breezy, the limo's here! It's already 6:45! We need to get to your grandparents before Harold's knees give out from standing in the driveway so long!"

I hurried and followed by parents out the front door where the limousine was parked.

Aunt Sharon and Paul pulled up in her Triumph. I ran over to greet them.

"Hey, isn't the limo cool?"

My aunt nodded. "It's wonderful. I hope my parents appreciate it. You just never know with them."

Paul reached out reassuringly, caressing my aunt's shoulder. "I betcha they're gonna love it, hon."

Aunt Sharon smiled tightly at me and Mom. "This will be their first time to meet Paul. You know Dad can be a bit judgmental. I just hope they're polite to him."

It was my turn to reassure. "Oh, Aunt Sharon, I'm positive they will!" My own affection for Paul had been growing with each time I was around him. He didn't seem to be trying to steal Aunt Sharon from me after all and Paul had been good about including me in some of their dinners and outings. I hated to see her feeling insecure. She was the one who was supposed to be strong and confident and full of positive energy. I needed to figure out at what age we got to put all our fears and doubts behind us.

Sharon added, "I did call ahead and told Mom I was bringing a date. She didn't act too surprised. I also asked her to warn Dad not to bring up the situation with Moose. I told her that was touchy at best, and definitely not a good birthday discussion." Aunt Sharon was right, but I didn't want to be reminded of Moose spending his nights alone in jail. Father said Moose was innocent and that meant that there was still a killer somewhere nearby. Which would be worse? For someone innocent to be locked up or for someone to be free and guilty?

This was going to be a bad night if I didn't readjust my thinking. I looked over at the limousine. I didn't know anyone who had ever ridden in one. I took a deep breath and held it in to the count of ten. The chauffeur opened the door and I felt very important as I climbed into the back. There was a bar, a sunroof and a tape player. We were in way good shape!

Father seemed indifferent about the fact that we were actually riding in a limousine. Mom seemed as impressed as I was. She had made a rare appointment to get her hair done and had bought a new dress. She looked younger and definitely happier. Even overweight I could see the pretty young girl she had once been.

As we pulled up in front of their house, my grandparents' faces lit up with disbelief when they realized the limousine was for them. The chauffeur got out and flamboyantly opened the door for them. It was just the way I had imagined it.

"It was my idea to get you guys a limo. Do you like it?" I asked.

Grandpa reached over and hugged me. "I love it, pumpkin."

Mom reached past me and patted his knee. "Happy sixtieth, Daddy."

My grandfather said, "You surprised me. The last limo I rode in was during Uncle Karl's funeral. Is this supposed to be the practice run for mine?"

My grandma suggested, "I think that was a hearse, dear."

"Aw, same difference."

My father snorted.

Aunt Sharon introduced Paul to my grandparents and they seemed genuinely happy to meet him.

We had reservations at the nicest restaurant in Englewood. Tanglewood Inn set back from a busy street in the older part of town, with big trees shading the parking lot and the rambling structure. We rarely ate out, so this was a big deal. The restaurant had cloth table linens and glass goblets on stems. I knew I was gawking like a tourist as I took in the crystal chandeliers, the beveled mirrors and grand piano. All of us dressed up in our best clothes, riding in a limousine and dining out at an exclusive restaurant, combined to give this evening a fairy-tale feeling. I just hoped I didn't spill anything.

At first I was surprised when Father ordered four bottles of Ernest and Julio Gallo wine with dinner, but then I remembered no one had to drive home. He was an experienced drinker, but I had never seen my mom drink before and she was noticeably tipsy. Dinners at home would often be very quiet, but tonight the conversation stayed lively and animated with each bite of steak and each sip of wine. We may have even been a little loud, but all I knew was that I felt very warm and very happy.

At Mom's request, the restaurant had prepared carrot cake, my grandfather's favorite. After dinner and dessert we sat visiting, Father and Grandpa Harold were savoring after-dinner drinks. Grandpa Harold was getting a little argumentative; probably the alcohol taking effect. After my experiences at the slumber party, I pretty much knew what he was feeling.

"Geoff, Dorothy tells me you allow Bree to run around the neighborhood unsupervised. She rides her bike to Sharon's anytime she wants, and the park, and God only knows where else. You have a responsibility to protect your family. Look at what's happened this summer. There was a murder, for God's sake, practically in your own backyard. You owe it to Bree to keep her safe even if it means keeping her home all the time."

I looked at Father, who frowned as he said, "That's enough, Harold. I have no intention of letting anything happen to Bree... or Dorothy for that matter."

"Yeah, I know, I know. You have all good intentions, no one ever thinks it could happen to them."

"What could happen?" I wanted to know. But of course I knew. I already wished I hadn't spoken. I didn't want to be reminded of Rachel. First the evening was almost ruined by my thinking about Moose, now it would be ruined by my thinking about poor Rachel. I needed a key to lock my mouth and my brain.

My grandpa looked surprised that I had spoken, he'd been so intent on convincing my father to lock me up indoors. "I'll tell you what could happen, pumpkin. This world is not the world of my childhood. There are evil men out there, serial killers, evil men who want to murder little girls, killers who won't stop until the police catch them and throw their sorry butts in prison! That's why kids have no business running around as if nothing's happened. It's a changed world... "

"O.K. that's enough." my father said flatly.

Grandpa was right though. I had known all along that the killer was still out there. I was only pretending that I was not scared.

My mom and grandma were both staring at their plates. I realized how alike they truly were. Aunt Sharon and Paul looked more fascinated than upset by the discussion. Father's best authoritative voice didn't deter Grandpa Harold from continuing his rant. I was starting to get that really uncomfortable feeling that I now recognized as the beginning of an anxiety attack.

"We all get comfy in our middle class lives. Nothing in the news pertains to us. No, sir! Well, I'm here to warn you, you better be petrified. If you're not scared to death, you're badly informed!"

Maybe Grandpa had heard about my visits to a psychologist this summer. Maybe I could use that to dissuade him from continuing this line of conversation. "Grandpa, I am scared! Just listening to your predictions of a serial killer is raising my anxiety level pretty rapidly," I said.

Father was looking really angry. I wanted my grandpa to stop. I wanted Father to just agree to keep me indoors so he *would* stop.

"Bree," he was addressing me again, "you need to be prepared. What would *you* do if you were plucked off the street by a serial killer and thrown into the back of car? Huh? Do you know what you would do?"

I shook my head no. I felt tears well up in my eyes. Don't cry, don't cry, I said to myself. When I first saw Rachel's body I was so sure I would have been able to escape. Bree Grant would have done something! Something remarkable and effective that would have saved her life. Since then, I'd had my doubts. There were just too many uncertainties in life. Too many sources of evil. Too many children who have been unable to escape from whatever evil or horror threatened them. The tears began to fall, heedless of my wishes.

Father looked at me. "Damn it, Harold, you're making Bree cry! I want you to shut up!"

Grandpa Harold got up out of his seat. Everyone in the restaurant was looking at us now. "It's my birthday, and I'll say whatever I please! Bree needs to know the truth about this world, and so do you!"

Father stood up himself, knocking over his chair. "Not if it upsets my daughter!"

His look was more menacing than I had ever seen in him. He didn't even look like my father.

I was way past upset. I knew it would help if I could stop crying, but my anxieties were completely out of control now. I wanted so much to be able to say, "Please, don't fight," but I couldn't find my voice. All I could do is sit there and watch through tear-blurred eyes as our beautiful evening disintegrated into shambles.

My father's sanctimonious voice. *"Come! I looked, and there before me was a pale horse! Its rider was named Death, and Hell was following close behind him...* Is that the truth you want her to know?"

Grandpa Harold walked around the table to my father. He poked him in the chest, whispering, "You really are one screwed-up guy, Grant. Vietnam left its mark on you, son. I'll shut up for now, but only for little Bree's sake. As far as you're concerned, however, my message remains."

I stared at the two of them and thought they were either a little crazy, or maybe, a lot crazy. The fact remained that Father had been genuinely upset by my tears and had stepped in to protect my feelings. Even without keeping me indoors all summer, he would never allow me to do something that put me at risk. I felt like it was entirely my fault the evening was ruined.

Mom looked really confused about what had happened. Grandpa and Father wouldn't look at each other and Grandma kept patting her husband's hand as if she were a mother saying "there, there" to her child. We were all ready for the evening to be over.

As we were walking out of the restaurant I was startled to see a big man getting out of a red Firebird. I grabbed Father's arm, "Is that the guy that lives in the brick house down the street from us?"

Father squinted and looked over. "I don't know. I don't pay much attention to who lives in our neighborhood."

"Ugh. Just look at that car, I see it all the time!"

"Maybe he does then." He was clearly distracted by trying to load his slightly tipsy family into the limousine. Grandpa was having the most trouble but refused to let Father help him. I decided to take advantage of this diversion.

Leaving Father in front of the limo, I ran over to the big man. Something about the adrenalin of the evening made me brazen.

I yelled, "Hey!" He turned around. I ran up to him, out of breath and with my heart beating wildly I asked, "Do you live in my neighborhood? We need to talk."

"Who *are* you?" He asked incredulously, but with a half smile.

"Sorry, I'm Bree Grant, I live in the weird shaped house on the corner of Briarwood and Cherokee." I was starting to feel a little foolish. I knew I looked very young. I felt pretty embarrassed, but I wasn't really scared and I needed to know.

"Oh, OK, then yeah, I guess we do live close to each other."

I asked as pointedly as I could, "Why have you been following me around the city?"

"You're nuts kid. I have no idea who you are…" Then a flicker of something in his eyes. "Are you the kid on the green bike I see riding all over? And the same kid who keeps ringing my doorbell and pounding on my door about once a week?"

I folded my arms in a defensive pose but didn't answer. He was the one who should be answering questions.

After scratching his head and studying me for a second he added, "It *is* you isn't it? Look kid, you're lousy in traffic, no offense, when you get your driver's license please warn me so I can move to a safer city. And please stop coming by my house trying to sell whatever you're selling. I'm not interested. I told you that night I saw you hanging out at the shopping center— to buzz off."

Could that be true? Maybe he wasn't trying to kidnap me in front of the theater but wanted me stop ringing his door bell? I ignored his lecture. "Answer this one question and I'll never come by your house again…where were you on the evening of May 24?"

"Why, did someone let the air out of your bike tires that night? I wouldn't be surprised, I've considered doing that to you myself—now how am I supposed to remember back several months ago? And more importantly what business is it of yours?"

"I've been investigating the murder of Rachel Carter…"

He interrupted, "And they caught the guy who did it…"

"Just tell me where you were and I promise you won't hear from me again." Which was true. Once I knew he didn't have an airtight alibi, he wouldn't hear from me because I would be turning over my information to Detective Hines who could take it from there. The guy's girlfriend or wife was following our conversation with bemused interest from the front seat of the car. I was beginning to feel like someone *was* letting the air out of my tires all right—that awkward feeling you get when you know you're about to look like a complete fool.

The big man sighed and rubbed his face. "Well if you must know, I was working. I work nights and sleep all day. Except… for when someone rings my doorbell in the middle of the day, then I don't sleep so well." I recognized the heavy use of sarcasm and glared at him. "Anyway…" he continued, "on that particular night I was most certainly working because I remember hearing about the missing girl on my way home from work on the car radio. Not that it's any of your business but I have a time card that is punched when I come and go at the factory, proving I was there all evening. Satisfied Nancy Drew or whatever your name is?"

Father was yelling my name. I knew I had pretty much just embarrassed myself. I waved to Father and quickly blustered my exit by telling the big man I would scratch him off my list of suspects—after I checked out his alibi of course. I saw him roll his eyes. Before I turned to walk away, I noticed the man's colors were shades of lavender and violet. If Diana was correct, then his colors told me he wasn't so bad after all.

Why had I gone and completely embarrassed myself after such an emotionally embarrassing scene in the restaurant? I knew why. Because I knew the killer was still out there. For weeks I had been in denial. I didn't want to think about it because the vague sense of responsibility still hung over me like Poe's pendulum.

The ride home was shrouded in stony silence, except for Aunt Sharon's stilted attempts to lighten the mood.

I was glad when the evening was over and we were back home. Later, Father stopped me before I made it to my room. I could smell the alcohol on his breath. "Bree, I'm sorry your grandpa upset you tonight."

Somehow, I still felt the evening was ruined because of me. I wished I hadn't started crying. What a baby I was! Alcohol sure seemed to be the cause of a lot of trouble lately.

"It's O.K. I shouldn't let him get to me... uh, Father?"

"Yes."

"I'm sorry I cried. I imagined myself trapped in a car, not able to escape. I couldn't stop thinking about all the children killed in wars and tornadoes and earthquakes... the thoughts wouldn't stop. I kept telling myself I was safe and you'd keep me safe. I know you were just trying to protect me tonight."

Father reached out and rubbed the top of my head. With slurred speech he replied, "That's what fathers are for, Breezy. Your colors told me how upset your grandfather..." He stopped midsentence realizing what he had just said.

I wasn't sure I heard correctly. "Colors? Father! You see colors too? And...and the shadows! Do you see the shadows?" I grabbed his arm as tears welled up in my eyes. "Do you?" I was excited but I was also shocked and confused. If emotions were sounds then I would go deaf from the cacophony. I wasn't alone. He knew. My father knew what I was seeing.

He was trying to back track over his words but suddenly became aware of what I was saying. He now knew I saw the colors. It was no longer a secret...for either of us. He reached out and put his hands on my cheeks. I thought he was going to say something reassuring, something to explain our gift. But instead he looked devastated. "Bree, oh God, Breezy, I'm so sorry, I had no idea." His voice cracked, "I thought I was the only one cursed. What could you have done at your young age to deserve this?"

This wasn't what I expected him to say. I thought he was going to hug me, but then he trudged onto his bedroom shutting the door behind him, but not before his shadow slipped in through the door trailing red behind him.

I stayed frozen to the spot where he had left me. I felt both reassured and rejected at the same time. There was so much that I didn't understand. I now knew my father and I had a lot to talk about. Maybe he didn't feel like talking about it tonight, but tomorrow we would make the time.

Later that night I wrote in my diary, why did Father say I was cursed? I didn't feel cursed. I pondered the fact that Father could see the colors too. Maybe it would help him to meet Diana. She could explain to him how the colors are good and not a curse. As I went over in my mind all I learned from Diana a thought occurred to me, she seemed hesitant to tell me why Father's colors vibrated, but now I knew, it was because our bright lights bounced off each other. I wondered what my colors must look like to him.

I also thought about the colors I saw around the big man. I had been very suspicious of the big man but now I could see how maybe, just maybe I had been wrong. Out of my confusion I got on my knees and decided to give prayer another chance. "Dear God, please forgive me for being suspicious of everyone, forgive me for messing up my grandpa's birthday. Also, please forgive me for drinking liquor the other night. Please help me stop worrying about things I can't control. Also, please help me to know how to help my father, he needs to know our gift is good. And remember, if Moose is innocent, please help set him free. Amen."

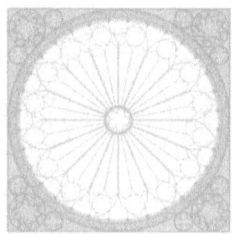

CHAPTER TWENTY-THREE

THERE HAD BEEN no nightmares and I awoke thinking about my father. A weight had been lifted with the confession of my secret, our secret, the night before. I was comforted with the knowledge that he and I shared the gift of seeing auras and I realized that I did view it as a gift now. Why didn't he? I had so many questions and I didn't want to wait for the answers.

After I dressed I entered the kitchen expecting to get my own Pop-Tart, but Mom was scrubbing down cabinet doors and offered to stop and fix me a real breakfast. While she fixed chocolate chip pancakes at my request, I made a glass of Tang and set at the table watching her at the stove. Did she know about Father's ability? For some reason I didn't think so. I kept my secret carefully guarded and he had been doing that for even longer than me.

It was so good to eat a hot breakfast and Mom sat down with me and had her usual black coffee and cigarette, reaching over to stab a bite or two of my pancakes. We made small talk about the night before, but avoided any mention of the scene Grandpa had made. She seemed to want to concentrate on the facts that her dad had been surprised and the meal was good and it was nice to be with family. I kept my mouth full of warm pancakes and gooey chocolate chips and let her ramble on while I considered whether to go back to Diana's.

Diana had said I needed to talk to my father, but first of all, he didn't seem to want to talk about it, and in the second place, she had actually said it was for *him* to discuss with *me*. I wondered if she had known we shared this gift. I had a feeling it was more important to talk to Father first and then maybe I would go see Diana again.

"Well, you get the clean plate reward this morning, Bree." Mom was smiling at me with a very pleased expression. She was usually happy when I enjoyed her cooking, or when I made all A's, or when I cleaned my room. She was relaxed this morning and I knew getting out the night before had been good for her. I didn't care if she was overweight, she was still pretty. I smiled back at her, glad she was my mother, and said, "I think I'm going to surprise Father at the studio. Do you want me to take him anything?"

She immediately jumped up and retrieved a plastic baggy of fresh oatmeal cookies she had made. "Riding your bike that far means you have to be very mindful of the traffic, but if you can find a way to take these to your father, I know he'll be happy to see you and the cookies. You're both his favorites." We smiled together at this little joke and I gave her a hug. "I love you," we each said at the same time.

It was only a couple of miles downtown to the studio but mostly busy streets and I was careful as I rode along the curbs thinking of how to approach the subject of gifts and auras. Should I make small talk first and ease into what I wanted to ask. What did I want to ask? Well, how long had he been seeing colors? Why did he see it as a bad thing? Had he known or suspected that I shared this ability? We had a lot to talk about. I just didn't know how to start.

Twenty minutes later I entered the back door of the studio and watched quietly for a moment as Father finished up a phone conversation. "Yes, I will be here Saturday. No, you don't have to bring the entire church committee. Yes, first we will discuss what you want and your budget. We can take care of this when you come in. Thank you. Goodbye."

Well, it sounded like we wouldn't be hurting for money this month. I was sure Father probably needed a good job right now to help pay Moose's attorney. Still not sure of how to announce my presence, Father turned, startled at first and then a look of concern clouded his face. He spoke first.

"Bree, I'm so glad to see you. You were on my mind. We need to talk."

Wow, this was going to be easy. "I thought so too. Here's some cookies Mother made this morning. They're oatmeal with raisins and still a little warm from the oven." I held out the baggy but he ignored the cookies so I laid them down and pulled up a stool by him.

"Breezy, I'm so sorry. I never knew. I wouldn't wish this on anyone, let alone my only precious daughter. I have so much to apologize for. I don't know where to begin except to let you know right off how very, very sorry I am."

"But, Father, I don't think you need to be sorry. I'm so glad I don't have to keep my secret anymore. I used to think it was a curse too, but now I see it more as a gift. A very confusing and untrustworthy gift, but still something special. I just don't understand it. There was a time when I thought it showed me the truth about people but now I'm wondering just what it shows."

Father was quiet for a moment and took a sip of coffee from his cup. I let him think while my own thoughts and questions bounced around in my head. Finally he spoke again.

"I was very young when I first saw the colors around the people in my life. I didn't know it was supposed to be a secret and one night at dinner I tried to describe these rainbows, these vivid apparitions to my parents. I didn't know how to describe them very well and my parents thought I was possessed or something.

"They tried to get me to deny I could see them. I know now that it scared them because they didn't understand what I was trying to tell them. My dad beat me. He whipped me hard. And every time after. If he even *thought* I was staring at someone he gave me a beating. I learned to keep quiet about what I was seeing, but Dad kept beating me just to make sure I never mentioned it to anyone else again."

Grandpa Grant had died before I was born and I was glad I had never known him. He didn't sound very nice. I could see how upset Father was at the memories and I reached out and touched him on his knee.

"Bree, I swore I would never hit my children if I was lucky enough to have a family. And I feel like the worst father in the world for spanking you. I don't know how I could do the very thing I hate. Sometimes I feel like I'm standing outside my own body and watching someone else do these horrible things. I love you so much. There is just no excuse for using a belt on a child as dear as you." He reached over and pulled me close to him. I felt so warm and safe in his embrace.

"Is that why you think the colors are a curse? Because your father beat you?"

He took a deep breath and I saw him shudder. "Maybe that. That and the war. Bree, you could never understand. I hope you never understand. I spent my life seeing the colors surrounding everyone around me. Color was everywhere. In spite of the beatings it was beautiful."

He took another deep breath before continuing. "In Vietnam the colors kept going dark. Everywhere I looked I would see colors erased, extinguished, in the blink of an eye. There was darkness everywhere I looked. It was almost worse than seeing the lifeless bodies."

I had seen Rachel's body without her colors and could imagine a little of what he was saying. I couldn't imagine that scene multiplied by scores.

Father seemed to regain his composure. "I've seen Death. I've witnessed what happens when the light goes out and the colors disappear. *The Spirit himself bears witness with our spirit that we are children of God, and if children, then heirs—heirs of God*"

"Then you do believe in God," I asked.

"I believe in The Power. I don't believe in a wise and loving Being sitting on a throne in the clouds. What I believe is that there is Power that is ours for the asking. Power to overcome that demon Death that wants to rob the world of all its color. The colors are a curse. It means we're weak. It means we're vulnerable to the Thief who would rob us of their beauty. You must do everything you can, Bree, to resist being weak. You are now my only prodigy. It is up to you to find the strength to resist the lure of trying to fathom the auras. It will only bring you grief."

He was agitated now but it was so good to be talking to him about these things. I wanted so much to help him. I wanted him to help me too. I didn't want to be weak but I wasn't sure I knew what he was talking about. I didn't feel that weak. Well, maybe a little.

"Father, you said *now* I was your only prodigy, I think that means only child. What did you mean by now?"

He didn't look at me at first, then he moved further away and said, "She was weak. Not strong like you. She never could have made it in this world. Death took her, The Thief stole the one that hadn't breathed her first breath, who hadn't received her colors yet."

I wasn't sure I fully understood. Was he talking about a baby, an unborn baby? I had been right when I told Mike that I thought I almost had a brother or sister. Now I knew it would have been a sister. I had so many questions still but I felt drained and sad. I decided to save any more questions for another day. We were both quiet for a while and then Father announced he had to get back to work. He gave me a small hug and said he would meet me home later. I grabbed one of his cookies before heading out the door but it didn't taste as good as I thought it would. Maybe I was coming down with something.

The next morning I awoke to find Mom sitting on the side of my bed. That never meant good news. Her new hairdo had been undone by a couple of nights in bed and she looked tired and really upset. I quickly sat up and asked what was wrong.

"Bree, dear, Moose's attorney called first thing this morning." She took a long drag off her cigarette.

"What?" I wiped the sleep from eyes, knowing I needed to focus on the bad news that was coming. Mom never sat on the edge of my bed to deliver good news. Her very presence so early in the morning sent my anxiety to its highest level of alert.

She looked really nervous. She'd either been crying or was about to cry. She took another deep drag on her cigarette. This was not going to be good.

"Apparently Moose hung himself last night in his cell."

I began to cry as Mom held me against her chest. She rubbed and patted my back like she had when I was little, making soothing noises. I think she was crying too. I wanted her to hold me like this forever. I let myself melt into her chest and breathed in the scent of the smoke. It was all familiar and comforting.

So he had been guilty and could no longer live with himself. It broke my heart to imagine what his last thoughts must have been. Having killed Rachel in order to bring back his daughter Jennifer, how deep was his agony when he finally realized it had all been for nothing? I knew Moose was intrinsically a good person. Had he stumbled through so many losses and was hopelessly lost in a maze of despair, that he was unable to find his way back? Maybe my prayers had been answered. Whether Moose was innocent or guilty, he had been set free. Isn't that what I'd prayed for? But it wasn't the answer I had been seeking. With his death, without a trial, we would never really know the truth.

Mom seemed to sense I'd need time alone to absorb this latest loss and she quietly left my room. After an hour of lying in bed doing lots of thinking and using coping techniques to lessen my anxiety, I made a decision.

I was 12 and about to enter junior high. I wasn't a little kid anymore. Moose was gone and like Diana said, I would learn through my own experiences how truly strong I am. I thought back to what Dr. Bryan had said about people creating an imaginary world to deal with life's events and how kids use dolls to work out emotions. But I wasn't a kid and I could deal with my anxiety in a more mature way. I knew what I had to do.

That morning, up in the attic, I took a long, reflective look around my secret sanctuary and told my mannequin friends a painful goodbye. Their clothes and makeup were needing attention, little mendings and touchups that I hadn't noticed this past summer. It no longer mattered but I felt a bittersweet tug at my heart when I noticed their neglect. Part of me, the part that was having a struggle letting go of my childish ways, didn't want to leave them imprisoned in the dark again, but there was a part of me that was looking forward to walking away into the light.

I straightened their arms and legs where they had been suspended in awkward poses. They stared at me blankly and silently as I gathered up my personal belongings and shut the door to the attic for the very last time.

PEOPLE ARE LIKE STAINED GLASS WINDOWS:
THEY SPARKLE AND SHINE WHEN THE SUN IS OUT, BUT
WHEN DARKNESS SETS IN, THEIR TRUE BEAUTY IS REVEALED
ONLY IF THERE IS A LIGHT WITHIN.
ELIZABETH KUBLER-ROSS

CHAPTER TWENTY-FIVE

THE PAST FEW days had been a dull gray blur. I stayed close to home listening to music and reading a little. Lori had called once and Mike had called twice but I told my mom to tell them I wasn't available and to my surprise she did. I didn't feel like talking to anyone. Father was in his studio at all hours and Mom and I just moped around the house avoiding anything resembling a schedule or balanced meals. I had heard Mom on the phone once with Dr. Bryan and twice with Aunt Sharon, but she kept the conversations short. I figured we were of one mind regarding any intrusion into our grief.

It was the morning of Moose's memorial service. My mom was waiting by the door with her handbag, nervously wringing her hands. "I don't know what is taking Geoff so long, we really don't want to be late, I need time to get my bearings before everyone arrives." I tended to agree so I went in pursuit of finding my father so we could leave for the chapel. As I turned from the kitchen, I could hear his voice. I felt confusion and glanced at the phone table but he wasn't there. I followed the sound of his voice to his bathroom. The door was ajar and I could see him—standing in front of the mirror—talking to himself.

I feel an intensity and suspect something remarkable is about to happen. He looks at me differently, I need to confront him—but like I said before, I'm afraid of this man...

"I'm leaving now," he announced suddenly and without preamble. "You are on your own, but you don't have to be afraid. You have everything you need. I've always told you how talented you are. You have to believe in yourself." He was still standing in the same spot but starting to fade like a familiar shadow on a cloudy day.

"We got through this just like I told you we would." His voice was growing fainter, barely a whisper now.

"Promise me that you'll remember me fondly," he intoned with the hint of a smirk. Then he was completely gone and I am left alone staring at my own reflection in the glass.

Father had been acting odd lately so I wasn't that surprised when I saw him talking to his reflection in the mirror. I touched his arm and he jumped slightly but then reached out and stroked my hair. I noticed he had a single tear running down his cheek. "It's time," he said, taking the words right out of my mouth.

We gathered at the chapel in the Jennifer Sullivan Drug and Alcohol Center at seven in the evening, the summer sun still burning bright. In spite of the warm temperature, most everyone wore black for Moose's memorial service. The room was full to overflowing and I recognized some of the people but not all. I was surprised to see Mike and his dad behind a couple I sort of recognized but couldn't place. I didn't think they had known Moose and I thought it was kind of sweet that they had come. I didn't see Lori or any other of my friends but they could have been behind me. I didn't want to swivel all the way around and somehow I doubted that they were there. I had the feeling that a lot of the mourners were there out of curiosity rather than sorrow but then I reminded myself I was too young to be so jaded.

Moose's girlfriend and ex-wife were both there and sat on the front row with Mom and me. Aunt Sharon had brought Paul; he was now a rather permanent fixture in her life. They sat on the other side of us. Grandpa and Grandma were behind us and I recognized Detective Hines and his wife toward the back rows and I wondered who was babysitting. I also wondered if Detective Hines felt he caused the suicide. It made me shudder with a sudden chill.

The past week had been a blur of strained routine. Father put in long hours at his studio and Mom and I tiptoed around him when he was home. He picked at his food, he drank too much and I often noticed him sitting in his chair staring at nothing. Both he and my mother had lost weight. Father especially looked gaunt, with dark circles under his eyes. I realized that he had been steadily losing weight all summer. I had been so busy investigating that I missed what was going on in my own home. After the service was over and things got back to normal, I planned to take Father over to meet Diana, who I knew could explain our gift better than I ever could.

Moose had been his best friend, maybe his only friend. He had stood by Moose when Jennifer died, spending that first week at Moose's house, never leaving his side. They often had lunch together and sometimes talked on the phone late at night. On some level, I recognized that Father had lost not only a friend, but a comrade in arms, an important part of his own history. The sorrow was etched in the lines of his face and the stoop of his shoulders.

Father had worked harder on the stained glass window he was dedicating to Moose than any other project I knew of. He poured all his creative energies and time into this final gift to his friend. Sleep and unnecessary words were all pushed aside, as this memorial took precedence over everything else in his life. He announced to Mom and me, before he even began the project that this was indeed going to be the 'perfect window'.

Watching Father now I felt confusion as I saw his entire aura had changed to the deep red once held only by his shadow. He now stood at the pulpit in the front of the chapel, behind him his dedication window radiating with the light from the setting sun. Father had left the house in the dark of the morning and installed his stained glass window earlier that day. Although not strictly religious, the scene depicted in the window had that kind of feel.

A wounded Roman soldier lay in an arid landscape, amid rocks and barren soil, clutching his side. Blood ran from between his fingers where he held his hand against his toga. His face looked skyward with a despairing look. Bending at his side was another male figure holding a flask of water to the wounded man's lips. The opalescent glass Father had used for the sky in the background of the picture was dark, streaked with intense blues and purples; a storm raging in the heart of night. Other, iridescent glass gave the illusion of light shining down from above the tempest.

I noticed how closely the figures in the window resembled my father and his friend, Moose. I thought maybe Father had tried to create a reference to the parable of the Good Samaritan; one man leaning forward to offer a bruised and bloody comrade a drink of water from his own wineskin canteen. That would be appropriate to the Center and to Moose's memory. As I sat staring at it, it occurred to me, that Father *had* finally created the perfect stained glass window.

Father looked every bit a minister, standing somber and grave in his dark suit. I hadn't seen him in a suit in years. Even with the weight loss and sorrow, he looked so handsome. He reminded me of the actor, Gregory Peck, who starred in *To Kill a Mockingbird.* That was my favorite old movie and if my father was Gregory Peck, that would have made me 'Scout', which I thought would be pretty cool, but they had their troubles too. Anyway, I knew it would be difficult for Father to deliver the eulogy. I felt a sympathetic lump in my own chest.

He began slowly, his voice barely audible, about how he first came to know Moose during the Vietnam War.

"As many of you know, Michael Sullivan—Moose to most of us—served with me in Vietnam. What most of you don't know is that Moose died in Vietnam."

I could see people lean forward to make sure they were hearing his words correctly.

"I'd taken five of my men, including Moose, to scout enemy positions and troop movement along the Ho Chi Minh Trail. It was a dangerous mission, and I was the only sergeant in our platoon who'd never lost a man in combat. I was determined to keep that record.

"We were ambushed that night by North Vietnamese regulars. Corporal Johnson took an AK round in the knee and another in the upper thigh. I was applying a tourniquet when I saw Sanchez and Gibson both fall in a flash of machine gun fire. The enemy lobbed two grenades in our midst. I tossed one back, killing enemy soldiers, and I lay on the other to protect Sanchez and Gibson, waiting for it to explode, praying that it would not. God answered my prayer." He paused dramatically. "And at that moment, God empowered me. He made me one of his own."

I heard a gasp to my right. I started to feel uneasy. I recognized the beginnings of an anxiety attack. I took a deep breath and held it for the count of ten.

"The serpent of the enemy did not explode and my own hands blazed like the sun! God's wrath raced through me, killing the enemy, sending their souls to Hell!"

I could hear the ripple of murmurs swell through the mourners. Soft whispers hissed up the aisles. A chill shivered down my back.

"I patched up Sanchez and Gibson the best I could, but at first I couldn't locate Moose. Then Johnson called to me and pointed to Moose's bullet-riddled body. Johnson had already tagged Moose for dead, pocketing one of his dog tags and jamming the other between his teeth, so they could later identify the remains.

There was no way I could accept this catastrophic fate! God had entrusted the care of these men to my safekeeping! I would not fail!

"I screamed out for God to take the life energy from the souls of the Vietnamese devils we had just vanquished, and give life back to Moose. I prayed, as Jesus did to God at Golgotha, but God did not forsake me as he forsook Jesus. God gave Moose back to me. I pulled the dog tag from his mouth… and Moose lived!

"I breathed the breath of God into him! God gave me the power to resurrect Michael Sullivan."

I had been holding my breath, trying to follow Father's amazing story. All around me, people squirmed in their seats. You could feel the disquiet as apprehension rose en masse among the congregation. I noticed the sinews in the back of my father's hands as he fiercely gripped the podium. Sweat dotted his forehead but the circles were gone from around his eyes.

"Moose went on to do good works but was driven to take his own life by the lies told about him. I told him to have faith; I would set him free. But he wouldn't believe. *Let those who undid that done by God and me beware of our wrath!*"

An eerie sensation was engulfing me. So many small recollections were firing simultaneously in my brain. I felt like I was suspended above an abyss. My breath was caught deep in my chest. I've heard that sometimes your life will flash before your eyes. Countless memories were careening around in a kaleidoscope of colors. I remembered playing chess with my father, watching movies while curled on his lap, listening to him play the piano late at night, sitting on the porch talking while fireflies danced in the setting sun.

"I breathed life back into Michael Sullivan on that day because God gave me the gift to resurrect! *I want to know Christ and the power of his resurrection and the fellowship of sharing in his sufferings, becoming like him in his death, to attain to the resurrection of the dead!*'

But the enemy's souls wouldn't leave me alone, they haunted me, followed me, their colors and shadows hanging over all of you, trying to fill me with their pain!"

I felt myself caught in a bizarre free fall as my mind wrapped itself around a single unsettling thought.

It had been so easy to push aside what I overheard that night a few years ago, in the early morning hours. I could ignore it because Father had ignored it. So it had to be O.K., didn't it?

As I had tossed restless in my bed, I heard classical music and knew Father was, once again, sharing my night disturbances. The piano fell silent, the Brahms Sonata stopped, and I heard the clink of glass as my father took another drink of his single malt Scotch.

Suddenly, I heard my father crash his fists on the keys of the piano. I climbed out of bed to make sure he was all right. I could see him, head against the piano, crying, "Please forgive me! Return to your father! Forgive me for hurting you! I would never hurt you on purpose! So help me, God, I didn't see you!"

Now it made discomforting sense. My father must have been talking about Jennifer, I didn't realize it at the time. I remember him working on the right fender of his antique red Pontiac sometime after Jennifer had been killed. He must have been on his way to see Moose, as he did so many evenings back then. He wouldn't have known it was Jennifer on the road, not until Lisa called the next day, telling how Jennifer had been killed in a hit and run accident. Maybe he'd even thought it was a dog he'd hit. Surely, he hadn't known it was a person. If he had, I know he would have stopped.

My mind whirled, but the pieces of the puzzle were suddenly fitting into place, like one of my father's stained glass windows. Listening to him now, I realized Father truly believed he'd brought Moose back to life in Vietnam. Just like he seemed to believe Van Gogh would rise from the grave and return to him.

Did he actually believe he could bring Jennifer back by murdering Rachel Carter in some bizarre tainted version of a Vietnamese custom? All I had were a jumble of conflicting memories and thoughts. What did I actually know?

Father's diatribe continued. Aunt Sharon had her arms around my mom. Paul was on the edge of his seat. I could tell he was debating with himself whether to go up and stop Father. Most of the people probably thought he was crazy with grief and exhausted from driving himself mercilessly to complete the memorial window.

"When an evil spirit comes out of a man, it goes through arid places seeking rest and does not find it. Then it says, 'I will return to the house I left.'"

I wondered about the bugs that were found in Moose's building. Moose's building, which connects to my father's studio. I had a vision of the dark and musty basement.

When I was younger, I went down there ever so boldly, exploring with Father. I wanted to show him how brave I was. One of the rooms, probably once used for Sunday school classes, had a wall with a small plywood board nailed against it. Father pried off the board. He told me the dark hole went directly into Moose's building. I remember being scared, but Father thought it would be funny for me to climb through and surprise the guys on the other side.

"Go on, Breezy! They'll be surprised!"

"But it's dark, Father. I'm scared."

My father's reassuring voice. "I'd go with you, but I won't fit. Go ahead, just walk straight through and follow the stairs up to the office. Go on, now!" He'd given me a little shove.

If I could go through the wall to the next building, why couldn't bugs?

Father paused his rambling sermon, took a deep breath, and pronounced, "I tell you now, I witnessed the murder that May night, and I can tell you Moose did not commit that crime!"

The audience gasped.

My heart was in my throat. I felt myself getting very dizzy. Father witnessed the murder? Was that possible? It would explain so much, or would it? Something wasn't right...something was very, very wrong...

Father continued, "I have been afraid to confront this killer, this taker of life, but now God has given me the strength to face him! It's too late to save Moose but it is not too late to save myself!"

How many sleepless nights had I worried how I would handle knowing my father was a murderer? Yet, he says he *witnessed* the murder...something didn't make sense. Then I remembered my time in the library researching anxiety and coming across a chapter on something called 'Dissociation'. It explained this disorder occurs when someone develops split personalities after a traumatic event and in order to protect themselves from the horror of reality, the person may actually see someone else in the event rather than themselves. Could this be what happened to Father? Is this why he was talking to himself in the mirror this morning? I felt anger, sorrow, and confusion.

My thoughts were all out of control. I had to stop this all-or-nothing thinking. I tried desperately to replace my nightmare thoughts with logical ones. I frantically told myself I was adding two and two and coming up with five. I'd been through this before, suspecting my father of the unimaginable.

I was six years old, high up in the tree in our back yard. I couldn't get back down. I wanted to jump into my father's arms, where I would be safe.

I looked up at his face, so handsome, and tried to breathe deeply. Focus on something beautiful, I said to myself. I looked over Father's shoulder at the stained glass window into which he'd put so much work, and love, and tears.

The sun was slipping below the horizon, its dying rays illuminating the glass in a final blaze of glory. I concentrated on the intricate design, one man reaching out to another, God's blessing shining down. A simple act of human kindness, offering a drink of water to someone in need. But the Samaritan held something in his other hand too. The flask was in his right hand, extended toward the parched lips of the wounded soldier. Something else was being proffered with his left hand.

Father had reassured me. Jump, it's OK. Go ahead, Breezy. I'll catch you. Trust me.

Diana had told me to trust my own feelings. Dr. Bryan told me to remember when control goes up, anxiety goes down.

As he spoke now about how Moose saved souls through his work, I felt myself rise out of my seat there on the front row. Aunt Sharon grabbed my arm, but I pulled away. I was captivated by the object in the Samaritan's left hand. I walked up the steps, past my father at the lectern, never taking my eyes from the window.

I'm scared. I want to jump, but I'm scared, Father.

I heard Father pause in his eulogy. There was murmuring from the crowd, but I kept my eyes on the stained glass window.

I stood, mesmerized by the sight of a coin in the hand of the kneeling soldier. Depicted on the disc was Jesus, sitting on a throne, holding a Book of Gospels in one hand and a staff in the other. I saw what I'd assumed was a military medallion hanging from the wounded soldier's neck. Its design showed the Virgin Mary placing a crown upon the emperor's head. These small design elements were the exact replica of the coin that had been hammered between Rachel Carter's teeth.

I was so high in the tree that day, too high to free fall. I had to inch my way down to his soothing voice before I could allow myself to jump.

Only three people knew about the coin: Detective Hines, me, and the killer. Father had placed within the stained glass window a clue that only the killer could know.

I imagined Moose lying bloodied in Vietnam with his dog tag between his teeth and the photo of Rachel Carter with the coin between hers.

I looked out at my mother who had risen from her seat. Her eyes flitted between my father and me. She looked more concerned than confused. Mom was surrounded by her sister, her parents, and her future brother-in-law. It reminded me of that old song, *Stand by Me*.

Then I saw Detective Hines start down the aisle and we locked eyes. I didn't know how much he had figured out already, but he knew something. And maybe I knew the rest. Maybe I had always known.

I reached up and touched the window with my fingertips.

Father's voice thundered behind me. *"Now we see through a glass darkly, then we shall see face to face. Now I know in part; then I shall know fully, even as I am fully known!"*

I stepped to my father's side and linked my arm in his. Resting my head against him, I felt the tension flow from his body and breathed in his scent. In my mind I imagined our colors blending together, our auras mixing in a rainbow of hues.

There would be a time for telling Detective Hines all I knew and confessing what I had done when I looked through Rachel's file. There would be a time of having to face the publicity that would embarrass our family. There would come a time of making a different kind of life, a life without Father at our side. That would all come later. For now I lived in this moment.

That moment, that memory, would have to last me for a lifetime.

***

www.ingramcontent.com/pod-product-compliance
Lightning Source LLC
Chambersburg PA
CBHW020236180626
46810CB00006B/2224